CANOPY

D. M. DARROCH

ISBN 978-1-890797-20-1
Copyright © 2021 by D.M. Darroch

www.DMDarroch.com

Books by D.M. Darroch

Inventor-in-Training series

The Pirate's Booty

The Crystal Lair

Cyborgia

For young children

No, No, Nora

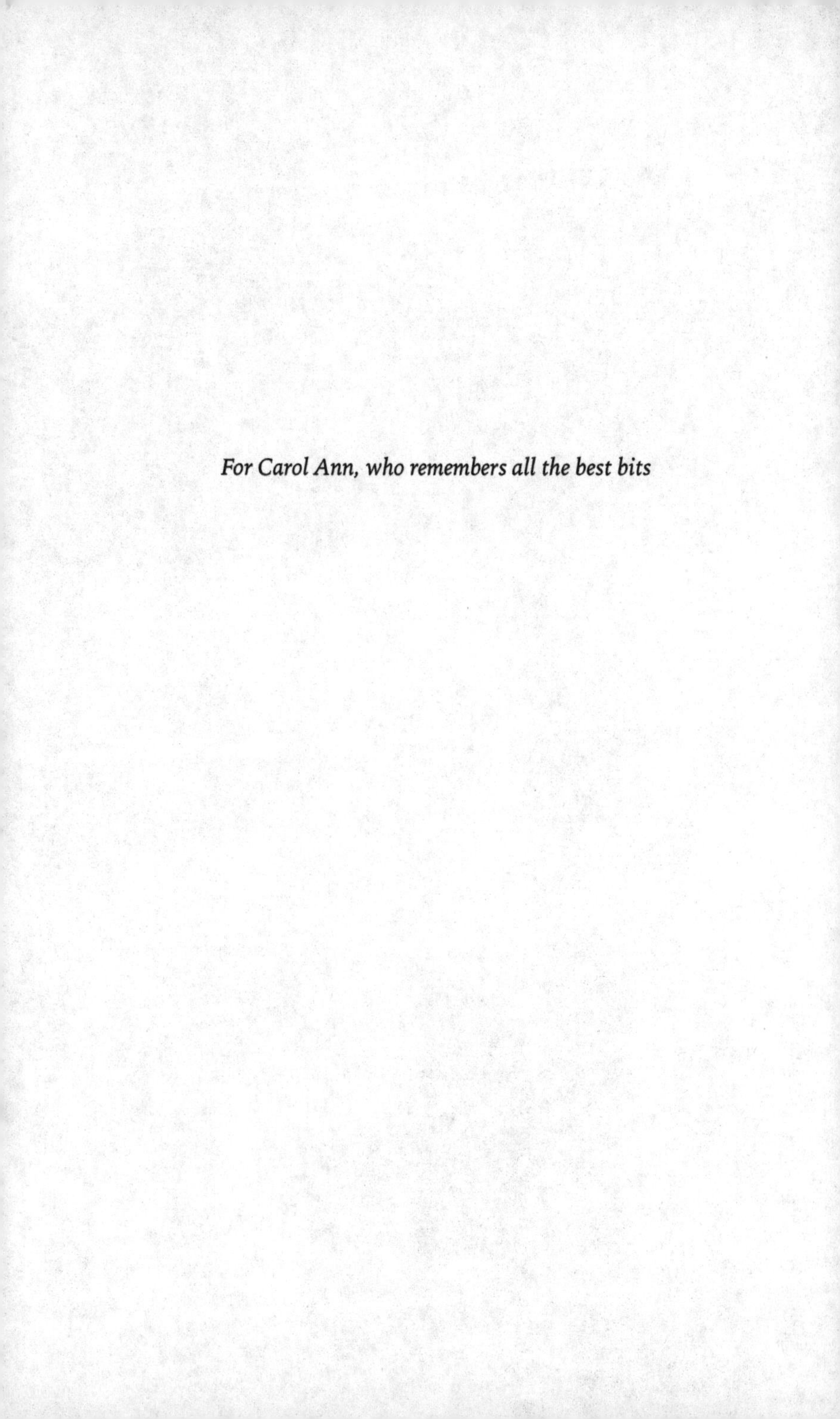

For Carol Ann, who remembers all the best bits

The Present

Spiders and their webs don't scare me. Actually, I quite like them. We have a lot in common: we're both silent and alert, largely solitary, stealthy and agile. Many species of spider devour their mates and others are known for their stinging bites; most are gentle if left alone. But the thing that really connects me and spiders is that even though we're both good for the community—they keep the insect population in check and I heal people—everyone loathes us.

The climbing boots in my hands are heavy, and I'm not entirely sure what I'm meant to do with the strings dripping out of them. The bottom of the boot is encased in thick metal spikes, brown with rust. I drag a stick across a spike and scrape away the brown to reveal a dull gray. These spikes will penetrate the Great One's hide. Will they stab deep enough to injure the tree? Will the tree be in pain? Will the tree bleed? Does a murderer worry about the pain of another? Even if that other is a Great One?

The Book of Silvanus commands that shoes never be worn, that the skin of a climber's foot always commune with the skin of the Great Ones—and I'm eager to try them on. I sink one naked foot, stained brown from years of running on pathways and climbing trees, a stain that washing fades but never removes entirely, into the depths of the boot. The hard shell imprisoning my foot is alien and slightly painful, pressing against my ankle bone, heavy on my toes.

I wasn't always The Blight. I once had friends, more or less. I once had a family. Those that have survived I'll never see again. Not in this lifetime.

The canopy hasn't felt like home for a long time. My childhood died with Joshua. I barely noticed when Yew left. My anger served to protect me from not fitting in, being set apart, feeling the resentment of the other climbers. I no longer need the anger; I'm not sure it ever helped. And I don't know what will help me where I'm going, but I'm fairly certain anger will be useless.

I was taught the climbers need us, we the special ones, the blessed ones, the healers, the descendants of Pseudotsuga, leader of the First Climbers. This mythology is passed from one generation to the next along with the expectation of cool reserve, scientific detachment, and above all, a perfection unattainable for the average human being.

Despite what my enemies think, I'm as average as they come. That is, if average means convicted of offending the Great Ones, dishonoring *The Book of Silvanus*, and breaking the commandments.

Most climbers never knew me, not really, and now they never will. It turns out I didn't know them all that well, either. But then, how well can we really know someone else's heart? Especially when we can't even understand our own.

The branch drifts in the wind and here I sit, my past and my future separated by an unimaginable climb.

From The Book

Once in the canopy, we discovered a vast world of flora and fauna unknown to humans. Upon discovering that huckleberry bushes, hazelnut trees, and salmon berries self-seeded and thrived in the nooks and crannies of the huge trees, we experimented with the seeds of other plants.

We learned to practice horticulture, planting vining crops, small fruit trees, and shade-loving vegetables among the leaf litter and needle detritus collected in the limbs and cracks of the mammoth trees. We planted herbs for every ailment: headaches, stomach aches, menstrual pains, arthritis. We planted herbs for recreation, relaxation, attention, and altered states: stimulants, depressants, psychedelics. And then we began to build.

Boughs of eight to ten feet across supported rough shelters and platforms. We linked the gargantuan limbs of the genetically engineered trees with hanging bridges constructed of cedar ropes and bark slats. We learned how high we could climb until the limbs no longer supported our weight.

We learned to hunt arboreal mammals, raccoons and opossums and all varieties of western squirrel, first with pistols, and when we ran out of bullets, by crafting short bows from the nurse-log maples.

We began to raise and train Cooper's hawks and sharp-shinned hawks to hunt small mammals in the trees and on land. We learned how to weave cedar strips by hand to make strong ropes. We crocheted hammocks and carved bowls and rain barrels. We experimented with plant fibers, hand sewing clothing with needles we fashioned from bird bones.

When we determined we had all we needed to live, we resolved never to set foot on the ground again. We resolved to live and die in the trees, far removed from the impending climate apocalypse, future resource wars, and pandemics threatening the earth far below us.

— PSEUDOTSUGA, *THE BOOK OF SILVANUS*

Chapter One

The afternoon light streamed through the branches above me, becoming brighter as I approached the sky. I'd climbed to the twelfth bough, far above the legal limit, and crossed into the Outer Reaches hand over hand, sweat flowing, adrenaline pumping, feeling every hair on my arms, legs, and scalp extend into the air as if to catch the breeze and float me between the trees like an orb weaver. But unlike those eight-legged creatures, I had no proteinaceous silk to catch me if I fell. No rope, no net, nothing but the roots far, far beneath the Great Ones, the giant Douglas firs that we lived among. Boughs and branches and twigs could compound my fractures, breaking fingers, arms, and thigh bones. They'd impale me, gut my torso, and break my head. Precisely this threat of danger, the adrenaline rush of tempting a painful death, pushed me onward.

Life had ended too soon for many others: frail kids sickened and died; elders withered; some of our parents even fed the Great Ones. Those were the unlucky others. Not me. I was smart and agile. I knew how far I could push myself, and

I rarely did anything stupid. The few times I'd gotten hurt, I healed quickly.

I sat leaning against an outer trunk, dangling my legs from the too-thin, weak branch, my heart in my throat as the wood creaked, bending beneath my weight. I repositioned my gangly self—I do physically resemble a spider in many respects—and hung from my legs, reaching out with my arms to feel for a stronger limb. I swung back and forth, gathering speed, then whooped and released, dropping down to a lower limb. The adrenaline buzzed through my brain, and I was breathless and happy.

I was the first one to arrive at our hangout spot, so I found an area where the needles grew thickly and concealed myself. To know the truth about anyone else, you must eavesdrop. Imagine all the secrets a spider hears from the dark corners between the branches.

I'm not saying everyone is a liar, but most people don't tell the truth. Some, like my poor excuse for a father, lie to save their sorry selves, but most people conceal things from you because they think you're too young, or they don't want to hurt your feelings. Maybe they themselves don't know the whole truth. Early on, I learned that the only one you can trust is yourself.

Wingnut wasn't coming to the Outer Reaches. He'd told us earlier that morning, but none of us ever expected him to join us. We always invited him, but he never came. Sorbus teased him about not coming along. He accused Wingnut of staying behind to flirt with the women of Bough Six. If I didn't know better, I might have thought Sorbus was jealous. Wingnut was tall, handsome, strong, and had charisma for days. He often entertained young women in his shanty on Bough Seven. I knew more about Wingnut's sexual encounters than I cared to—Salix made certain of that.

According to Salix, all of the Bough Six women were crazy

for Wingnut. And as quickly as the name of Wingnut's current lover changed, so too did the person that Salix and her friends shunned.

On the branch beneath me, I heard a loud grunt followed by laughter and some jocular cursing, and I knew that Mangrove and Sorbus had arrived. I repositioned myself and peered through the limbs over their heads. They were jostling each other roughly. Of course, like idiots, they weren't wearing climbing ropes. I wasn't wearing climbing ropes either, but I wasn't wrestling anyone on top of a twelfth bough, and frankly I was a much better climber than either of them.

Mangrove and Sorbus had been best friends since childhood, but they couldn't have been more different. Mangrove was wiry and quick. His curly light brown hair framed his sand-colored face like a pruned shrub, spirals of hair tightening as it grew. The springiness of his hair matched the tautness of his body. I wondered whether his limbs relaxed when he slept; I couldn't imagine what that looked like in him. He was constantly in motion, his brown eyes darting side to side beneath his thick brows, missing nothing. He leaned his back against a tree trunk, bounced a leg nervously, and picked fir needles from his curly hair.

Sorbus was short, dark, and stump-like. He lay face up on the branch, balanced on his spine, and stretched his muscular ebony arms and legs off each side. Black hair covered his arms like a pelt. Although in his teens like the rest of us, Sorbus already had a beard thicker than most the men twice his age. His long black curls had locked together as his hair grew, and he wore the thick tangles pulled into a sloppy ponytail. The long, thick mass of hair pillowed his head on the branch.

"Hey, losers! Give me a hand up. This limb I'm standing

on is groaning like it's about to break!" yelled a female voice below them.

"That's cuz you eat too much, fat ass." Sorbus rolled to his stomach and reached his massive arms down to haul up Salix. Slightly smaller and much less hairy than her brother, Salix was also short, dark, and solid. That was where their similarities ended.

"No more than you, tubby." She fluffed her halo of dark curls. Her eyes flickered toward Mangrove, who studiously ignored her. "Where's your sweetheart? Your squeeze?" She gasped, threw her head back, and uttered several suggestive, high-pitched sighs. "Your heart's true desire?"

"Shut up, Salix."

"Stood you up, did she?" Salix plopped down on the limb beside Sorbus and picked at a hangnail. "It's that rancid odor of desperation you give off. Keeps the girls away."

"Sorbus, can you do something about this? She is your sister, after all."

"Just because we shared a womb doesn't mean I have any control over her."

"Born two seconds before you. Means I'm the boss, possum-breath."

Sorbus swung his arms and legs off the limb again. "Ignore her. Eventually she'll go away. Like a fly."

"More like a mosquito. She'll bite us full of holes before she leaves."

"Aw, come on you guys. You know you love me. Who else is gonna tell you the truth? But seriously. Where is Ostrya? I haven't seen her all day."

Mangrove shrugged and looked away. Salix rolled her eyes and turned her attention to her brother. "How did your meeting go, Sorbus? Did you get the traineeship with Cedrus?"

"Yeah."

"That's great!" She punched his arm. "So, give me the details. What did he say? I mean, you certainly weren't his first choice."

"Thanks for the vote of confidence." Sorbus rubbed his arm.

"Come on, don't be like that. Tell me what happened! I need details."

"Four of us applied. Canopy needs builders, so they took all of us."

"Yeah, but how'd you get Cedrus? I'm sure the other three wanted to work with him. He's the best. Everyone knows that." Salix was a know-it-all. Even when she had no clue.

"Salix, geesh. Do you really think I suck that hard? That he wouldn't choose me?"

Salix pressed her brother. "Just tell me. How'd you get it?"

Sorbus rolled his eyes. "Cedrus chose last."

Salix whooped. "I KNEW it! You only got Cedrus because he had no other choice!"

"Mangrove, do you know how lucky you are NOT to have a sister?"

"I thank the Great Ones."

I'd been on the receiving end of Salix's needling many times myself. If she weren't my only female friend, well, I wouldn't have any. It was time to make my entrance, so I pretended I'd just arrived. "Hey! Are you guys down there?" I called.

"Hey there, Ostrya! Get on down here!" yelled Salix.

I swung out of the tree to Salix's far side. Mangrove stepped beneath me; his arms extended upward as if I needed help. Really insulting when you consider I could climb circles around him.

"You gonna move?" I shimmied down the tree trunk, my

thighs clenched tightly to its girth and my fingernails digging into the bark.

"I thought … an extra hand …," he said.

I snorted, kicked his arms away, and jumped down to the branch. I dusted off my thighs and blew my loose, tangled hair out of my eyes.

Mangrove's eyes roamed from my legs to my stomach, and then upward. When his eyes finally reached my face and I met them with a clear look of my own, he reddened, which of course set me off into a blush. I turned my head to find a seat and moved over next to Salix.

"So, how's everyone?" I asked brightly, hoping Salix didn't mention my burning cheeks. I had no desire to be her next victim.

"Yeah, so my dumb brother got chosen by Cedrus."

"Hey! That's great news, Sorbus," I said.

His eyes flickered over to me, and a hint of smile touched his lips.

"He was the only one left. Cedrus had no other options."

I shot her a look, but she ignored me. We both knew that when it came to treating brothers kindly, I had little to say. But Sorbus had talked about this traineeship for the past year. "Cedrus is lucky to have you," I said.

"Want to know about my traineeship?" asked Mangrove, staring at me.

"Sure, tell us," said Salix.

"I'll be answering to Maestro Hamamalis."

"Maestro Hamamalis heads up the agriculture crew. I didn't know you wanted to garden." Salix expressed the surprise I also felt.

"No, I won't be a gardener. I'm going to be a hunter."

"Do you need a traineeship for that? I mean, grab a spider stick and whack away."

Sorbus sneered. "Duh, Salix. When was the last time you

ate a spider? Where do you think the meat at the market comes from? A team of hunters supplies the meat for all us climbers. Hunters are the only ones allowed to kill prey."

"Well, technically we're the only ones allowed to take more than we need, because we provide for others," said Mangrove. "Any of you could kill to protect yourselves, like from a spider. And you could hunt to feed your family, but only your family."

When Joshua and I were kids, Yew had taught us to use slingshots on tiny prey. Anything we'd slain, we'd had to eat: All spirits are equal. You take a life only to prolong your own. Joshua had understood immediately, but I'd eaten a vast quantity of beetles before I learned my lesson.

"The hunters kill more than they need, so they report to Maestro Hamamalis, along with the gardeners," said Sorbus.

Salix shook her head. "I didn't know that. Did you know that Ostrya?"

"I knew Yew got the meat for the market from the hunters. I guess I never thought about who the hunters were. Seems silly, because we'd starve without them," I said.

"We wouldn't starve without them. We could always eat plants. Like Wingnut. He's a vegetarian," said Salix.

"Can't you go one hour without saying his name?" said Sorbus.

"I was just ... he's the only vegetarian I could think of."

"We couldn't all be vegetarians. Do you know how many plants we'd need?"

"If we were all gardeners—"

"It still wouldn't work. Not enough sunny places to grow as much as we'd need."

Salix's expression indicated that she was about to dig in for a great sibling debate, so I changed the subject. "So, Mangrove, who's your teacher?"

He grinned, thrilled to have the attention. "No traineeship. They tested my aim with the bow and arrow, my skill with the climbing rope, and boom! Done! I'm a hunter."

"I'm super excited," said Salix. "Wollemia chose me, out of everyone. Me. I'll be designing and making clothing."

"Really?" The word slipped out of my mouth and I instantly regretted it. I tried to explain myself, but I only made it worse. "I mean, I'm surprised you want to work on Bough One, all those old people and little kids—"

"So what? You're working on Bough One."

"I mean, I never thought, working fiber seems so, so … not like …"

"You know, Ostrya, some of us have to choose for ourselves. We don't all get to be a doctor because mommy says so. Not all of us are born into such an important family."

Her words stung. Her intention was to hurt, her tone was sarcastic, but all she said was true. And if I was being honest, my words had been insensitive and stupid. She was so smug and selfish dismissing Sorbus and Mangrove with a flick of her tongue. I guess I wanted to hurt her. But I couldn't stomach being the bad guy. "I'm sorry, Salix! I didn't mean it like that! Fiber is an important job—the entire community needs clothing and blankets, and—" I didn't know what else Wollemia's fiber team did. "What I meant was, you know, I thought you'd want something more, um, physical maybe? Up in the canopy, I don't know …"

Salix punched me in the arm. "Dude, don't hurt yourself. No need to apologize. I love working with fiber—and I'm good at it! I'm gonna learn everything. Wollemia can barely sew anymore, her arthritis is so bad. I'm gonna do all the fine work—so much more than the other trainees."

I barely heard her. My heart was pounding and my head was spinning, not the good turbulence like when I'm climbing, but the sick feeling I wake up with in the morning when I think of all the people I'll have to smile at and greet. Salix was my friend, and I didn't even know how to talk to her. How was I supposed to learn how to talk to patients?

Salix elbowed me in the side. "Hey, come on! You're gonna be a great doctor. You're smart. You're gonna learn all the bones and medicine recipes and, whatever, wicked fast."

I nodded and forced a smile. To my relief, Salix moved on to other prey. Her roommate Toona was pining after Sorbus, and this was apparently hilarious beyond measure.

The chartreuse larva of a Geometridae moth dropped from a small branch at my eyeline. I found it odd that they were called inchworms, since they were at least half a foot long. *The Book of Silvanus* classified the arachnids and arthropods living on the earth and in the trees. Generations ago, the Book claimed, insects and spiders were so small they would fit in the palm of your hand. The oxygen increases generated by the Great Ones had allowed them to grow ever larger; that's what my mother explained. Of course, she believed in the Book. But such small orb weavers and beetles and inchworms—I didn't believe they ever existed.

I bit a hangnail while I considered the worm drifting in the breeze. Blood welled up around my cuticle and I pressed my index finger against it to staunch the bleeding.

"Ostrya?" Mangrove had settled in beside me without my realizing.

I glanced at him and he reddened again, but he didn't look away. His direct gaze was unnerving, and my heart began to beat loudly in my chest. I was sure he must be able to hear it. His brown eyes were soft and concerned. "What's wrong? We're talking about our new jobs. You don't seem excited about yours."

"I don't get to choose, do I?" It came out more bitterly than I'd intended.

Salix stopped midsentence in her diatribe about her

roommate. "What do you mean, Ostrya? We all thought you wanted to be a doctor."

"No, not really."

"Oh? What traineeship do you want?"

"It's not about the traineeship. Or not only. It's about everything. All of it."

"Why do you have to make everything so serious all the time?" Salix fluffed her hair again. "You're too intense. Relax. It won't kill you."

I was sick of being considered weird, especially by her. She'd look at me in a pitying way and shake her head. It was infuriating. And anger made me honest for once. "Don't you ever wonder what else there is? Beyond these trees? Beyond these pathways? Outside of the canopy?"

"Ummm, earthwalkers and cannibals," she said. Sorbus nodded his head in agreement. Even Mangrove seemed puzzled by my question.

"Earthwalkers and cannibals. Really? You believe all that duff they tell us when we're little? Where's the proof?"

Salix stared at me. "You know what happened. Earthwalkers destroyed everything down below and there was nothing left to eat, no plants or animals, so they started eating each other. Our ancestors escaped into the trees. Anyone left alive down there, as unlikely as that would be, eats human flesh. So, what else do you need to know?"

I'd started with this honesty thing and there was no stopping whatever came tumbling out. "What's the point of it all?"

"The point of what?"

"We're caged like those fantastical animals in *The Book of Silvanus*. The elephants and tigers. But we've caged ourselves. We're both the zoo animals and the keepers. I mean, we're born in these trees, we live in these trees, we die in these trees. We're not allowed to climb past Bough Seven. We're not allowed to climb into the Outer Reaches. That's a pretty small area to live a life.

"And then, what do our lives look like? We figure out what job we want to do for the entire rest of our time in the trees, we do it every day until we're too old to do it, and then we fall out of the trees, or get high and jump. Our lives are no different than our parents' lives, their parents' lives, all the way back to the First Climbers. That's all our lives amount to. You want to see your future? Look at your parents."

Sorbus and Mangrove stared at me like I'd consumed the clinic's entire supply of psilocybin mushrooms. "You forgot falling in love and having sex and being partnered and having babies, though," said Salix.

"Oh, yeah. How could I forget? Life is so satisfying that we create more people to come after us and enjoy the same exciting life. Nothing changes for anyone ever."

"You're even more sunshiny than usual this afternoon." Salix rolled her eyes and stood up, signaling the end of the conversation as far as she was concerned. Sorbus stood, shrugged his shoulders, and the twins began making their way back to the legal limits.

Mangrove remained, dangling his feet over the branch. We sat in companionable silence, independently together, watching the inchworm descend on its invisible thread. After a while, he said, "Ostrya? What do you want? What would make you happy? If you could do anything?"

In that moment, it seemed as though the sunlight through the upper branches condensed into one ray and lit my heart with a warm orange glow. I turned my head and considered him, watching me with those needy brown eyes. He didn't look away. He didn't blush. He wasn't thinking of me *that way*. He was simply thinking of me.

I said, "I want to climb down."

Chapter Two

❧

The early morning rays dripped through the needles, waking each successive bough as they passed from the top of the trees to the forest floor. The lighter sleepers woke and roused their more deeply sleeping neighbors with the sounds of their early morning bathing, breakfasts, and waking children.

Every morning a flurry of activity ensued from the top of the canopy and spread down to Bough One. Beside each shanty was a large rain barrel, and people in various stages of undress splashed water on themselves and others. They gobbled food rations, got children ready for the day, and set off for jobs, traineeships, or school. Not a soul in the canopy was idle. From the youngest infant to the most doddering elder, every person had a responsibility to fulfill their duty to the community.

My regular morning routine consisted of squeezing my eyes tight when my mother called to wake me, rolling over in my hammock, groaning, and trying to sleep for another three counts. When my mother's voice rose to alarming, violence-threatening levels, I opened my eyes and blinked about the room, feigning innocence.

I simply could not wake in the early mornings. My mother's voice blended into my dreams, coloring the chase sequences or punctuating a somnolent argument with sleep phantoms. She would tell me after, when I finally awoke, that I'd been carrying on an entire conversation with her. I had shambled from one end of the shanty to the other, bleary-eyed and mentally unfocused, allowing her to guide me with simple commands: Brush teeth! Comb hair! Eat something! Once she was confident I was thoroughly awake and would not slip back into dreamy unconsciousness, she recited a list of my morning rounds, and then left for the clinic. In the beginning of my traineeship, we split home visits to members of the community recovering from injuries or illnesses. As she became more confident in my abilities, she visited patients only on Boughs One and Two, leaving the upper boughs to me. Her knees were beginning to fail and the pain of climbing up and down stairs furrowed her brow and puckered her lips by evening.

One morning several months into my traineeship, Sorbus's voice booming through the shanty awakened us both. "Good morning, sorry to disturb! We need a doctor on Bough Seven. Wingnut did something to his arm—it's hanging there—he can't move it—he's in a ton of pain."

"Ostrya, quickly," yelled my mother. "Sounds like a dislocated shoulder! The longer the arm is out, the more difficult it will be to fix. Up! Now!"

I rolled out of the hammock, caught my big toe in the webbing, and bounce-tripped across the shanty floor toward my clothing balled in the corner. It was a relief to strip off all my clothing at night and swing in my hammock, my skin kissed by the night air. Our shanties only had doorways, no windows. They were hot and close, and sleeping was a sweaty business. I felt the crisscrossing pattern across my back where I'd lain on the hammock netting.

My mother scolded Sorbus, still hovering in the doorway, "Turn your head, young man. Nothing to see here!" He obediently turned his back to us. I smiled to myself. Like most of the adults, she didn't realize that Sorbus was about as interested in me as he was in Salix's roommate, which was not at all.

I squelched into my squirrel leather climbing shorts and bandeau, and then threw on a cedar fiber shirt, and then pulled my rat's nest of hair out of my face, dug the sleep from my eyes, and scrubbed my teeth with my dogwood brush.

While I dressed, my mother drilled me. "Now, you remember how I showed you last time? Talk to me. What are the steps?"

"Bend the elbow ninety degrees. Grip the elbow, apply traction," I said.

"Good. Next?"

"Hand to forearm, externally rotate the elbow. Maintain traction of the elbow with other hand."

"Yes. Two vital things?"

"Ummm, elbow, forearm, traction—" I couldn't remember what else. "I said ninety degrees, right?"

"Relax and pain. Make sure he's relaxed and stop whenever he feels pain."

"Yeah, duh. Of course, I know that."

"If you don't say it, I don't know you know it. Last? The sound?"

"Popping. The ball of the humerus has to go back into the socket."

"The socket?"

"The glenoid cavity."

"Good! My hope is you won't need to do any scapular manipulation." She chewed her bottom lip. "We haven't gotten to that yet, and you can get up there much quicker than I can."

"Don't worry, Michelia. I've got this." She'd told me never to call her Mom at work. Even though we were in our shanty, this definitely qualified as work.

She squeezed my arm and faintly smiled. "I know you do. No more wasting time." It was probably the humidity that warmed my face.

I grabbed my spider stick—I loved spiders and didn't like killing them, but only someone courting sepsis sets out in the early hours without their spider stick—and then Sorbus and I set off running side by side for the stairway to Bough Seven, swinging our sticks in front of us.

In some earlier age, the adults had designated the upper boughs for unpartnered youth. We were told that in the beginning the entire community lived on the wide branches of the first and second boughs where it was possible to walk four abreast. As the population grew and spread upward, the adults decided the younger climbers would have an easier time among the higher, narrower boughs than the older climbers. Maybe the adults simply preferred having the loud, hormonal youth as far from the general population as possible. For some reason, most young women were assigned shanties on Bough Six and young men were assigned to Bough Seven. Non-binary and gender fluid climbers were interspersed across both boughs.

Unlike the other trainees, I still lived with my mother on Bough Two. It was closer to the clinic on Bough One, so it technically made sense. That was an easy explanation for others.

Sorbus and I were racing up the stairs when someone grabbed my elbow, yanking me to a stop. "Hey! Where you two off to at such a pace? Late from a tryst? Better hope Mangrove doesn't find out you're two-timing him, Ostrya." It was Cedrus, the most sought-after builder-trainer who happened to be both Sorbus's mentor and my sister's annoying partner.

I shook myself free. "Shut up. Me and Mangrove aren't a thing."

He snorted. "That boy definitely has his eye on you!" He nodded at Sorbus. "You ready to take him on? You could certainly hold your own man to man, but Mangrove is a hunter after all, and a great shot to hear Maestro Hamamalis brag about him."

It always amazed me how clueless the adults of this community were. I rolled my eyes at Sorbus. He winked back. "Ostrya's not interested in me."

"Ha! You must learn to read between the lines, my young friend. If men waited for the women, this community would have ceased to exist long ago."

I stared at Cedrus wondering, not for the first time, what my sister saw in him. I knew that he was teasing me, and I hated being teased, especially by him. "You certainly can't be suggesting that men should chase women who aren't interested in them? More specifically, that Sorbus should chase me? Because that would make you sound like a grubby earthwalker. And you remember what happened to them."

Cedrus laughed gleefully. "Oh no! Little sister's getting mad!"

"Cedrus, let me explain this in simple terms you can understand. You and me, we're not family. Cassia and I are sisters only because we share the same loser dad. She spent more time with him than I ever did, poor thing. Might explain her terrible taste in men."

"Ouch!" said Cedrus. "That was harsh."

Sorbus didn't meet my eyes. He knew how I despised my father. "That was mean, Ostrya."

He was right. Cedrus was annoying and forever antagonizing me—he claimed to do it out of affection for Cassia's little sister—but he was no Yew. Yew, who'd broken one of the commandments by fathering three children, who'd walked out on Cassia's mother before walking out on mine, who regularly swindled both buyers and sellers at the market, who abused whatever mind-numbing agents he could find, who loathed me nearly as much as I loathed him.

I should take back my words, I knew I should, but I couldn't apologize, not to Cedrus. I wasn't a child to be teased. Better that he thought me heartless, cold like my mother. No one dared tease Michelia.

I sniffed, glared at Cedrus. "We done here? Cuz, if you don't mind, I have an urgent case waiting for me." Cedrus stepped aside.

I took the stairs two at a time, feeling my thighs scream with the strain. I closed off my mind to pain, either feeling it or causing it, and I didn't slow my pace until I'd rounded the fir on Bough Seven. Sorbus scrambled up the stairs behind me and took the lead. I followed him across the main bough, brushing past a cluster of drowsy men and leaving a chorus of angry voices behind us. Our feet pounded across a bridge, our pace causing it to swing wickedly. I was having difficulty keeping up with Sorbus; his thick legs sped on and on. I hadn't realized before how fast he was. My lungs screamed in my chest and then, all at once, we arrived. Wingnut leaned against the side of his shanty, rocking back and forth, cradling his immobile arm.

I'd known him forever; he was as familiar to me as my own hands. And yet, his physical beauty astonished me each time I looked at him after not seeing him for a while. His broad chest rose and fell with each shuddering breath, and the sweat glistening on his golden skin accentuated his muscular abdomen and biceps. His sculpted face, set off by clear blue eyes, was drawn and pale with pain, and I set to work, trying to ignore the curious onlookers by mentally reciting the steps Michelia and I had reviewed. I squeezed my eyes shut, took a deep breath, opened them, and then he whimpered, ground his teeth, and it was done. I adjusted a sling around his shoulder.

"Well? Better?"

His breathing was shaky. "The horrible pain is gone. It's still sore though."

"Yeah. It will be tender while it heals. The sling will keep your arm in place. Let the shoulder heal. Come to the clinic later, let Michelia check it out."

"Sure. I'll do that." He reached his healthy arm out toward Sorbus, grasped his hand. "Thanks, man. Thanks for getting Ostrya."

Sorbus's eyes flickered away. He looked at his feet, pulled his hand away. "No problem. You'd have done the same." He cleared his throat, met my eyes, and smiled weakly. "I'd better hurry to get to work. Cedrus will be waiting." He turned, squared his shoulders, looked at the few young men who lingered. "Come on, guys. Excitement's over."

Before I could follow them, Wingnut touched my arm. "Come in for a sec. I've got something for you."

"Uh, yeah. Sure." The truth was, I was in no hurry to get to the clinic today. I hadn't seen much of Wingnut since I'd started my traineeship, and I enjoyed his company. It wasn't his physical appeal, though there was that certainly, but something else, something deeper, truer. I could be myself with him. He understood me somehow, like we shared a secret.

I was certain he would never make a move on me. Nor did I want him to.

His shanty stank like body odor and stale weed smoke. His shanty mate, a scrawny, sunken-chested boy, snored loudly from his hammock in the corner.

"How did he sleep through all the excitement?" I asked.

Wingnut pointed at the floor beneath the hammock. I squinted in the dim light. "That looks like ..."

"Yup. The most glorious bud you've ever seen. He's a gardener too, been at it longer than me. Scored that yesterday. Smoked a good bit of it. He's dead to the world this morning."

"Is that allowed?"

He snorted. "Allowed? Technically, no. But gardening hurts a body, and sometimes you have to self-medicate. And what Maestro Ham doesn't know won't hurt him. You know, gardeners share with their friends. Go ahead, take some. He won't notice and it's the least I can do to thank you."

I shook my head. "No thanks. I appreciate the offer and all, but I've seen what it can do to people who don't need it."

"Yew."

"Among others."

"Feel like sitting down?" He bent to pick up a wood stump.

"Don't you dare. Not with that shoulder. I'll get it." I pushed two stumps, remnants of old apple trees the gardeners had removed several seasons ago, around the table and sat on one of them. He sat down across from me.

"How've you been?"

I shrugged. "You know. Hanging with Michelia." I rolled my eyes.

He chuckled. "Come on. You make her out to be some ogre. Honestly, you're lucky to have her."

My own words slapped me in the face. He'd lost his mother when he was young. Spiders.

Orb weaver bites were bad enough; that's why early risers and late evening workers never walked the pathways without their spider sticks. Orb weaver bites were probably the most common ailment among the climbers. The webs were easy to miss in the dim light of the lower boughs and especially plentiful across the pathways. The hand-sized orb weavers strung their webs from limb to limb in the dark hours and feasted upon the flies, mosquitoes, and moths while we slept. They performed a valuable service: Without them, both our crops and our skin would have been devoured by the flying beasties. But the bites of the orb weavers itched and swelled. The spiders weren't poisonous, but they were large and their bites likewise. Without appropriate treatment, the wounds could quickly go from abrasions to infections, or even become septic, and lead to ugly skin scarring or amputation. Few climbers made it to an advanced age without one or two spider scars. Scarred faces and missing fingers were a common sight in the canopy.

Wingnut's mother hadn't been so lucky as to meet with an orb weaver. She had met her end by jumping spider. The average climber was less likely to encounter a jumping spider than an orb weaver because the jumpers were usually off, chasing prey. They were smaller than orb weavers but harder to avoid. Spider sticks were virtually useless against them. By the time you saw one flying toward you, it was already too late to swing.

But the Great Ones help you if you ever stumble upon a sleeping cluster of jumping spiders—they often hibernate in groups of twenty or thirty. I'd only heard about it: the ambush, spiders pouncing one after the other, the stinging bite of one hairy, striped predator after another. Thirty jumpers: That's how many they estimated attacked Wingnut's mom. It was an ugly, tragic death, and one that Wingnut had been old enough to remember.

Wingnut's father never re-partnered, and Wingnut became his father's sole reason for living. To say that Wingnut's father was proud of his handsome, strong boy was an understatement. Wingnut was encouraged to be loud and vocal, adventurous and daring, to show no emotion but happiness.

Wingnut had confided to me that he was choosing an agricultural traineeship in the hope it would provide him the solitude he'd always craved, the ability to be alone with his thoughts.

If only. I wondered how that would feel.

"How's life as a gardener? Is it everything you hoped for?"

"Well, there's the free weed." He grinned.

"Yeah, that is something. But that's not all, right?"

It took him a moment to answer. "I'm quickly realizing it's not as quiet as I thought. Who knew gardeners were such party people?"

"Probably has something to do with the perks."

"Yeah."

"Maybe hunting? You'd get to spend time alone then."

He stuck out his tongue and crossed his eyes at me. "Yeah. That's not going to work."

Wingnut could never take the life of another creature. We all knew he was a vegetarian. I suspected he took the greatest care not to harm even an earthworm. Despite what had happened to his mother, he said once that he never went out with a spider stick. He couldn't bring himself to injure them, and as someone who was drawn to spiders, I admired that about him.

"So, what happened? How'd you pop out the arm?"

"I'm not entirely sure. I got up this morning and did my normal workout."

"Which is?"

"Arm strengthening. Chin-ups. I love the pull in my biceps, the stretch in my hips. I heat up the muscles pretty good before I really get going. It's a great core workout too. After that, I run."

"How many? Chin-ups, I mean?"

"My goal for this week was one hundred a day."

"That seems like a lot."

"I don't know. I can do ninety no problem. I figured, what's another ten? I was sore today though; Maestro Ham worked us hard yesterday hoeing and hauling. We harvested apples and prepared the planting area for the next rotation."

Gardening in the canopy was not for the weak. New areas had to be prepared all the time with composted earth hauled from limb to limb with ropes and pulleys. Low-hanging branches and twigs were always being cleared, the detritus saved for the builders, clothing makers, or cooks, and hauled by the gardeners to construction sites, the tailor workshops, or to communal cooking areas.

When Wingnut had signed on for this traineeship, he'd probably dreamed of quiet days spent alone with birds, insects, and plants for company. I'd thought of gardening for that reason myself when I still believed I had a choice. I imagined the sun on my face, the smell of fruit and flowers in my nostrils, the soil under my fingernails.

"So, gardening?" I asked.

He scratched his neck beard. "Turns out, it's less about growing things and watching the birds than about reorganizing nature. Weeding and pruning. So much weeding and pruning." He nodded toward his snoring shanty mate. "And far too many of his type."

"Yeah, shouldn't he be at work?"

"Not my problem."

I knew how he felt. So many loud-mouthed types in this canopy. My job had me dealing with far too many of them. And my sister had gone ahead and married one. "So, what went wrong this morning? How'd you hurt your shoulder?"

"I don't know. I was sweating heavily. My left hand

slipped from the limb and I was dangling from my right hand, which shouldn't have been a problem."

"But it was."

"Apparently."

"Well." I slapped my thighs and stood. "I should be getting on. Visit Michelia today. She'll probably write you a medical excuse from work. You won't be able to do any heavy tasks until that shoulder heals."

"We'll see what Maestro Ham says about that."

A loud snort from the corner startled us. Wingnut waggled his eyebrows and I laughed. He was one of my favorite people. Too bad we had no interest in each other. I turned and left the shanty.

A familiar voice called out, "Does mommy know you're spending time on Bough Seven? What would the doctor say if she knew you were alone in a boy's shanty?" Salix stood sentry outside Wingnut's shanty, arms crossed.

My face burned. I knew too well that this would be fuel for Salix's gossip machine. The last thing I needed right now. I stammered, "I … I was checking … it was nothing …"

Salix narrowed her eyes and crossed her arms. "One lover isn't enough for you? Only take what you need, Ostrya."

I hid my face behind a wall of hair and rushed down the stairway. I knew the lie that I'd slept with the Wingnut would spread like fire throughout the canopy. Salix would see to that.

Chapter Three

"In the beginning, humankind roamed the earth. The earthwalkers ate of the plants that sprouted from the soil and consumed of the flesh that roamed alongside them. They drank of the rain that settled in the ponds and the lakes. They built their dwellings of the clay and the rocks and the trees which the earth provided and warmed themselves of the fuels dug from the earth and gathered from the plants. They covered their fragile bodies with the leather cut from animal hide, coats woven from animal fur, and delicate coverings made of plant fiber."

Cassia's voice was mesmerizing, her presence commanding and calm. She held the attention of the children in the palm of her hand.

I slouched in the doorway of the school shanty as unobtrusively as I could. A few of the little kids saw me. The red-headed girl, Zelkova, smiled and waved. I smiled back, and then motioned toward my sister with my head. Cassia would be unhappy with me if I distracted her students. Erica, the cute brown girl and Cassia's not-so-secret favorite, listened attentively to her teacher, despite having heard this story countless times. We all had. Even so, Cassia continued the pretense of reading the history of the climbers from *The Book of Silvanus*. She must know the words by heart. I sure did.

"The earthwalkers lived in communion with the earth, taking from her only that which they needed and returning their bodies to her when their time was done. They woke when the sun rose above the trees and slept when it sank away again. The earthwalkers planted and gathered and slept in concert with the seasons. And, for a time, life was in balance.

"The earth provided for human needs, and the earthwalkers flourished. They multiplied and ruled over the plants and the animals and built great wonders upon the earth. The earthwalkers realized prosperity and discovered ambition. They wanted more."

Her voice emphasized the word "more," and she lifted her eyes from the book. Cassia looked at each child in turn before turning the page and continuing with the lesson.

"They summoned their great thinkers, their philosophers and engineers and learned to bend the earth to their will. They grew only the tastiest vegetables and the tenderest meats, stealing the soil and water from those plants and animals they deemed undesirable, whose flavors were unpleasant, habits unsuitable, or appearances unseemly. They built ever larger dwellings, burned more fuels, and turned day into night and night into day.

"And as the earthwalkers dominated the earth, flora and fauna vanished. Human activities heated the air, clouded the skies, and dried the ponds and the lakes. Yet earthwalker cities continued to grow, and earthwalkers continued to take. They began to know hunger, thirst, and more homelessness.

"The earthwalkers summoned their great leaders and made war upon each other. The strong absorbed the soil and water, inhabited the dwellings, and burned the fuels of the weak. And still, the earthwalkers multiplied and devoured the remaining plants and animals. They enslaved the earth."

Cassia's voice became more strident, her reading pace quickened. She spit out the words, her anger and resentment palpable.

"The earth began to resist. Her floors rumbled and split, her skies burned and wept. She whipped humankind with hot winds, drowned them with her polluted seas. And the earthwalkers summoned their leaders, engineers, and architects to battle, to conquer the earth. Earthwalkers ate and drank and burned and warred, yet the earth was resolute. She would reclaim her authority. She would shake off the grasping, greedy fingers of the earthwalkers. She would protect the denizens of her forests and oceans, her avian, arboreal, terrestrial, and seagoing creatures.

"The earth went to war with the earthwalkers. She raised up her forests and recruited her animals. She drowned and burned and starved those who would kill her. Those she did not destroy ended themselves."

Cassia slowly closed the book and reverently stroked the leather cover with a gentle hand. She raised her eyes to the children once more, her voice gentle yet strong.

"We climbers alone survive. We climbers who have forsaken the old ways. We climbers who dwell within the protection of the Great Ones."

My sister was everything I was not. Soft, feminine, beautiful. She was short and full-figured, her smooth mahogany skin shining with health. Our father's Y chromosome had done little to lighten her complexion. She was one hundred percent woman, unlike me who danced an androgynous line between child and adult, my height the only physical characteristic setting me apart from the little kids in her school. My tiny acorn chest was ridiculous; Cassia had always owned the curves, more pronounced now that she was pregnant.

"You always tell us the same story, Cassia." Zelkova's voice was slightly muffled by the finger buried in her nose.

I could have hugged that filthy little stinker. Kids are great that way: honest, direct, unafraid. I don't know when we start to lose self-confidence. Growing up sucks. She dug deeper, and then pulled out her finger and inspected the sticky black substance she'd unearthed.

"Don't pick your nose, Zelkova." The command was uttered with the bored sigh of an adult who reprimanded a child for the same offense day after day with no improvement. "And why do you think that is? Can someone tell us? Why do I tell you all the same story over and over again?"

"It's the only one you know!" yelled a wiggling boy whose light skin and corkscrew hair were difficult to see beneath the grime.

The other children laughed and I cracked a smile.

Cassia saw my expression and scowled at me, turning her attention back to the class. "Very funny, Tung. How about you, Erica? What do you think? Is it the only story I know?"

She smiled encouragingly at the shy little girl, bright yet bashful. Her mother, one of Wollemia's weavers, created beautiful garments for her daughter. Cassia had told me she would dress her own daughter just this way if the baby turned out to be a girl. Erica raised her eyes to meet Cassia's, and then looked down again quickly.

"Erica, why do I tell this story?" coaxed Cassia.

"So we know where humans came from," whispered the girl, so softly it could have been a light breeze rustling the cedar branches.

"Yes, and what else?"

"So we don't make the same mistakes the earthwalkers did."

"Yes! Exactly! I will keep telling this story and reading to you from Pseudotsuga's words until you all know *The Book of*

Silvanus by heart. One day, you will be adults—maybe even the teacher—"

"Noooo—" groaned Tung, sending the other children into giggles again.

"—and you will tell the story to your children or students," said Cassia. "Now, Tung, since you are so tired of hearing me talk, how about you tell us the commandments?"

Eager to have the eyes of the classroom on him, Tung scrambled to his feet and recited, "Number one, take only what you need. Number two, produce only to replace. And number three—" A glimmer of mischief flickered in his blue eyes. "All spirits are equal, except for girls."

Discord erupted as the girls booed and the boys hooted and slapped a dancing Tung on the back.

"Okay! Okay! Enough. Children. Settle down," said Cassia. "Of course we all know that the third commandment is 'All spirits are equal.' And that applies to all children, Tung. But it also applies to squirrels and huckleberries, and parents, and crows and blue jays. We all are spirits, and we all deserve respect and fair treatment."

From the corner of my eye, I saw a movement off to the left. Cedrus was descending from the upper boughs. He swung down to a wide branch, his lean muscles rippling, and smiled at me, all white teeth and amber eyes. I was still mad at him from the morning, so I turned my back on him. He stuck his head over my shoulder and grinned at Cassia. Her dark cheeks took on a purplish glow. She was blushing ridiculously like a stupid teen, even though she was almost a mother! She smiled at him and said to her students, "That's enough for today. Now all together, let's have our closing prayer and you can go home for lunch."

The children stood and sang together, "The Great Ones shelter and clothe and feed us. Protect us while we live, oh Great Ones, and when we die, we will feed you." I stepped lightly out of the doorway. Cedrus moved stupidly into the space I'd vacated and was nearly knocked over as the young ones barreled out of the classroom.

Cassia called at their backs, "No running or shoving. Single file. Take care going home!" I snickered at Cedrus as he tried to regain a tough, masculine swagger. He and Cassia were absurd when they were together.

"Little monsters." Cedrus opened his arms. Cassia smiled and buried herself against his chest. What was she doing now? Inhaling him? Gross. What must he smell like? Sweat mixed with pine resin and a hint of hickory? She peered up into his face. He leaned down and pressed his lips to hers. Clearly, they'd forgotten I was standing there. Or they remembered and simply didn't care.

"How's our little swimmer?" His lips grazed her head.

"She's been busy all day. Kicking from one end of my womb to the other. Ow! There she goes again."

Cassia let go of Cedrus and rubbed the sides of her bump with both hands.

Cedrus reached out a tentative hand. "May I?"

"Here." Cassia took his strong hand in hers. "There, feel her?"

His eyes widened. He looked at her and barked a laugh. "Wow! He's really something!"

"She."

"We'll see about that." He squeezed her tightly to him.

"Careful." Her protest was dampened by a hard kiss.

I cleared my throat. They were getting carried away, and the last thing I needed to witness was my sister and her idiot partner canoodling. They'd done that already, which was the reason I was here. I was supposed to be checking on Cassia's progress.

Cassia pushed Cedrus gently away and began organizing her classroom. He helped her roll up the children's woven bark mats and pile them in the corner of the lean-to. She picked up the broom to sweep.

"Dammit. This broom needs to be retied. The cedar fronds are all dried out."

"Let me do it." Cedrus took the broom from her hands.

She settled herself on the pile of mats and watched him pull the dried needles from the broom before unwinding and retying the rope around its neck. His large fingers were nimble, probably from twining rope for hanging bridges. I took the opportunity to examine her. "How've you been feeling this week?" I asked.

"A bit tired and annoyed. I'm constantly hungry, but I can't fit anything into my stomach. And I have to pee constantly." She turned to Cedrus. "Were you at the south side again this morning?"

"Yup. Maestro Drypetes is desperate to find a crossing. The distance is farther than we've ever built, and I'm not sure if our materials are up to the challenge."

I pulled a pressure cuff and stethoscope from my satchel. I wrapped the cuff around Cassia's upper arm, pumped it, and then set the earpieces into my ears and listened closely. Her pulse was a bit quick; I blamed Cedrus's presence for that. I placed the stethoscope on Cassia's abdomen, moving it first to one side of her bump and then to the other. Two heartbeats? How had Michelia missed this? Or had she merely neglected to tell me?

"Ummm, Cassia? Something is weird," I said.

"And there's only one way across?" Cassia ignored me. She was usually attentive and caring, not such a bad sister, until Cedrus showed up. It was as if no one else existed for her when he was around.

"Only one way across the low branches. Plenty of overlap in the upper branches, but Maestro Drypetes wants the crossing open to the whole community, not only the young ones."

Cassia nodded. "That makes sense."

"Cassia, I found something interesting." I moved the stethoscope around her abdomen again. Had it really been two heartbeats?

"Yeah, which makes it even more important that I figure this out, and soon. Maestro Hamamalis wants his crews to create a new skygarden."

"Wow. I did *not* see this one coming," I said, louder.

"Oh?" Cassia was responding to Cedrus's construction news. She seemed to have forgotten about me, though my stethoscope was probing her midsection.

"Yeah, that's why we're looking for a crossing. Since the last storm a lot of the overhang was cleared out. There's good sunlight on the south side."

Having finished retying the broom, Cedrus made a few practice sweeps across the floor planks. Cedar needles spilled from the broom, and he cursed.

"I'll take this with me. The brush is shot. I'll get one of the trainees to fix it."

"This is *very* surprising. But then, perhaps you knew and simply didn't tell me," I announced.

That got her attention, sort of. She looked at me briefly but then turned back to Cedrus. "Why does he want to plant over there? Is there a food shortage?"

Cedrus shrugged. "Don't think so. I haven't heard anything. Would be good to have multiple garden areas though, not just the west end, right? I mean, spread out our gardens. If anything ever happened, an infestation or crop blight—"

"You know what *The Book of Silvanus* says about food and population," said Cassia.

I pulled the stethoscope from my ears and glared at

Cassia. "Don't you even care about your examination? About what I heard?"

She stared at me as though my presence were a surprise. "Just a minute, Ostrya. This is important." And then she was back to Cedrus. "What if there's a cull?"

Cedrus dropped the broom and pulled Cassia to him.

I'd had enough. If she didn't care that I'd heard dual fetal heartbeats, why should I? I packed my tools back into my satchel and said to Cedrus, "Can you make sure she gets to Michelia tomorrow morning?"

It was like I was both invisible and inaudible. He was positively crooning over her, kissing her head and inhaling her hair. "Stop it. You're overreacting. You're the teacher. You know that's a child's story, nothing more. Maestro Drypetes and Maestro Hamamalis are only preparing for the future."

"But we're bringing another mouth into the community," said Cassia.

"Two," I said.

"Two what?" asked Cedrus.

"Oh, so you can hear me? You can see me? Thought I was invisible or something," I said.

"Two what?" he demanded.

"Mouths. To feed. You're having twins. Go see Michelia."

I spun on my heel and left the school.

Michelia would have been appalled at my lack of professionalism. But every medical assistant has her limit and I'd reached mine.

And if I'm honest, it felt good.

Chapter Four

It was shortly after lunch time, and Bough One bustled with activity. Old folks gathered in the carved recesses of the smaller trees. Young parents, babies strapped to their backs, were already traipsing toward the market to trade for the evening meal. I slouched along the thick branch, its surface smoothed from ten generations of gripping human feet. No danger of splinters on this level. The soles of young feet like those of Cassia's charges had plenty of time to toughen before they were allowed in the higher levels.

"Leave her alone, you nasty little crows, or I'll tell your mothers!" scolded maestro tailor Wollemia where she sat gossiping with her life partner Thevetia.

Erica wiped tears from her eyes and rushed past me. Tung stood giggling, his tree-sap sticky ringlets standing straight up from his scalp. Zelkova jeered and laughed at the fleeing girl. Erica had better toughen up quickly, I thought. There was no getting away from the ghouls in this canopy. It was either grow a thick skin or become like me and Wingnut, always needing to be alone.

As I walked to the clinic, I worked my fingers through my

tousled brown hair, flinching as I tugged at the knots. Thevetia pushed herself to a standing position. Her rounded shoulders and dowager's hump were a testament to the unforgiving work of the gardens. Michelia had told me Thevetia had once stood eye-to-eye with the tallest of the men. She'd climbed trees and hewed bark and hauled branches, dirt, and plant material with the strongest of them. To look at her now, gray and bowed and fragile, was to look at my future. And that of Wingnut, Sorbus, Salix, Mangrove. There had to be more. I needed to believe that.

She hobbled over to me. I could practically hear her bones creaking. "Sweetie, I wanted to tell you … that magic potion you made for my knees isn't working."

"It's not a magic potion, Thevetia. It's a poultice, and you just started using it. It takes a few days to work."

"The pain, sweetie. You don't know how it hurts. Especially in the mornings when I first wake."

"I understand, Thevetia. But you have to give it some time to help you feel better."

"How much time? I really can't take this pain. I'm so stiff."

"Remember what I told you? Yesterday? It may take up to two weeks for you to feel the full effects. But it will start feeling better in maybe five days."

"Two weeks?"

"For full effect, yes."

"Are you sure you made it right? Are you sure you have the right recipe? Maybe you cooked the potion too long—"

"No. It is the right recipe. It's Michelia's recipe. And it's not a potion. It's the same poultice Maestro Wollemia uses on her knuckles and Maestro Drypetes uses on his back. Michelia even uses it." I appealed to her partner who was watching all this with an amused expression. "Tell her, Maestro Wollemia. It works, right?"

"Sure. After a fashion," said the maestro tailor, Salix's boss.

"Hmmm." Thevetia considered this. "Well, I simply don't understand why my knees still hurt."

"You've only just started using it. If you don't feel better in two weeks, come tell us at the clinic."

"Two weeks? Why so long?"

I took a deep breath and silently counted to ten while braiding my hair. I'd forgotten to bring a tie, so I coiled the braid tightly to the back of my head and scrunched the end into the hollow near my scalp. That should be neat enough to suit Michelia. The last thing I needed was another lecture about hygiene.

"Thevetia. Two weeks. Then come see us."

She blinked at me vacantly.

"Hi, sweetie. I wanted to tell you something ..." She sighed. "Oh, now I can't remember what it was. My memory, you know. Not what it once was. Oh! Now I remember. Wollemia told me about some magic potion that makes her aches go away. Could I get some?"

I smiled brightly. "Sure! It will take about two weeks for us to brew the potion and chant the incantations. Why don't you come see us then?"

"Yes, I can do that. Two weeks. Thank you, sweetie."

I turned and walked briskly toward the bridge that connected the central tree with the clinic tree, but not before seeing Maestro Wollemia cover her smile with an arthritic hand.

Great Ones, take me before my mind goes.

Chapter Five

Without raising her eyes from the scales upon which she was measuring herbs, Michelia said, "About time you found your way to work. You know, if you don't take yourself seriously, no one else will either. The community depends on us to keep it healthy and to have the answers when members are sick or injured. If they see you shirking your responsibilities and behaving like a juvenile delinquent, they aren't likely to take your healthcare guidance."

I just got here. Geesh. Can you leave the lecture for five seconds? That's what I thought of saying, but all that came out of my mouth was: "Yup, sorry." The arguments ended faster if I simply agreed. I shut the door behind me. The clinic and the council office were the only two shanties in the canopy that had doors. In the case of the clinic, it made sense. We locked up the various medicines and tinctures every night to keep them safe from nocturnal visitors, both four- and two-legged. You only needed to look at my father—or a raccoon, not much difference there—to understand that reasoning. I didn't know why the council office was locked. I could have asked my grandmother Butia, but at that point in my life, I didn't care.

"Really? Is that all you have to say for yourself? Sorry? Sorry doesn't cut it when you give a patient the wrong medicine. Sorry doesn't mean a thing when you pull the wrong tooth or forget the anesthetic when you're stitching a laceration. Where were you until—what time is it? The sun is heading into the west. We're well into the afternoon. And me here, alone, taking patients and mixing medicines. How long were you up on Bough Seven? You know I don't like you spending time up there. You should have fixed that shoulder and come right back down here."

Michelia was exaggerating, again. It was shortly after lunch, not well into the afternoon. Which reminded me that I hadn't eaten—so I grabbed a piece of my mother's mainstay, dry-as-dirt nutloaf. Besides, I'd fixed Wingnut's shoulder, examined Cassia, and counseled Thevetia. If I'd had a bit of a nap in between all those visits, so what? I wasn't sleeping so great at night and with this new schedule, I had to wake up way too early. I knew fighting with her wouldn't work, but I'd been studying under my mom's tutelage long enough to know how to guilt someone.

"You want to know who I was with?"

She stopped what she was doing and mirrored me. I hated when she did that. It made me feel ridiculous. She was all defiant, sticking out her chin, one hand resting on her jutted-out hip. Is that what I looked like to her? "Yes, I would really like to know."

Self-conscious now, I adjusted my stance, dropping my hand and relaxing my hip. I pulled my chin back in and tried to relax my face. She did the same.

Though my mother was nearly fifty years old, only the furrows on her brow and the light dusting of gray through her short brown hair hinted at her age. A full head shorter than me, she stared back at me, strength emanating from her eyes, one blue and one green. Same as mine—allegedly every doctor in our line going all the way back had inherited Pseudotsuga's heterochromia. Unafraid of conflict, my mother had no favorites when it came to chastising patients. She scolded everyone for their bad choices, regardless of age or rank. A grown man was as likely to get a tongue lashing about his poor hygiene as a five-year old boy. A wise maestro and a green trainee were equal in her eyes.

Yet, despite her uncompromising ways or perhaps because of them, my mother was if not beloved certainly respected throughout the community. She was the picture of help and care. Hers was the first pot of soup to reach a sick family, her touch on the feverish forehead cool and comforting, her control of the blade exact. Observing the effect of stress on young parents—the constant vigilance required to keep their children safe in the trees took its toll—it had been her idea to start up a community school. She had pushed for the construction of an elder shelter on the lower bough by gathering support among her patients and their families. It had been completed three months ago, and elders like Thevetia and Wollemia were relinquishing the upper boughs to the sinewy youths, improving their quality of life, and it was to be hoped, their longevity.

"I fixed Wingnut's arm," I said. "I told him to come down and see you."

She nodded her head. "He was here an hour ago."

"Oh, okay. How did I do with the shoulder?"

"Great actually. I tightened up the sling for him. A little more practice and I think you'd have it. What else?"

I couldn't exactly tell her I'd gone back to our shanty and taken a nap, so I lied. "I checked in with a few of the new mothers, made sure their babies were gaining weight." To make my story more plausible, I added, "The stinging nettle hasn't increased Acacia's milk supply. We may need to consider blessed thistle."

She nodded. Great, I'd sold that one. How much time would that have taken? Did I need to invent another home visit? If I invented too many, she'd see through my charade. It would have been unlikely for me to climb back up the stairway again after descending from Bough Seven all the way to Bough One. I'd better stop while things were still believable.

"Then, I stopped in to visit Cassia. Cedrus will be bringing her to see you tomorrow. And, I would have been here sooner, but I was waylaid by Thevetia, who doesn't remember her visit here yesterday. So, I've been busy."

Michelia turned back to the scale and continued measuring herbs. Sighing, I bit into the nutloaf and chewed. And chewed. And chewed. It was dry and bland, but the fat and protein of the ground hazelnuts stopped my hunger pains. I moved to the opposite side of the table and began tying bark strips into packets. I figured I wouldn't receive an apology, but I knew the conflict was over.

"Are you sure about Acacia? Our blessed thistle is running low, and it will be at least four months before we can harvest more."

I hedged. "She can probably wait another day. I'll check her again tomorrow."

"Okay. But if her milk doesn't come in with greater quantity, the infant will need to nurse with another mother. We can't put future babies at risk, not with four more deliveries expected this month. How is Cassia progressing?"

"Why didn't you tell me she was expecting twins?"

The scale clattered as Michelia swung around and stared at me. "What?"

"You didn't know? I heard something odd this morning. Two heartbeats."

"How could I have missed that? Impossible. Are you sure?"

"I listened multiple times. The beats are on opposite ends of the uterus."

"Twins then. How in the name of Pseudotsuga did I screw that one up? Never, not even when I was in training, have I ever missed a multiple."

"It explains her rapid weight gain, her early fatigue."

"How did I miss it? My concentration hasn't been great. Damn menopause brain." Michelia scratched her head. "This means she'll deliver earlier than we planned."

"Definitely. She's huge."

"Did you tell her she's having twins?"

"Yes. She knows."

Michelia nodded. "Good."

Good? That was debatable. But she wouldn't hear the details from me. "I told her to come in tomorrow and see you."

"Yes. Absolutely. That was the right thing to do."

I blushed, feeling the foreign warmth of praise envelop me. It was short-lived.

"Why didn't you bring Thevetia with you? I should examine her again. Perhaps we need to start her on rosemary supplements or ginkgo for that memory? Here, scoop these piles into the packets. We've had a run on St. John's Wort this week."

"It's this dreary weather. So dark these last few weeks. It depresses everyone."

"Well, the elders and the mothers, at any rate. Bough One has many benefits, but sunlight isn't one of them. After you've packaged the herbs, you may leave. You've had a busy day. Be sure to visit the market on your way home. And stand up straight. Your posture is atrocious."

As I left, I remembered what day it was. The anniversary of Joshua's feeding. That would almost explain why Michelia was picking at me. Almost.

Chapter Six

The west end of Bough Four was my sanctuary. A smelly sanctuary, to be sure, but the odor of the ginkgo fruit guaranteed that the likelihood of meeting anyone else was nil. During harvesttime, workers wrapped squirrel pelts around their noses and breathed through their mouths before approaching the western fourth. No one, not even my mother, especially not my mother, knew of my sanctuary.

Even though it would be many months before the trees dropped their fruit, so essential for enhancing the cognition of our elders and combating other ailments, the air was lightly tinged with a vomit smell. I gagged a little until I adjusted to the stink and then rested my long frame against one of the ginkgo trees that was cradled in the armpit of a Great One.

I tilted my head back and looked through the ginkgo branches to the sparse needles of the Great One and the gray sky beyond. The sky threatened rain. When I was younger, I'd been told stories about the beforetimes, when the sky still rained white and cold for many months, a time called *Winter*.

Winter had been one of the four times grouped into *Seasons*. The main difference among the Seasons was that the temperature changed and the earthwalkers couldn't grow food while Winter reigned. But then the earthwalkers started the war to control earth and earth fought back, and the first things to die were the Seasons. The Seasons fought among themselves. Winter was the weakest, and it was killed first. Spring and Autumn were the next to die. I can't remember the difference between those two Seasons; earthwalkers planted in one and harvested in the other. For a while, it looked like Summer had survived the war between earth and the earthwalkers. It stopped raining. And it was hot, so hot. And then the rains started, and Summer drowned. The war ended with earth victorious, the earthwalkers vanquished. And we, the climbers who lived among the Great Ones, survived.

When I was little, I imagined what white, cold rain might feel like. *Snow*. I loved the droplets on my skin when the rain was coming down hard. The first wave of a downpour was cool and refreshing and I imagined snow would feel like that but last longer. For within seconds of a hard rain, my skin grew used to the temperature and the water felt tepid and clammy, and my clothes were soggy and bloated like the moss on the northside of a limb. *The Book of Silvanus* told how earthwalkers in the north used to live in houses of ice. Some of them even *froze* to death. I'd never understood what freezing meant. Maybe stiff and hard like a day-old squirrel carcass but without the smell. That was difficult to imagine. There were odors everywhere in the canopy, some fragrant like overripe apples and flowering currants, some unpleasant like baby bottoms and corpse flower, most cloying like sweat and feet and raw meat. What would it be like to live in a world with no odor? To feel snow on your face in a frozen Winter world?

I used to sit like Erica in school, listening with wide open ears, eager to learn about the earthwalkers. As I grew older, I began to understand that our holy book, *The Book of Silvanus*, was nothing more than a collection of fairy tales meant to keep us docile and content in the treetops. Because, after years of indoctrination in the so-called "truths" of Silvanus, why would anyone sane choose to leave the canopy for an earth ruled by cannibalistic earthwalkers?

I knew the book was a lie. All of it. I wondered how many of us knew the teachings were untrue but said nothing about it. I was sad that there had never been Seasons though. I really would have liked to have seen white rain.

I embraced the gloom of the gingko grove. It matched my mood. I was exhausted, my reserve of quiet battered down by the faces, the inquiries, the existence of other people. Assistant to the doctor was not a position that lent itself to solitude, and unlike my mother, I had no desire to nurture other souls. I resented the sick and the elderly. I resented the pregnant women and the injured workers. I resented the children with their splinters and the women with their monthly pains and the men with their pulled muscles and smashed fingers. They could all feed the Great Ones, for all I cared.

I'd never wanted this job. Doctor. I didn't want to turn out like my mother, bitter and jaded and responsible for everyone else. I crawled over to the edge of the bough and looked down. There were no boughs beneath the gingko grove. Though the first fruits wouldn't have dropped until long after the First Climbers had fed the Great Ones, they had anticipated the future stench when they planted the trees. They had planned for the generations that came after them. If the fruits weren't harvested, they fell over two-thousand feet down to the forest floor where they exploded and fed the Great Ones with their vomit-stinking flesh.

It was a special kind of planning, of thoughtfulness, to

care about the happiness of people who weren't yet born. The First Climbers imagined us following them after several generations and planted the trees so they wouldn't drop their stinking fruits on our heads. I know where I'd plant gingko trees—on Bough Seven, right above the heads of Salix and her minions on Bough Six. I giggled to myself imagining the ripe gingkoes landing on their gossipy heads. It cheered me up a little.

I leaned over the bough then and imagined the ending of everything. One little slip, that's all it would take. I could share the path of the ginkgo fruit and disappear forever from the responsibility, the gloom, the people, the boredom of this place. I closed my eyes and imagined the fall. The breeze rushing past, my hair flowing behind me, a clear path to the leaf and needle-strewn ground beneath, no branches to break my bones or slice my skin. And then, silence. My end. Sustenance for the Great Ones. In my imaginings, it suddenly felt real. I could hear the whistle of the wind in my ears, the sweat whisking off my brow, and then the soft thump as my body met the earth for the first time. And the last.

Bile rose in my throat when I finally opened my eyes. My death by falling felt all too possible suddenly. I pushed away from the edge, my head buzzing with adrenaline, blood surging from my hands and feet to my racing heart. I curled into a ball beneath the stinking ginkgo and drew in deep breaths of filthy humid air scented with vomit. I knew I was being melodramatic. Mom always told me I was too emotional, too intense. But sometimes it felt good to push myself to the brink, to the very edge of reason, and then, at the last second, pull myself back.

My heart quieted and my head cleared. I stood and walked through the grove, picking my way carefully along the rough pathway. My calloused feet, immune to the rough edges of the rarely walked path, gripped the branches.

When I reached the largest ginkgo at the center of the grove, likely the original planted by the First Climbers, I stopped. I pulled myself up into the gnarled tree's arms and peered into the center. An orb weaver had covered the opening with a large, sticky web. I hadn't brought my spider stick, so I broke off a dead branch from the gingko and poked it into the web to be sure it wasn't currently inhabited.

I imagined getting bitten by the monster who'd woven this web and snorted with dark humor. I could hear Michelia if I needed a hand or foot amputated: "How could you have been so careless? I don't have time to cut off your leg this morning. I have to pack poultices."

Alerted by the movement of its web, a bulbous brown creature dropped by a thick filament of string to the web's center. I jumped back and swung at the spider. The stick connected with a soft thump. The spider tumbled out of the tree hollow and swung wildly from its drop line. I ducked away to avoid touching the creature and swung again. The spider ejected a line of sticky string from its spinnerets and dropped down, far below the branch. Too late, I realized that at nearly two inches in diameter, the spider would have made a tasty snack. Much as I disliked killing this creature I identified so strongly with, Michelia's nut loaf had worn off and my stomach had started complaining.

"Take only what you need. All spirits are equal," I recited, a habit I'd started in childhood whenever I missed a target with my slingshot.

I pulled the web off the tree, pulled the sticky bits from my fingers, and rolled it into a ball. Spider fleece was a treasured commodity. It could be used to bandage and clean wounds, to block night noise in close and cramped quarters, or when wrapped on a twig, to brush teeth or clean ears and noses. In large quantities, spider fleece could even be spun and woven into lacy undergarments, but I had no use for those.

No creatures would have survived the spider, so I plunged my hand into the tree hollow and pulled out the project I had hidden inside. Soon, it would be too large to fit in this hollow, and I'd need to find another place to hide it. Not that anyone would find it here—not until harvest time, at any rate. I plopped down at the base of the tree and unwound the hank of rope I'd been twisting in secret over the past several months.

Only cedar harvesters were permitted to gather cedar for the community. Cedar trees were interspersed among the Great Ones. We traveled and lived among them, as we lived among the Great Ones. Because cedar bark was resistant to rain, it was essential for clothing and housing our community. To prevent over-harvesting the interior cedars, individuals were forbidden to take the bark for their own purposes. Only tailors, builders, and fiber workers had license to use the bark.

I hadn't broken the law—not that law, at least. I had crossed beyond the boundaries of the community, beyond the ginkgo grove, to harvest my own bark. It was forbidden to go to the Outer Reaches; locations beyond the canopy boundaries were deemed unsafe for all but the hunters if the builders had not constructed a path from one tree to the next. Of course, that rule never prevented me or any of my friends from climbing where we wanted. If no adults found out, it was like it never happened.

We hadn't climbed together since our last hangout in the Outer Reaches before we'd begun our traineeships. We were all busy learning our trades. Besides, I didn't want to hear how wonderful Maestro Wollemia was or how talented Cedrus was. Especially not Cedrus—it was bad enough that

Cassia was crazy about him. I certainly didn't want to listen to Sorbus go on about him.

I especially didn't want to hear about Mangrove's wonderful trade. He got to spend his days entirely alone in the canopy with his thoughts for company. That sounded like perfection to me. No, I'd rather commiserate with Wingnut. He was as miserable as I was. Well, nearly. I doubted his soul was as dark as my spider girl soul. If only I could weave iron silk from my butt and drop out of this tree like the orb weaver, I'd escape my destiny of boredom.

As far as I knew, I was the only one who crossed into the cedars from the gingko forest. So much cedar to the west was unharvested—plenty for everyone to have two, three rain cloaks and shingles over all the pathways. But telling anyone about it would have been admitting my crime and worse, revealing my sanctuary.

I ripped a hunk of bark into strips and began braiding. Last year, I'd watched a builder braid cedar bark for a bridge. Pleased by my interest, he taught me that many thin strips twisted together made a rope far stronger than one wide strip alone. I began stockpiling my own secret supply of cedar. By my measurements, I'd braided nearly fifty feet of cedar rope over four months. My nimble fingers could rip and twist quickly. I figured I'd have one hundred feet of rope in four more months, just in time for my birthday that marked seventeen gloriously dull years of living among the Great Ones.

I couldn't think of a reason for my rope habit. I didn't need more rope. I didn't even use what I had for climbing. I'd lost all control over my obsession. I felt a burning need for more feet of rope, more cedar bark to make the rope. I wasn't sleeping well lately because my mind never quieted. I lay awake at night thinking of harvesting cedar; when I was asleep, I dreamed of braiding rope. For some reason, I was happier when I was making rope.

While I braided, time stopped, and that afternoon I became aware of the darkness creeping around me only after my pile of cedar had been exhausted. I wound the three feet of rope I made that afternoon around the hank and tucked it back into the old gingko's hollow. My feet gripped the rough bark pathway and I sprinted toward the market.

Chapter Seven

The fat drops began falling as I ran down the rope stairway that twined around the massive fir at the center of the Great Ones. At Bough Two, I brushed past an unshaven builder rank with the stench of heavy labor, his sweat captured in his woven tunic. He yelled, "Watch it!" then recognized me and bowed his head. "Joshua's feeding day. May the Great Ones protect you."

"Thanks," I mumbled, nodding stiffly, and then continuing down the stairway. I landed on the pathway of Bough One and sped east, running as fast as I dared across the pathway. My hastily tied up hair had come unbound somewhere along Bough Three and, having narrowly avoided colliding with a woman tossing mop water from her shanty, I ran through a damaged sprig of needles that joined with my hair and arrived at the market along with me, five minutes before closing.

The market was a shanty with three walls near the central stairway. A large cedar slab counter displayed the plant harvest of the day and any birds and animals provided by the hunters. Every family in the canopy was given an allotment of food tallied daily by the market keeper. No money exchanged hands because we had no need of money. Every able adult had a responsibility to the canopy and to each other. The canopy continued to function because everyone did their duty.

So proclaimed *The Book of Silvanus*.

But the way the market functioned was that if you had something to trade, something of value to the market keeper, he might forget to log your rations or might offer you items that weren't displayed on the cedar slab. A transaction between you and him, a wink here, a sly look there, something hidden in the dark corners behind the counter, out of sight of the Council of Elders.

Pulling the sticky twigs from my hair, I panted, "What ... have you got ... left?"

"Got some huckleberries. Not the sweet season, but they fill an empty belly," yawned Yew, keeper of the market, sometime thief, substance abuser, and my father. "You're late tonight, Ostrya. Thought I might not see you, Joshua's day and all." He blinked quickly and cleared his throat. "You and your mom busy at the clinic these days?"

Yeah, like he cared about Joshua. "Haven't stopped all day." I wiped the rain off my face and squeezed water from my hair. "Is that really all you've got left?"

"We had some fresh chard earlier. I gave away the last of the broccoli just five minutes ago. Hold on—I may have a bit of miner's lettuce left." He handed me a bundle of limp, weedy-looking greenery. "Throw it in some water, should refresh it. Squirrel meat, you know, this time of year I can't keep it in stock. You let me know, I can maybe set some aside for you. Against the rules, but ... if I could maybe get some of that ... mmm ... you know ...," he coughed into his hand, "magic mushroom?"

Any other parent would have set aside some of the good

food for their family, against the rules or no. But not Yew. We got the leftovers. It wasn't that he was a rule follower. He wasn't. He simply resented my mother that much.

"You know I can't get you psilocybin. Michelia administers that in select psychiatric cases under close supervision."

"Aw, come on. A little something for your old dad. She won't notice—"

I glared at him. "I'm not even allowed to touch it. Don't bother asking." I knew he was winding me up. He'd wheedle and complain, throw on a guilt trip, sprinkle in some anger, and a dash of show-some-respect-I'm-your-father. He was a user and a loser. My using loser.

Yew had gotten Cassia's mother pregnant when they were teens. Realizing he wasn't cut out for fatherhood from almost the moment Cassia was born, he began chasing my mom around the canopy. She initially encouraged his attentions to spite her own mother, councilor and all-around badass Butia. Butia and my grandfather, the previous doctor, had hated him. Mom hadn't liked him much either, but that hadn't stopped her from falling in love with him. My mother was a little older than me at the time—nineteen, I think—and Yew had allegedly been a good-looking, charming, bad boy. Laughable if you saw him now. Occasionally you could catch a glimpse of handsome, well-hidden beneath whiny, grasping, neediness.

Nature took its course, and Yew had two more children with Michelia, the maximum allowed for a partnered couple. One for each of them. Produce to replace; one of the unbreakable commandments. Cassia replaced her mother. My brother and I replaced Yew and Michelia. Yew's interest in us, me and my baby brother Joshua, had lasted longer than with Cassia, probably due to pressure from the power couple, my grandparents. My mom was a babe once upon a time, so she kept his attention for a while. She's almost fifty now, and I see how some of the older guys watch her when they think she doesn't see. She could get another partner easily if she wanted one. I think she's done with men; Yew saw to that. After several years together, our family crashed and burned leaving my mother separated from my father and me responsible for the marketing.

"Do you even know how dangerous mushrooms are? You could feed the Great Ones while you're tripping."

"Okay, okay. I hear you." He leaned in closer and I could smell his unwashed hair and stale breath. "I don't really want the mushrooms, you know. Just a little drop of that apple juice you got locked up at night. Quench my thirst. That's all I need."

"No way! You know that apple juice is alcohol we need for sterilizing instruments and cleaning wounds. It's not for drinking. And you're a diabetic! You can't drink that stuff!"

He scowled at me. "I don't need no lecture from a kid. Pseudotsuga's balls! You're as bad as she is! Take your huckleberries." Our interactions had been like this ever since he left, me the adult and him the spoiled child.

I opened my satchel and dumped the huckleberries inside, beside my blood pressure cuff and stethoscope. "How's that foot?" I asked, more gently. "Giving you pain?"

He grunted in response and carved a notch in the log that he used to keep track of ration allotments. He'd turn a blind eye on trades that would benefit him personally, but where Michelia and I were concerned, he never forgot to record even the smallest item we received from the market.

"You know where I am if you need a debridement." I picked up the wilted miner's lettuce and turned away.

"I didn't charge you for the lettuce."

"You're a real prince."

He snorted. I looked over my shoulder at him. His grin revealed several gaps that used to hold teeth. For a fraction of a second, I saw a glimmer of what he once had been. He chewed on a hangnail, pulled the loosely woven fiber curtain across the open wall of the shanty where he also lived, and the image was gone.

My mother was going to love this. Squished sour huckleberries and wimpy weeds for dinner after laboring how many hours at the clinic? She'd wonder why dinner was so meager, and I was going to have to think up something. Another lie. I was getting good at them, but it made me feel even worse than I already did most days. Maybe I could try a new tactic: silence. Simply not answer the questions? How would that work? Mom would tell me I was being rude, ignoring her. Didn't matter. I could either feel bad for lying or feel bad for keeping my mouth shut. I'd lose no matter what I did.

As I slumped back up the rope stairs toward Bough Two—our shanty was on the eastern side—I heard Mangrove calling my name. I climbed to the landing and watched him crest the stairway. Sparse, scruffy hair dusted his cheeks and chin. He was trying to grow a beard, unsuccessfully. Three small black carcasses dangled from his right hand.

"A great day of hunting, but Yew closed up shop already."

"Oh? You've been hunting all day?" Was it possible that he hadn't heard the rumor about me and Wingnut? Mangrove and I weren't seeing each other, but I'd have to be both blind and stupid not to know how he felt about me. And the rest of the canopy assumed we were together. "Is this the first you've been back in the canopy?"

"Yeah. It was a great day out there. Hey, I only need one bird, two if I share with Salix and Sorbus." He bounced from one foot to the other, nervous, not meeting my eyes. "Joshua's feeding day. May the Great Ones protect you. What are you and the doc having for supper?"

So he hadn't heard yet. But he would by the time he sat down to eat with Salix.

"Um, thanks Mangrove. I've got some huckleberries. Miner's lettuce."

"Well, I got three ravens. You and the doc can have one." He thrust a drooping black bird at me with a shy smile.

"No, thanks. I couldn't. I don't have anything to trade. Unless you want the miner's lettuce."

"No, you keep that. You and the doc need your vitamins. I don't expect anything. Especially not today. One day, maybe, you'll have something that I need." He blushed and stammered, "I mean, like extra food or, um, medicine, or something."

I knew Mom and I could use the protein. I was regretting not having eaten that orb weaver when I had the chance. Coming home nearly empty handed from market would be difficult to explain. I didn't relish the thought of my mother having one more thing to yell at me about. I knew she'd heard the Wingnut rumor by now; I didn't look forward to that conversation either. But if I brought home fowl for dinner with those huckleberries? I might survive this day after all. I didn't feel right taking from Mangrove though. Especially knowing how he felt about me and the lies he would hear from Salix shortly—that would be cold-hearted. I must have something I could trade.

"Sorbus snores, doesn't he?"

"Like two ash trees moaning in a storm wind."

I dug my hand into my satchel until I felt the soft, sticky spider fleece. I pulled it out and gingerly picked a huckleberry from the web. "How about stuffing this in your ears so you can sleep?"

"Whoa! That's a serious hunk of spider-fleece! You've got yourself a deal. Though, really, you could have just taken the bird."

Our fingers brushed as I took the dead raven. I felt heat

rise to my cheeks and I avoided his eyes, pretending to be interested in the carcass.

"It's a big one." Stupid. Stupid! An idiotic thing to say, the sort of comment admirers probably chirruped to Wingnut.

But Mangrove beamed with pleasure. "Yeah, I think that's the biggest of the three. But, I mean, you and your mom should have the biggest one. There are two of you. Three of us will share the other two. That seems fair. Nothing will go to waste." His eyes sought mine. They were warm and kind and searching.

My stomach was fluttering now. I bit the inside of my cheek, trying to draw blood, focusing on the pain, not the red heat in my cheeks or the sick feeling in my gut. I balled up the spider fleece and shoved it jauntily in his ear. "Here's your spider-fleece. Does it work?"

He laughed happily and pulled the fleece from his ear. "Huh? What'd you say? I couldn't hear you with this spider-fleece in my ear!"

"Okay, then. I've gotta get going. Michelia will strip the hide off me if I'm late. Um, listen. Don't believe everything Salix says, you know? She doesn't always get it right."

He snorted. "Tell me something I don't know." His face grew serious. "You know, she only eats with us because she's Sorbus's sister. I, um, don't have a thing for her."

I nodded. "I know. I really have to go, okay?"

"Sure thing. See you, Ostrya."

"Bye, Mangrove.

I walked along Bough Two a few paces. I knew I should have said something, warned him about what he was going to hear, but it was all too stupid. Wingnut and I were friends. Same as me and Mangrove. It wasn't Mangrove's business who I spent time with—he didn't own me.

But I remembered how he'd sat with me the day we all

found out about our traineeships that day in the Outer Reaches. How he'd stayed with me after Salix and Sorbus had left. How he'd really listened to me, really cared, and now I knew I needed to tell him. Or at least prepare him for Salix's vicious gossip. I turned back around. To my surprise and our mutual embarrassment, he was watching me walk away. He flushed bright red and ran up the stairs. This was getting serious.

Chapter Eight

A half section of moon glittered between the upper boughs, lending a pale light on the path. I slouched along the eastward boughs toward home, my wet hair pasted to my face and dripping down my neck. The main thoroughfare, a thick Douglas fir branch, split off into three rope-and-slat bridges. I jogged along the left-most bridge, as the bridge pitched and swayed with each foot strike. I closed my eyes and stretched my arms as I ran. I was a raven, a red-tailed hawk, a bald eagle soaring high above the forest. Admittedly, I was a little old to play this game. I felt foolish after a minute and opened my eyes before I reached the threshold to the adjoining fir. I'd stubbed my toe and skinned my knees on this very crossing more than once.

The first time I tripped over the threshold to the connecting pathway, I broke my pinky toe. I stumbled home, my lower lip quivering, determined not to cry, and I hadn't shed a single tear. My toe had been pointing sideways, bent backwards from the impact. My mother had taken one look at it and tweaked it back to its intended direction. I whimpered from the blinding pain, but I kept from crying by biting my thumb. I only cried afterward when my mother yelled at me, demanding to know why I'd been so stupid as to run with my eyes closed. She'd told me she was too busy for my nonsense.

I could hear her words as clearly now as I had all those years ago: "Ostrya, don't I have enough to do taking care of the entire canopy without having to clean up your messes, too? Stupid, stupid, Ostrya. Get your head out of the clouds and think with the brain you've been given!" And when I began to cry, she had shaken her head disdainfully and turned her back, muttering that I'd better stop blubbering or she'd give me something real to cry about.

I'd been seven years old then and I hadn't cried in front of my mother since. I also learned to mend my own injuries.

Our shanty was three firs east of the central Douglas fir, the Great One that connected all of the other Great Ones and nurtured and protected us.

I passed shanties to the left and right, crude one-room structures of hemlock and fir with cedar roofs. Open doorways faced the branch-sheltered path. We set the doorways off to one side of the structure to guard against the invasive stares of curious eyes. Some climbers draped furs or blankets across the entryways, but most of us didn't. The structures were small and close, home to a minimum of two roommates and a maximum of a family of four. Any breeze passing through the close inner air was welcomed, not barred from entry.

Some homes were fastened to the trunks of trees. In a strong storm wind or during a torrential downpour, these were the sturdiest shelters. For this reason, many shanties encircled every trunk without much distance between them. If your neighbors argued, or snored, or got along *really well*, you heard everything. People who wanted more privacy lived in shanties fastened to platforms that extended off the wide pathway. The construction crews reinforced the platforms with joists beneath the boughs. The platform shanties were quieter, but if the canopy was hit by a storm, they creaked and groaned frighteningly. The third type of home, only permitted on Boughs Three and below, was the hanging shanty. These homes were suspended over the bough pathways from thick ropes that looped around over-hanging branches and encircled the shanty like a net. The ropes were checked by the construction crews every six months and replaced every two years. The hanging shanties required fewer resources to build than the platform shanties, but there were fewer of them because most climbers felt unsafe swinging from the boughs in a fierce wind.

I adored our hanging shanty. I wouldn't live anywhere else. The frequent windstorms that frightened the dwellers of the trunk and limb shanties barely registered with me. I'd lived in this hanging home my entire life and the swaying of the trees soothed me, lulling me to sleep. So long as the rope was sound, our shanty wasn't going anywhere, no matter how hard the wind blew. I wasn't begging my mother to let me move to Bough Six. I didn't want to live on a platform, or worse, crammed against a tree trunk with Salix and her mean friends.

Our shanty was dark when I arrived; no light welcomed me home. Mom hadn't returned from the clinic yet. A late evening for her, then; she'd be tired and grumpy when she arrived. I grabbed hold of the floor swinging over the bough —our shanty was suspended about three feet above the tree limb—and pushed my body up, curling my legs beneath my torso until both feet connected with the floorboards. I ducked my head before standing so I didn't hit my head on the ceil-ing. I hadn't been able to stand up fully in our shanty since I was fifteen. I tipped my head out the doorway and squeezed water from my hair. I wiped the rainwater from my face, arms, and legs so I didn't drip all over our ten-by-ten-foot room.

The interior was dim; the pale moonlight was too weak to give much light through the thick overhead branches and couldn't penetrate the cracks in the walls of our home. I reached into my satchel and wiggled my fingers until they brushed against my flint. Sparking it, I lit the tallow candle on the table in the center of the room, arranged the dead raven and the miner's lettuce on either side of the candle so they'd be the first thing Mom saw when she got home, and then I dumped the huckleberries into a carved wooden bowl and plunked it down on the table.

The candle flickered and spit, illuminating the small room with a warm yellow glow. My toes caressed the floor, the rough-hewn fir limbs warm and soothing to my feet. My big toe bumped against the cedar rope that was wrapped and twisted around the floorboards to hold them together. During a three-day rainstorm, Joshua had invented a game we played on that floor to distract ourselves from the sideways blowing rain. Something with pinecones and intervals between each rope. I couldn't remember the rules now—it had been ages ago—but we'd played it while the storm raged on, our shanty rocking in the updrafts and downdrafts of wind, the sky dark for days.

The candle threw shadows at the walls, cedar planks stacked tightly and secured to the floor with mortise and tenon joinery. No effort had been wasted on crafting windows, but the cracks in the walls beckoned visiting breezes to come in and stay awhile. Cedar roof shingles, fortified by a stuffing of fir needles and pine resin, guarded the interior.

A simple table, three pieces of bowed scrap wood wrapped in subpar rope, faced our uncovered doorway. Built-in warped wooden shelves stretched along the left wall. Two intricately plied and crocheted plant fiber hammocks stretched across each corner of the right wall. Between the two hammocks, a small cedar bark doll and an unlit candle rested on a tiny shelf. I reached for the candle, held it to the taper I'd already lit, and then cupped it with my hands while I stuck it in its own soft dripped wax beside the doll. My satchel slipped from my shoulder and dropped to the floor, and I rolled into my hammock with a deep sigh.

The exact moment my eyelids fell shut, my mother's weary voice called out: "Hello, Ostrya? Give me a hand up, will you?"

My mother had a difficult time getting into our shanty these days, especially after a long day standing around the clinic. The wetter the air, the more her knees bothered her. I swung myself out of the hammock and padded to the doorway. I knelt and grabbed her by her two bent elbows, and then leaned backward and used my body weight to lever her into our hanging shanty. Anyone passing by would have wondered what in the name of Pseudotsuga's balls was up with us, but our method worked.

"Ow." Michelia groaned to her feet. "Damn these rusty knees! I can hear the moisture snapping inside them, trying to get out. I brought some more nettle poultice. Thought I'd give myself a knee massage tonight." Her eyes flickered over the table. She sighed.

"Is this all you were able to get us for dinner?"

"Yeah, that's all Yew had left."

"He didn't clean the bird before you bought it? I'm supposed to pluck a bird before we can eat dinner tonight? That man is as lazy as he is stupid—"

"Well, I didn't exactly get the bird from Yew."

Mom raised an eyebrow. "But you did get the huckleberries from Yew."

"Yeah, that's all he had. And the greens."

Her nose wrinkled. "Those are inedible. He'd already sold out by the time you got there? I let you leave early. What did you do all afternoon?"

I met my mother's stare and lied brazenly. "He was picked clean early. I guess food's a little scarce these days."

"Golly, I'll say. So who'd you get the bird from?"

"I ran into … a friend."

"A friend, huh? Was this a female friend? Or a male friend?" She said this like she didn't really care, but we both knew she did.

"Does it matter? It's food, and we wouldn't have it if my friend hadn't given it to us."

"A man then. I figured. What'd you give him for it?"

"I had some spider fleece."

"Where'd you get that? Did you take it from the clinic? Just because you're my assistant doesn't mean the supplies are free for the taking!"

"Of course I didn't take it! You don't honestly think I'd steal from the clinic, do you?"

"I don't know half of what's going on in your head these days. You're more work now than when you were a baby. I have to watch you more closely now than when you were little, that's for sure."

Evidently, I wasn't the only liar in the family. She'd barely watched me at all when I was little because she'd been working all the time. I knew I shouldn't fight with her—it was Joshua's day—but I was getting triggered. "What is that supposed to mean?"

"You know exactly what it means, my dear." The word *dear* was uttered with sarcasm. "Watch out for those men. They're only after one thing."

So she'd heard about Bough Seven and my visit to Wingnut. Of course. Salix would have raced down and told Maestro Wollemia, first thing. And Wollemia's fiber shanty was only a bridge away from the clinic. Those fiber workers loved a good rumor to fuel long hours at their backstrap looms in the company of the other weavers. And the doctor's assistant, the daughter of that high and mighty family, was allegedly swinging in a hammock with the notorious Wingnut. A juicy story like that had to be shared.

I had two choices. One, I could honor my mother with the truth: I'd skipped out of work briefly to have a conversation in, gasp, Wingnut's shanty. So deeply sorry. It would never happen again. Two, I could emulate my esteemed father and become outraged and insulted, and thus deny any wrongdoing. Even though we'd both know I was lying.

In many ways, I was my father's daughter.

"I can't believe you! What do you think, I'm going to hook up with some random guy for a raven? Do you know how insulting that is?"

"I'm just saying. Last thing we need is another mouth to feed."

"You'd know more about that than I would," I shot back.

"Hey! I was partnered before I had you."

"Barely."

"That's enough! I'm your mother, after all."

"You started it."

"I don't want you to make any mistakes you'll have to live with the rest of your life."

She was starting to back down, but I was only warming up. "So I'm a mistake now, am I?"

"That's not what I said or meant, and you damn well know it!" She glared at me.

I crossed my arms and glared back. "No, you just implied I was prostituting myself to put dinner on the table."

"Ostrya!" Mom closed her eyes and took a deep breath. She opened them again and shook her head. "I know you've got a good head on your shoulders. Just watch out for those men. Since whoever you got the bird from didn't bother to clean it, that will be your job."

"Noooo." I really worked the whine. I didn't mind cleaning fowl, but she didn't need to know that. If she did, she'd find truly odious ways to punish me.

She thrust the dead raven into my hands. I faked a disgusted look, and then grabbed our knife and a cedar basin off the shelf and climbed out of the shanty. Ten feet along the pathway was our family water bucket. The rain had diminished to a fizzling mist; it beaded on my forehead and mixed with the dewy sweat on my face. I crouched down, balanced on my toes, and scooped water from the wooden bucket to the basin.

Beginning at the dead raven's vent, I plucked a handful of feathers, sneezing as one floated up to tickle my nose. I placed the carcass on the branch and stuck the sharp blade into the bird's vent, making a cut all the way to the ribcage. Plunging my fingers into the carcass, I scooped out the bird's entrails, lungs, and heart, and carefully set them to one side.

Next, I sliced into the raven's neck and removed the windpipe and crop. Splashing water from the basin, I washed the fowl. The remaining blood and entrail bits dripped on the branch.

By then my legs were beginning to cramp. I stood and stretched, the gutted bird in my left hand. I plucked feathers with my right, moving methodically from neck to tail. In this climate, moist air was a constant, but the rain slicked my fingers to such a degree that the feathers clung to them and my hands looked more like a bird now than the naked avian carcass. I had trouble pulling all the pinfeathers, so I left a few on. I figured the fire would burn them off.

I streamed water from the basin over my palms and rubbed my hands together. I poured more water on the fronts of my hands, but the water didn't quite remove all the feathers. I wiped the stragglers on my bare calves, then crouched again, placed the naked bird on the branch, and chopped off its wings before the first joint on each side. I cut off the feet, leaving drumsticks. After cutting off the head, I scooped more water from the bucket into the basin and drizzled it over the fowl, and then over my hands and legs.

"Ostrya," called Mom from the doorway of the shanty. "How's it going?"

"Just finished." The butchering had taken time and my emotions had cooled. I barely remembered what we had argued about. But then, we argued about everything, so what did it matter?

"Thanks for doing that. I hate cleaning birds. I'll be out in a second." She disappeared from the doorway for a moment, and then reappeared wearing a rain cape woven from cedar bark. "Help me down." She sat on the edge of the swinging house.

I walked to the doorway, and Mom placed her hand on my shoulder and eased herself to the branch. "I don't trust myself with this rain and these knees. Let me see the bird."

I handed her the plucked and cleaned carcass and watched as she examined it thoroughly, inside and out. Pursing her lips, she opened the flap of the bird's wing stub and pulled three stray feathers. She inspected the other wing stub and found the same.

"That was a fair job. You missed quite a few. Don't forget to check under the wings next time. Now hand me those innards. Wash up the huckleberries and then dry off. We'll eat when I get back." She sighed while looking at the meat in her hand. "Raven needs to cook slowly. Coated in raccoon lard. A couple hours at least. I can't wait that long though, can you?"

I shook my head. I was starving.

"Guess we'll live with it." She turned and headed toward

the common fire where she would cook our dinner. "And throw away that rotting miner's lettuce. I hope Yew didn't charge you for it."

We were getting a late start on dinner and she hurried to cook our meal before the cookfire burned out. Climbers brought their family's protein to the communal fire for cooking. Each cluster of shanties around a Great One lit a cookfire in a large, hollowed out and mud-coated firepit for the evening meal. For both safety and convenience, communal fires were essential in the canopy. The firepits were made from huge, carved out stumps of fruit trees and coated in fresh mud before each firing. They were lit in the most open areas of the lower boughs so the cookfires wouldn't set fire to the cedars and smaller trees of the canopy.

In the beginning, according to *The Book of Silvanus*, there had been no rainfall, and it had been far too dangerous to light fires in the treetops. The First Climbers were like the animals, eating their protein raw and bloody. Yet more proof that *The Book of Silvanus* was a collection of lies—it rained so frequently that we often had trouble starting fires because it was too wet, not too dry. And the Great Ones were largely immune to fire, even though their needles would smolder and smoke.

I scooped a basin of water from the rain bucket and returned to the hanging house, carefully setting the basin on the doorsill before hauling myself up. After placing the basin and the knife on the table, I wriggled out of my wet shirt, shorts, and bandeau. The shorts twisted and tangled on my thighs, and I tugged them off, cursing. Such a gross feeling, wet squirrel leather on wet skin. I draped my clothing over the edge of my hammock. The water dripped and pooled before rolling down the cracks between the planks. The animal hide would stiffen and shrink as it dried. My shorts would be tight, uncomfortable, and itchy. My bandeau would fit for once. And my cedar fiber shirt would dry quickly and feel softer than it had before.

Like all the younger climbers, I owned a minimal amount of clothing. The fiber workers made all our garments by hand, and climbers didn't amass multiple outfits until they were adults and had stopped growing. We made do with leather shorts and fiber tops. Most women added tightly-fitting leather bandeaus for extra support. Ever try to climb trees with your chest banging around? Mine is smaller than most, but I still wouldn't do it. If it was a breezy day or a storm was blowing in, we might wrap ourselves in a fur squirrel blanket.

The older adults covered their bodies with loosely fitting tunics, capes, and boxy pants woven from plant fibers. Hamamalis was the only maestro who still wore the leather shorts; gardening required him to be agile and pants got snagged on limbs. Everyone went barefoot. *The Book of Silvanus* forbade coverings for the feet because material objects prevented our communion with the Great Ones. Besides, shoes would have been far too slippery and dangerous for crossing tree limbs.

I closed my eyes and wrapped my arms around my body, feeling the shanty sway in the wind. My hips had widened since my last birthday, but my breasts were the same hard acorns I'd had since I'd begun my monthly bleeding, nothing at all like Salix's firm round breasts or Cassia's voluptuous globes.

I couldn't care less. Not really. What use were breasts if you had no infant to feed? They got in the way when you were climbing and swinging in the Outer Reaches. Women with large bosoms complained of pain in their backs and the ogling eyes of men. My breasts didn't stress my back muscles or make anyone look twice. Well, except for Mangrove.

I grabbed the soft squirrel rug from my hammock and wrapped myself in it. After I'd dragged my fingers through my wet hair to untangle knots, I went back to the table and began rinsing the huckleberries. My mother returned sooner than I expected.

"Ostrya! Help me up!" She set a plate of steaming meat on the door sill. I fastened the blanket so it wouldn't fall off me, moved the meat plate to the table, the tantalizing odor teasing my nose, and then hauled Mom into the house.

"I ran into your grandmother," she said. "When Butia saw what we were having for dinner, she shared some of her market meat with me."

I waved my hand over the plate, wafting the delicious aroma closer to my face. My cheeks pinged as the saliva began to flow. "Ummmm ... it smells like ... ummm ... raccoon?"

"Yes! Raccoon! Now tell me, how does Butia come by raccoon meat and all we get tonight is huckleberries? Yew hates her even more than me."

I shrugged and handed the knife to her. She closed her eyes for the blessing. I gazed at the raccoon meat one second longer before closing my eyes while she prayed.

Mom cleared her throat. "We thank this raven, this raccoon, and these berries for giving of themselves so that we may live. One day, we too will give our bodies so that others may live. All spirits are equal. Protect us, oh Great Ones."

I opened my eyes and watched my mother guide the knife into the bird's flesh, dividing the bird into two portions with the precision of a trained surgeon. My mouth watering, I waited for the knife to carve the raccoon meat, but Mom set the knife on the table and picked up one of the bird halves and set it on my plate. "Joshua always loved raccoon. Put it by his place, would you?"

I stared at her. I was so hungry. I opened my mouth to argue, but one look from my mother, and the words dried on my tongue.

Reluctantly, I picked up the juicy hunk of meat, carried it to the tiny shelf, and placed it in front of Joshua's doll. The candle flame wavered when I removed my hand. I licked my fingers, savoring the fat and juice before returning to sit across from Mom at the table.

The bird was dry and chalky in my mouth. The breast meat stuck in my throat. I choked it down and ate a few huckleberries, wet and tangy on my tongue. I picked up the bird's liver, lightly warmed from the fire. At least this part of the bird was soft, even if it was gritty and had an acrid after-taste. I gazed longingly at the raccoon meat growing cold by Joshua's doll.

"Don't covet Joshua's dinner. There's more bird if you're still hungry. Remember, take only what you need."

"I know, Mom."

All spirits are equal. Even the dead ones.

Chapter Nine

❧

I watched Tung skip along the pathway toward Cassia's school. He was the age Joshua had been—

—but he looked nothing like Joshua had looked. Tung's hair was bean vines on the compost heap at the end of the season, curled tightly around and around. Joshua's hair had been fir cones dropped in spring, shiny with rain, straight and chopped short. Tung's eyes were round, gray, wide open. Joshua's had been squinty, oblong, narrow at the edges, the color shifting with his mood. Tung skipped and bounced with the impetuous energy of a chipmunk. Joshua had crept and tiptoed, silent, stealthy like a barred owl, seeing all, taking his time, thinking it through.

"I know you." He stopped suddenly, staring at me. "You're the doctor."

"I'm the doctor's helper."

"What's your name again?"

"Ostrya."

"Why are you eating your hair?"

I hadn't realized I was chewing on my hair, a nervous habit my mother was always nagging me to quit. I pulled the sodden hank from my mouth and pulled it behind my neck. Tung stared at me, awaiting my answer, and then forgot the question and raced toward Zelkova with a yell. She ran away from him, giggling, and an impromptu game of tag ensued, to the displeasure of Wollemia emerging from the elder's area with Thevetia.

"Watch where you're going!" She wrapped her arm protectively around the waist of her friend who smiled vacantly. "You trying to knock us down? Ostrya! Do these belong to you?"

I pushed myself off the school wall I'd been propping up and, my mother's voice in my head, stood up straight for once. Wollemia was old as forest duff, but she was nearly as commandeering as my mother. Salix admired her, not that she needed someone to teach her how to be even more domineering.

"No," I answered, slightly intimidated.

"Well, where's Cassia? She knows we can't have these youngsters scrapping around over here. It's dangerous. They could knock someone over. Tell her to get out here and gather her pupils."

"Oh, sorry, I guess it is my job. She's not here. I'm in charge today." Under Wollemia's imperious glare, I ran after the two children. I grabbed each of them by the hand, Zelkova skipping along beside me and Tung trying to yank free.

Wollemia grunted and raised an eyebrow. "Better take them in hand quickly. Show no fear. Especially not with the boy. That one's got the mischief of a new-hatched raccoon." She guided Thevetia to a bench and helped her to sit, then sank her wide bottom onto the seat beside her. I felt her eyes on me as I hustled the wayward children into the school shanty.

I was subbing for Cassia because she and Cedrus were at

the clinic. Michelia would do another exam of Cassia, make sure both babies were healthy, and update her estimated delivery date. I had gotten the job of looking after the little kids until lunchtime. Lucky me.

Five more children entered in fits and spurts, some on their own, some ushered in by protective parents. Erica's mother kissed her daughter at the doorway; both were unusually clean for climbers, their hair neatly braided.

"Good morning, Miss," Erica said quietly as she entered the shanty, studying her feet.

"Good morning." I understood why she was Cassia's favorite. Of the seven children who entered the school that morning, this young girl was the only one to say hello. She smelled faintly of sarcococca blossoms, their floral vanilla scent preferable to Zelkova's odor of hickory smoke and dirt. Tung's stench was far worse.

Erica wandered to the side of the room farthest from her boisterous classmates and rested on a cedar mat, greeting none of the other children. She watched them silently, missing nothing, attentive as an owl. Like Joshua.

"Hey, kids. Quiet now." Erica turned her head to look at me. The other children continued giggling and talking. I remembered Wollemia's advice and shouted, "I SAID QUIET! NOW!"

That did it. They stared at me, mouths hanging open.

"Now, for those of you who don't know me, my name's Ostrya, and I'm the teacher today. I'M THE BOSS. Got it? You're not the boss." I pointed at Zelkova. "You're not the boss." I pointed at Erica. "You're not the boss." I pointed at a tall, thin brown boy. "None of you are the boss. Got it? You, Tung! Who's the boss?" I suspected if I got him to follow, I'd have no difficulties with the others.

"You're the boss," he said, staring with his wide gray eyes.

"That's right. Remember that, and we'll get on just fine." I stretched to my full height, the crown of my head bumping the ceiling, placed my hands on my hips, and jutted my chin forward in my best impersonation of an adult in charge.

They wouldn't dare mess with me. Everything I knew, I learned from my mother.

Thirty minutes later, the kids had recited the alphabet in their sing-song voices so many times I thought I'd dig out my own eardrums. We'd counted to twenty-five with varying degrees of success: Zelkova had broken down in tears after ten, and Tung had showed off by counting to one hundred by fives. Next on Cassia's list was reading to the kids from *The Book of Silvanus*—the part about the cannibals. The kids ranged in age from about five to maybe ten. Most of them were at the young end. The adults indoctrinated the next generation early.

Someone a long time ago had decided the sooner little kids learned that the earthwalkers ate each other, the better. *The Book of Silvanus* said we were something like two or three thousand feet above the surface of the earth, whatever that meant. I didn't understand distance, and I don't think any of us did, not even Butia. How could we? Except for the hunters, none of the climbers ventured more than a mile from their shanties. All I knew was some days the mist and clouds were beneath us, sometimes they were above. I suspected that even if a hungry earthwalker could have seen us in the upper boughs—unlikely because we were camouflaged from view by low-growing fronds and it was probably too dark in the forest to see much anyway—they'd have to figure out how to climb up two thousand feet or whatever in the dark. We'd see them coming long before they arrived, if ever, so, it was unlikely that we'd be attacked by surprise.

This was the text I was supposed to read to the kids: *The starving masses devoured the living species wherever they were housed, depleting the species' past recovery, and accelerating the destruction of the soil. Many unfortunates died from poisoning as they consumed toxic plants, animals, and fungi in their desperation to assuage their hunger.*

And for the first time I understood the meaning behind the text—we were never to descend. By the time we were mature adults, contributing members of the community, we had to think that it was our idea not to leave the canopy. My friends had all been brainwashed. Sorbus, Salix, and Mangrove—I wasn't sure about Wingnut. Oddly enough we'd never discussed it. They believed the duff we'd all been fed ever since we were as young as these kids: *The most plentiful, indeed the only source of nutrition for humanity was other humans.*

I'd never heard of any climber venturing to the forest floor or of any earthwalker climbing up. None of these little kids was in danger of climbing down a Douglas fir for fun. No way was I going to read from the book of lies. They'd hear it from Cassia another hundred times before they became trainees anyway. I crossed the task off Cassia's list and decided we'd play a game instead. "Hey kids, anyone want to play Squirrel, Squirrel, Raccoon?"

The jubilant cheers were proof enough that I'd made the right decision. I reminded myself what I'd told the kids: I was the boss today. We could do what I wanted, so we played games until lunchtime. And when it was time to let the kids go, I didn't make them say the prayer to the Great Ones. But I did have them recite the commandments, because even if *The Book of Silvanus* was a vast conspiracy of lies, those three rules were good guidelines for our community: take only what you need, produce to replace, and all spirits are equal.

When the last kid left—Erica had wisely waited until Zelkova and Tung were long gone—I was finally able to leave the school. I didn't know how Cassia did this job every day. I'd barely moved all morning, but I was exhausted. I was used to physical exertion. Most mornings I was climbing up and down stairs to do home visits, and I climbed into the Outer Reaches every chance I could. But this work, watching and guiding little kids, was more tiring than I realized. It wasn't that I liked working at the clinic, but I'd be happy to get back to my regular job.

I stacked up the cedar mats, grabbed my satchel, and stepped out the door. Cedrus was hurrying toward the school holding the broom he'd repaired. I'd neglected to sweep and didn't plan to start now, so I turned in the other direction to make my escape, but he called out, "Ostrya! Wait!"

I groaned and stopped. He tossed the broom into the school shanty and said, "Would you please talk with Cassia?"

"Sure. I'll stop by tomorrow." I was tired and hungry. I needed to eat and be alone for a while before my mother gave me her list of chores for the day.

"No, I mean now?" He looked past me to where two older weavers eavesdropped the way they do: feigning interest in the same old story they've been telling each other for a decade while their ears rotate toward the sound of younger voices and fresh gossip. He motioned for me to come closer and spoke quietly. "You know we were just at the clinic."

I rolled my eyes. "Yeah. I know. That's why I was babysitting all morning."

"We're having twins!"

"You don't say."

"Cassia doesn't seem to be taking it well. Could you come talk to her?"

I'd been working hard all morning and the last thing I wanted to do was listen to Cassia complain, but she was my half-sister and one of the few people in the canopy I actually liked. I nodded my head and sighed heavily so Cedrus would know he was asking a lot. I didn't want him around while I talked to her, and happily for me, he turned toward the central Great One and up the stairway to work.

Cassia was gulping back tears and rubbing her bump when I poked my head into her shanty.

"Cedrus said you wanted to talk to me," I said.

"Huh?" Cassia seemed surprised to see me. "I didn't say that. Oh, I guess he thought …"

"He said you were upset …"

She rubbed her bump and closed her eyes. I could see her taking deep breaths, and I imagined she was doing her birthing exercises. One. Hold. Exhale. Two. Hold. Exhale. She opened her eyes and said, "Cedrus is so happy we're having twins. You should have seen his face when Michelia confirmed it. I wish I could be happy, too. But how are we going to handle two babies in this tiny shanty?"

"A lot of families have two kids. They're small at first. They won't take up much room." What did she want from me? I wasn't the one who'd gotten her pregnant. Shouldn't she be talking to Cedrus about this?

"Two children are more than we need. It goes against the rules. I tell my pupils every day: Produce only to replace." She was talking at me. I might as well be a table or a hammock. She wasn't even looking at me. "And how am I going to raise two babies and continue teaching? I can strap one on, that's what I'd been planning on doing. She can nurse and nap in a sling. But two? How do I manage that and continue teaching? And Cedrus will be no help. Up in the limbs building bridges, wrapped in ropes and harnesses. He's not going to be carrying a baby around."

"Ummm, lots of parents do it."

Her eyes flicked over at me. Like she was surprised I was there. And once she remembered, she shot daggers at me. "I know! My mother did it! All alone when my father left us for Michelia!"

"And my mother raised me alone after he left her! What's your point?" I didn't understand why she was attacking me. I hadn't told her to get pregnant. And I certainly wasn't going to apologize for our father.

She burst into tears. My mother would have reminded me that the changes in estrogen and progesterone levels during pregnancy were affecting Cassia's neurotransmitters. But I imagined how I would have felt if I thought I was having one baby, being pregnant and having to raise a kid, ugh. And then, when I'd finally gotten used to that idea, being told that I was now going to have two poopers in my shanty. I'd be angry. But then, I never would have hooked up with Cedrus in the first place.

One of the main differences between me and Cassia—and there were plenty—was that she loved kids. I liked them okay; they were amusing, but I had no plans to make new ones. She'd chosen childcare and education as her life work. Why was she so upset about having two babies instead of one?

Awkwardly, I put my arm around her shoulder. It seemed like something one sister should do when the other sister was sobbing, but it felt weird. She hugged me then, hard, and I knew I'd made the right move. She sniffed and coughed and mumbled into my shoulder.

"What's that? I couldn't hear."

She cleared her throat. "Produce to replace."

"Yeah, so? Two babies. Two of you. One baby for you. One for Cedrus. You aren't breaking any commandments. You'll have two children to replace you when it's time for you and Cedrus to feed the Great Ones."

She looked at me, fear and uncertainty clouding her wet, brown eyes. "Three babies."

"What are you saying? Three babies? You're having twins, not triplets."

She wiped her eyes, and then shook her head. "I'm having two babies with Cedrus. But I already have one."

What was this? My sister had a child? Where was it? Who was the father? Did Cedrus know?

She walked to the wide hammock she shared with Cedrus and sat down, hands rubbing her bump again. She sniffed and forced a smile. "I wonder what happens to those who disobey the rules."

But we both knew. Joshua had paid for Yew's folly. Who was to pay for Cassia's?

Chapter Ten

It was quiet at the clinic, the way I liked it. My mother had stepped out immediately after I arrived, but not before giving me an old medical text to read through. Passed from doctor to trainee since it was carried into the treetops by the First Climbers, the book had probably been rebound ten times. The cover, stained dark and mellowed by the hand sweat of healers, was an amalgam of leather strips, most likely the hides of chipmunks and tree mice. The hard resin cementing the pages to the cover was no longer fragrant. I cracked open the spine to the chapter Michelia had assigned: "Medical Device Sterilization." I was in for a real snooze fest. One paragraph in, and my mind had already drifted away from the yellowing page.

So Cassia had a child. After telling me, her hand had flown to her mouth, as though she might grab the words and shove them back in, reverse time and prevent herself from uttering the truth. She had refused to give any further details and told me to get out of her shanty, but not before making me swear to never speak to anyone about what I'd heard. But someone must know. Someone must have helped her deliver the baby. How old would that child be now? Cassia was six years older than me. She would have lived with her mother until at least sixteen; she wouldn't have moved to Bough Six until she was trainee age.

I knew Cassia moved back to Bough Three after her mother had been diagnosed with the wasting disease. She'd partnered with Cedrus shortly after her mother died—two years ago now. If Cedrus had been the child's father, wouldn't she have partnered with him sooner? And if he'd known of her earlier pregnancy, he would have understood her upset and not asked me to talk to her. She must have been pregnant before she was with Cedrus, maybe as early as the beginning of her traineeship. But if she'd gotten pregnant while living on Bough Six, why hadn't she partnered with the baby's father?

Two mysteries. Who was the child's father? And more importantly, who was the child? He or she would be no older than five or six, maybe even be in Cassia's class now. How strange to think about that—Cassia's child, being taught by Cassia, not knowing that Cassia was their mother. But Cassia knew. Cassia spent time with her child every day. And if she had to give up her job teaching to raise twins, she'd no longer have an excuse to see her first child. That might be another reason she'd been upset.

I set aside the medical text my mother had given me and wandered to the corner bookshelf. I pulled out one book after another and opened the cover of each until I found one that looked like a guide to childbirth. I sat cross legged on the floor, the book open on my lap, and read about labor pains and cervixes and contractions. My sister was having twins. Surely this was more important to know about than sterilizing surgical equipment. Childbirth was also much more interesting.

The chapter on caesarean sections had drawn me in by the

time my mother returned. She stood over me and crooked her neck to see what I was reading.

"You won't be ready to do one of those for a while. But I might have to perform one, and I'd like my tools to be sterile when I do." She motioned with her head to the beginning medical text I'd abandoned. "Put those books back on the bookshelf and you can practice some interrupted sutures. Your technique is improving, but you're slow."

"Only because that bone needle you make me practice with is so cumbersome." I stacked the books.

"You know we don't have many surgical needles, and they all need to be sterilized after use. And my trainee hasn't yet finished her assignment on proper sterilization techniques."

I rolled my eyes and threaded the cedar fibers through the bone needle. In an actual patient, my mother used squirrel gut: It was more pliable and unlike cedar fibers, it dissolved in the body. I had just shoved some spider cotton in my nose to block out the stench of the half rotten crow corpse I'd been practicing my stitches on when Mangrove walked in. I quickly pulled the cotton out of my nose and palmed it.

My mother looked at him, looked at me, raised her eyebrows. Not subtle. "Hi, Mangrove. What can we do for you?"

"Spider bite." He stared at me. "My hand."

My mother took his hand in her own. "Redness. Swelling. I see the puncture holes. It was a big one."

"Yeah. Walked right into it."

"That's not like you. I don't think I've ever seen you here for a spider bite. Not in seventeen years."

Mangrove blushed and said, "Wasn't a great day of hunting. Thought I'd slay a spider. Bit of meat for the market."

"So did you?" I asked.

"What?" He was flummoxed and growing redder by the second. It was contagious; I blushed also.

"Slay it," I said.

"Yeah. Yeah, I did. But Yew wouldn't buy it. Said real meat or nothing."

My mother stood smirking, watching the two of us. I shot her a look and she stuck her tongue out at me behind Mangrove's back. "Ostrya, why don't you take this one? You can finish up your suture practice later."

I was nearly an adult! I was going to be the next doctor. I could do this. Clearing my throat, I gestured at one of the two examination tables. "Sit there."

Mangrove settled himself on the cedar table, smoothed and slightly bowed from a generation of patients. I poured warm water from our little burner into a bowl and gathered soft cedar bandages from the neat pile my mother had arranged that morning. I placed them beside Mangrove and grabbed the nettle astringent and the fir pitch.

I touched his swollen hand and he flinched. "Sorry."

"No problem. It's a little tender."

"Ostrya, three complications of an untreated spider bite. Go," said Michelia.

"Now? Really?" I gently washed Mangrove's hand with the warm water. "Swelling."

"Yes, we see that. Next?"

"Blisters. Cellulitis."

"If a blister opens?"

"Possible infection."

"Leading to?"

I dabbed the nettle astringent on the puncture marks. I knew the answer to this one. Everyone in the canopy knew the answer to this one. Did I really need to say it?

"Michelia, really?"

"Infection leads to what?"

Glaring at my mother, holding Mangrove's injured hand. "Later."

Loud. Stern. Insistent. "Now."

Quickly, looking at the floor. "Sepsis. Amputation. Blood infection."

Mangrove audibly gulped. I looked at him and he smiled, almost.

"Symptoms of sepsis?"

"High temperature. Chills."

"Both?" asked Mangrove.

I nodded. My mother said, "Spider bites are no joke. Certainly not worth chasing spiders to sell at the market. What else, Ostrya?"

"Umm, red patches on skin. Tender to the touch."

"My hand is tender to the touch! Do I have—"

"No," my mother and I said simultaneously.

"Maybe we should continue after our patient leaves?"

"The more our patient knows about the risks of spider bites, the better able he'll be to recognize if he needs to come back to see us, and the less likely he'll be so reckless next time."

"Confusion. Lightheadedness. High pulse." I stroked the fir pitch on Mangrove's hand and thought for a moment. "Did I forget anything?"

"The worst one. Low blood pressure."

"Oh! Yeah! Septic shock."

Mangrove's once red face was ashen. His voice shook. "What's that?"

This symptom was interesting and easy to remember. The grisly ones always were. I gulped and recited, "Chemicals released by the body to combat the infection can cause widespread inflammation that fatally damages the organs. Septic shock is when the blood pressure drops because the body's own chemicals cause the blood to clot and reduce the flow to limbs and internal organs. The lungs, liver, and kidneys can fail, leading to death."

Mangrove fainted.

"He won't be hunting spiders again anytime soon," said my mother. "Wrap that hand and then we'll bring him around."

I tied the cedar strips around his wound, bent his arm at the elbow, and rested his hand on top of his chest. My mother patted his cheeks and called his name. I sprinkled some water on his face. His eyes fluttered open and he gazed around the room in confusion.

"What happened?" he asked.

"You passed out," said my mother. "Can you stand?"

He jumped off the table, wobbled backward, and sat down again.

"Give it a second. Ostrya, get the willow bark tea." She touched Mangrove's shoulder. "Drink the tea when you get home and twice more before bed tonight. If the swelling gets worse through the night, come see us tomorrow. You might need nettle tea as well, but probably not."

I handed Mangrove a small cedar satchel of the tea. He dipped his head bashfully and wobbled out the door.

When he was out of sight, I whirled on my mother. "Did you know he would faint?"

"Of course not! What do you take me for, a sadist?" Her eyes turned solemn. "Don't answer that. This is a teaching clinic, and how else are you supposed to learn? If he didn't want to hear about sepsis, he shouldn't have put himself in that position."

"What position? He was legitimately bitten!"

"By a spider? Mangrove? That boy never misses a thing. He's alert and careful. I've never witnessed him do anything remotely reckless." Clearly, she had no idea about our journeys to the Outer Reaches. "When all the rest of you had your bumps and bruises and splinters and stitches, that boy remained uninjured. I swear I've only seen him in this clinic for the occasional cough."

"It almost sounds like you like him."

"Of course I like him! He's a good kid, if myopic where you're concerned."

"What does that mean?"

"Do you honestly believe his story? That he just happened to walk into a spider web? In the middle of the day?"

Now that she mentioned it, it didn't sound like him at all.

"Isn't it more likely that it was a deliberate act? An injury that would give him an excuse to see you?"

"What!" Why would anyone choose to put their hand in an orb weaver's web? They struck quickly, all fangs and hairy legs. I'd only been bitten once, but it was a pain I'd never forget. I doubt Mangrove would forget it either.

Her eyes were direct and hard. "He's clearly heard who you've been spending time with."

"Nothing happened between me and Wingnut. We don't like each other that way. Salix is a liar."

"That girl is not your friend. Ostrya, I know there's only friendship between you and Wingnut. Mangrove needs to hear it from you. Or he's bound to do something even more dangerous to get your attention."

"But I'm not with Mangrove! He's not my boyfriend!"

"Then he needs to hear that, too. Now, enough personal talk in the clinic. Get back to your suturing." The scale clinked as she began measuring herbs for prescriptions.

I shoved the spider cotton in my nostrils again and twiddled the bone needle between my finger and thumb. She was going to be in a good mood. She'd just given me advice and I listened. That would make her feel important, relevant. I might not get another chance for a while.

"Mom? I mean, Michelia?"

"Umm hmmm."

Part of me knew I shouldn't do it. I'd been sworn to secrecy. Cassia was afraid for her life and the lives of her babies. I knew that, but I also knew my mother. I could trust her. Though she didn't know it, my sister could, too. Part of me wanted to know, needed to know. Why else had Cassia told me if she didn't want someone to share her secret? That second part of me, the part that had to know the truth no matter the consequences, blurted out, "Did you know that Cassia already has a child?"

The scale clanked loudly. "Who told you that nonsense?"

"Cassia."

"Oh." She was silent and I glanced up from the decomposing crow I was suturing. She was staring into space. She shook her head and said, "Well. That's news to me. And you should keep it to yourself."

She went back to measuring herbs. Our conversation was over.

Chapter Eleven

❧

The hanging house swayed back and forth as the wind kicked up. The squirrel blanket dropped from my shoulders when I bent to sit on the edge of the door sill. I dangled my legs off the edge as I used to do when I was much younger, relishing the cooling effect of the wind on my calf muscles. This was my favorite time. The world was asleep. The only wakeful beings were the night animals and me.

My mother slumbered in the corner hammock. She'd had a double draught of her nightly sleep remedy, a tonic of Passiflora and St. John's Wort that usually knocked her out for the entire night, and then clung to her mind through the morning like the tendrils of the vine she crushed to distill it.

She drugged herself awake in the morning with Gynostemma and mint. Did all adults need depressants and stimulants to get through a day, a night, a life? And others—Yew was a prime example—looked for a complete escape from reality. Why would I ever want to live my entire life in this canopy? Why would anyone?

A large gust buffeted the tree limbs. Our house leaned

precariously, sending the wooden bowls clattering to the floor. Still, Michelia slept on. She'd been having more difficulty sleeping lately; her insomnia grew worse heading into spring, the anniversary of Joshua's feeding. I didn't like to think of it. I spun my body around and climbed to my feet.

Joshua's raccoon meat from the previous night had fallen to the floor with the gust that knocked the bowls down. I bent and picked it up. The fat had congealed, leaving a white film along the edges of the cold, hard slab of meat. After a night and a day and another night in the persistent heat, it was no longer appetizing, yet I still felt the urge to bite into the flesh, rip it with my incisors, and leave teeth marks all over the wretched piece of meat. I scowled at my mother's immobile body on the hammock and knew that I wouldn't dare. I put the meat back on the shelf and straightened Joshua's doll, then gathered up the bowls and placed them on a low shelf. The house rocked again, nearly knocking me off my feet while patters echoed on the roof. The Great Ones were dropping their cones.

This was certainly no night to be out. The perfect night for me though. I grabbed my satchel off the floor. Gripping the door frame, I waited until a powerful gust receded, the house still rocking, and then jumped down to the branch path and began gathering pinecones. The wind whipped my hair around my face. The air smelled of ozone and I pulled it into my lungs and laughed joyfully. The rain hadn't started, and when it did, so what? I was alive and no one else was awake and who was going to tell me no? I walked away from the shanty, stuffing cones from the path into my satchel.

My satchel was soon full of the useful commodity. We used pinecones for kindling in the community fires, building blocks for children's toys, and ammunition for future trades. I climbed the spiral stairway, no destination in mind, but I wasn't tired and didn't feel like lying in my hammock staring at the ceiling. The wind picked up energy and water coursed down the tree trunks. Wrapped around the trunk of a Great One, the central stairway offered more protection from the elements than the pathway. I climbed around and around the trunk, past Bough Three, onward to Bough Four. The wind howled around me and rain spattered my head and shoulders. I tipped my head back and opened my mouth to catch the cedar-flavored water, sharp and cleansing. I closed my throat and allowed the water to fill my mouth and trickle out the sides. I was a waterfall, a fountain. How I loved the rain, life-giving water.

The Book of Silvanus described a lifetime when there had been water on earth, great pools of fresh rain gathered in earth's crevices. I imagined it to be like how my ears collected water in the rain or when I washed my face. The book described water surrounding the earth on all sides, as though earth had been floating in its own great water barrel, special brackish water, called *ocean*. Before, humans had dried ocean water for its white residue, *salt*, and used it to season food. We dried lamb's quarter for our seasoning, so I supposed it made sense. But how had salt gotten into the water in the first place?

Reading those stories, I often wondered what it would have been like to have lived then; that is, when I'd thought the stories were true. If only they were—I would have given anything to see such vast quantities of water held by earth, to taste that mythical ocean with my own tongue.

Having gathered water in my cheeks, I snapped my lips shut and spewed the water out the corners of my mouth. Now I was a water god, a cloud, a source of life. The heavens split above me with a burst of light and a jarring boom followed by an unnatural stillness, the silence broken only by the patter of rain drops on the tree limbs and needles and a high-pitched whimper.

My ears perked up. The whimper was a human sound. I leaned over the edge of the stairway, holding tightly to the rope handrail as the wind pushed and pulled, and I looked down. The lightning lit the night sky again followed by crashing thunder, and I could see clearly down the trunk fifty feet or more. The stairway was empty, as one would expect in the middle of the night during a storm. Yet, I was certain I had heard something, and I continued climbing up the staircase in the black night, the moon hidden behind storm clouds.

Clutching the handrail, I approached Bough Five, feeling my thighs now. Climbing in the darkness and rain was tiring. The sky illuminated with lightning and was accompanied by a crashing boom. A soft sobbing immediately followed. There on the landing at Bough Five, Zelkova shivered and huddled against the Great One's side.

She gazed down at me with wide, wild eyes, her red hair plastered to her head. I crested the bough, and she wrapped her arms around my legs, nearly knocking me over. I crouched beside her and squeezed her small body to me. "You're okay. You'll be fine. I'm here now."

She let out a wail and hid her face against my chest, her snot and tears mixing with the rain dripping down my body.

"What are you doing up here, Zelkova? You don't live up this high? You're not old enough. Where are your parents?"

Between sobs, Zelkova said, "Hahaha … hoooome. A … a … asleep."

This redhead looked nothing like me, yet in this moment, it was difficult not to feel the kinship between the two of us. When I was a little girl and Joshua was alive, when Yew still lived with us, I used to lie quietly in my hammock, swinging above the double-wide hammock of my parents, and listen to the night sounds. My father would fall asleep almost the second he settled into the hammock, but my mother took longer to relax. I waited for what felt like hours until my mother's breathing slowed and deepened, and I knew I was safe. In that moment, I stretched out my right leg and pushed against the wall, swinging my hammock wide over my parents, and then rolled and jumped, clearing their sleeping bodies by mere inches. I waited to be sure no one stirred—no one ever did, though my father's nocturnal snorting would make my heart stop—and then I tiptoed out the doorway, jogged up the stairway, and climbed into the upper branches. They never found out until that last time.

Tonight, Zelkova and I were both adventure seekers, out in the rainstorm alone, no adult the wiser. I was having the time of my life, but she was terrified. I needed to get her home. "Let's get you back to your parents, okay? They're probably worried about you. Where's home?"

She opened her mouth to respond when a huge gust buffeted us, knocking me to my knees. I grabbed Zelkova tightly to my chest and wrapped my thighs, arms, and body around the main trunk, the child smashed between my chest and the tree. The limbs shuddered and the stairway rocked precariously back and forth. Another boom followed by a blaze of light, and a series of sickening cracks and crashes resonated through the trees, and then all was still once more. The only sounds that continued were Zelkova's whimpering and the pitter-patter of the rain through the trees.

I released the tree trunk. Zelkova wrapped her arms around my neck and I stood, holding her against my bosom, my adrenaline pumping. This was a storm to remember, and I needed to get up to the top to witness it. If I got up to Bough Seven, I could watch the storm with Mangrove and Sorbus, and I was already on Bough Five. I could get up there in no time if I hurried. But I had a little girl to look after now; I couldn't take her with me. I'd need to take the kid to her shanty first. My mother was sedated for the night; she'd have

Chapter Twelve

✤

By the time I made it back to Bough Five, the storm had increased in intensity. I clambered higher, excitement pushing me forward. Bough Seven was the very top of the habitable area—we hadn't built shanties any higher because of storms like this one. Most of the shanties at this level were clustered around the central Great One and the surrounding firs on all four sides, the most sheltered locations. Far fewer platform shanties were built here than on the lower boughs, and no hanging shanties at all. Those who lived in the highest limbs benefited from the most sunlight, but during the frequent and unpredictable windstorms, they had the most to fear.

The full force of the downdraft struck me as soon as I released the stairway handhold. My spine grazed the rough tree trunk and I bent over, forcing my shoulders into the gale and hitting resistance. I dropped to my knees and crawled along the pathway toward the west.

The west end was not a good place to live, especially on Bough Seven. The needle cover was sparser there than anywhere else in the canopy—a result of the storms blowing no idea what time I returned. She didn't even know I was gone.

"Where do you live, Zelkova? Which bough? Bough One?"

"Bough One is for babies." She sniffed, fear forgotten amidst her budding pride. "Erica lives there. That's why me and Tung hate her."

"Bough Two, then? That's where I live. No babies there."

Zelkova nodded and I put her down.

"My legs hurt." She reached her arms up.

"Ride on my back?"

She rubbed her eyes and nodded at me, so I boosted the soggy little kid onto my back and returned the way I'd come as quickly as the wind and rain and rocking stairway allowed.

in from the west. The thin overstory allowed more sun to pierce through, ideal for crops, but it often grew hot by day's end when the sun angled through the limbs. The new trainees got the least desirable shanties, and somehow Mangrove and Sorbus had scored one of the most precarious sites I'd seen. A dangerous place to live, but the best view of the storm.

Earlier in the evening, hearing pinecones drop inside my snug shanty on Bough Two, I craved the excitement of a storm. On the stairway at Bough Four, my yearning for adventure had only increased. Even at the landing of Bough Seven as the treetops bent and moaned, I still thought it a great idea to scramble to the west end, the only worthy vantage point for storm-watching for an adrenaline junkie like me. But over the wailing of limbs bent to their limit, I heard the human yells and curses drifting from shanties. The young men on Bough Seven were awake and on the move. Eyes gleamed at me in the dark. Someone grunted, pushed me to the side, scrambled past.

A disembodied voice. "Stairway's the other direction!"

And a little later: "Bridges are out that way!"

The farther I crawled away from the central stairway, and the nearer to the canopy edge, it finally hit me: They were fleeing. And then it became obvious. I needed to get to Mangrove's and Sorbus's shanty. I had to wake them. Get them to safety. Not only did they live the farthest west, they lived in a platform shanty—an old one that had survived many storms—but how many more would it outlast?

Were they already awake? Already on their way out? I mean, who could possibly sleep through such a storm? I stopped crawling for a moment, dug my fingernails into the pathway, lay flat against the tree limb, and allowed the air to gust over me. The wind tickled and taunted my back. It didn't feel that bad, not such a terrible storm, not when you were horizontal. I was more than halfway to the west end. No point in turning around now. As I rose to my knees again, a gust slapped my face, hard. I bent my head, gritted my teeth, and moved on.

The rope bridges linking the Great Ones and the firs and the slightly smaller cedars pulled taut then slackened abruptly as the wind whipped the treetops. I wrapped my arms around the hand ropes and crossed slowly. In the event of a bridge collapse, my chances of survival depended upon how securely my arm was fastened to the dangling debris. Untethered, and the Great Ones would be feasting on my lifeless corpse within moments. That was the lesson Cassia's kids needed to learn—not the fantasies perpetuated by the book. But kids would learn that only by climbing into the Outer Reaches, by living outside of the canopy boundaries.

The moon's glow bled through now, outlining the angry clouds scudding across the sky. Darker, lighter, blocked. But I knew my way, moonlight or no, eyes closed or open. Every inch of this canopy was mine and had been since I was a kid climbing by night as everyone else slept.

I crawled to my friends' shanty and the moon appeared again, in time for me to see the tree limb that held the shanty platform, the same limb I was kneeling on, bend downward. I stretched my body across the limb and clung to it like a crab spider. The wind released the limb, and I heard a thump from inside the shanty.

"Son of a baby-flesh-eating-cannibal! Sorbus!"

I crawled the final few feet to the shanty and poked my head into the doorway. A shadow rested on the floor, rubbing its head. I lay across the doorsill catching my breath.

"Huh? Whaa?" Sorbus's voice. "Whacha doing on the ground, Mangrove?"

My hands glowed as the moon came out from behind a cloud and Mangrove saw me. I watched him grab a pair of shorts, turn his back to me, and quickly pull them on. The hut shuddered and he fell to his knees again.

"By the roots of the Great Ones, that is some storm brewing," said Sorbus. "Need a hand up?"

"I've got it, I've got it. Thanks for your concern." Mangrove blinked at me, rubbed his eyes, and blinked again. "You're really here, right? I'm not dreaming?" He reached for a shirt.

"We need to get out of here. Now. This is a bad storm."

"Sorbus, Ostrya's here. I think. Can you see her, too?"

A throaty snore came from the darkened corner. A tremendous gust bent the branch again, released it, and the shanty upended, knocking Mangrove to his knees again and tossing Sorbus from his hammock. Sorbus hit the floor with a grunt. He sat up, red-rimmed eyes blinking and said, "Oh. Hi, Ostrya."

With white knuckles, I clung to the doorsill.

"Why's Ostrya here?"

"Storm. She wants us to leave." A deep, ominous crack through the shanty punctuated his words. I sat back on my heels. "Guys?"

"We gotta get out—NOW!" yelled Mangrove, grabbing Sorbus by the shoulders and hauling him off the floor.

"Wait a minute! My clothes!" Another gust rocked the shanty and my friends stumbled and fell.

Mangrove was the first to his feet, and he tugged Sorbus toward the door, shoving him at me. "No time! Out!" I grabbed Sorbus's arm and dragged him, all skin except for his native furriness, out the doorway. Mangrove jumped from the shanty, his hand clenched around something, and then he was screaming, "Run!"

Mangrove wobbled, regained his balance, and raced from the shanty. I stumbled behind, Sorbus bringing up the rear. A widow maker tumbled from the heights as if out of thin air and impaled my friends' home.

It was as though the dead tree limb had ripped open the clouds on its way down. A torrent of hail blew sideways, wickedly pelting our heads and bodies with tiny, painful shards. Under the assault, Mangrove dropped to his knees and crawled toward the central trunk of the tree. His back propped against the trunk, he pulled his knees to his chin, and then made room for Sorbus and me. We joined him, and the three of us stared wide-eyed and dripping at the rocking shanty and the ten-foot spear sticking out from its roof.

Sorbus took his clothing from Mangrove's shaking hand and dressed quickly. "Guess we won't be feeding the Great Ones today," he said, a little too soon.

The tree groaned and pitched sideways. We three clutched the trunk, the limb, and each other. The squall had the tree and us in its grip. The wind was blowing so hard, it bent the top of the tree nearly to breaking. We couldn't possibly move without falling off. I grasped the limb with every ounce of strength I had, legs and arms wrapped tightly around the only solid branch in reach.

Mangrove's eyes glittered wildly in the dark. Lightning flashed, revealing his wiry body, pink and blotchy from being pelted with pinecones, hail, tree debris. Sorbus's tangled coils writhed about his head and his eyes were clenched shut.

"We're going to die," he said.

"No we're not," I said. "Are we, Mangrove?"

Mangrove gripped my hand so hard his fingernails left indentations in my skin. He stayed silent.

"Mangrove. Tell Sorbus this is only a storm. We're not going to die!"

Sorbus and Mangrove stared at each other. If not for Mangrove's hand clamping mine, I might have thought they'd forgotten I was there. Sorbus was gripping the tree trunk with all he had, every muscle in his body tensed. "This is it. This is when we feed the Great Ones."

"Yeah, I think it might be," said Mangrove.

"Shut up!" I yelled. How could they be so convinced they were about to die, so willing to let it happen? We'd climbed all over the Outer Reaches; we could hold on to this limb in this storm as long as we needed to.

"I've got something I've been meaning to tell you—" said Sorbus.

"Right now? You know how to pick your moments," I said.

But he wasn't talking to me. "If this is it, if this is when we die, I want you to know the truth."

"Some deep, dark secret? Doesn't matter."

"No, it does. I need you to know—"

"Nothing you need to say. You're my best friend. I don't wanna die, but I'm glad we're going out together."

"Mangrove! Shut up! I need to tell you—"

Thunder boomed directly overhead, interrupting Sorbus midway through his revelation.

"—I love you, Man!"

Lightning crackled in the sky and I saw the shock radiating across Mangrove's face. I was certain Sorbus saw it, too.

The wind released the limb we were clinging to then. Mangrove let go of my hand and grabbed Sorbus. "I love you, too!"

"I don't want to die without you knowing—you're my best friend!"

"And I don't want to die, period." I unwrapped myself from the tree trunk. "We've got to get away from here."

They crawled along the pathway behind me in single file, all of us trying to duck from the punishing wind as we headed toward the safety of the center and the stairway that would take us down lower in the tree. Another jolt of electricity lit the sky then, but none of us was prepared for the concussive explosion that followed. When I opened my eyes, Mangrove knelt bleeding above me, his forehead wrinkled with anxiety. Sorbus sat on the pathway, picking splinters out of his shoulder. Mangrove's mouth was moving, but all I could hear was a dull ringing. He pointed over my shoulder and I turned. Behind us, the platform shanty once occupied by Mangrove and Sorbus burned. The fire caught the needles of the westernmost tip of Bough Seven and danced across the surface of the limb. We watched in frozen horror as the wind stirred the fire and the burning structure collapsed, taking the widow maker and smoldering limb tip with it. The flaming branch, shanty, platform, and widow maker crashed down through the canopy. Shredded bark and scorch marks on the thick tree limb were the only evidence that the shanty that once housed Sorbus and Mangrove had been there.

Chapter Thirteen

⁂

"Well," said Sorbus, a macabre grin breaking through the horror, "I guess this means we're homeless."

Mangrove wiped a wet lock of hair from his eyes and gaped.

"Look out!" I pulled Mangrove back from a blazing limb falling from the sky.

Mangrove seemed dazed at first, and then glanced at my hand resting on his upper arm. He smiled goofily and I let go. Finding my voice, I said, "That was close."

Sorbus started to giggle. Mangrove got swept up in the laughter. The sight of the two of them, disheveled and rocking with hilarity was contagious and I joined in. The three of us, bleeding and splinter-ridden, sat giggling on the edge of that broken-down fir tree while red embers fell around us. I think we were momentarily insane. Group hysteria or something. I felt tired all of a sudden, my adrenaline seeping away. Our situation had been dire. I hadn't realized how dire. Fear and stress poured from me with each wave of laughter until I began coughing. The smoke rising from the wet wreckage was acrid and growing thicker. I waved my hand to clear the air and backed away from the edge.

"We have to get to safety," I said, the hilarity ending as suddenly as it had begun. "Do we go to the center? Or do we get low?"

"We can shelter at Salix's shanty," Sorbus said. He and Mangrove often took the short cut to Salix's shanty, a quick climb down the tree trunks from their shanty to Bough Six. It took far longer to walk to the central stairway, climb down, and walk the same distance again toward the west end of Bough Six than to simply climb down the trees.

"In this storm? Safer to use the stairway." Mangrove tried to stand, thought better of it, and began crawling back the way we came.

"Hold up Mangrove," said Sorbus. "The stairway might not be there anymore. The storm probably ripped it away."

"Ostrya came up that way."

"That was an hour ago," I said. "But there are a lot of bridges between here and there." The trees, giant though they were, were being whipped side to side by the gale force wind. The bridges had been precarious the first time I'd crossed to the west end. I didn't want to cross them again in even fiercer wind.

"Think we can make it down the shortcut?" asked Sorbus.

"Worth a try," I said.

Mangrove gripped the trunk with his muscular thighs and dug his fingertips into the cloven bark of the Douglas fir. He took a deep breath and clasped the trunk with his feet while he moved his hands down the trunk until he found a deep handhold and shimmied his feet down the trunk. Once he had moved several body lengths down the tree, I followed. The tree was moving in a circle, pushed in one direction by the wind and returning to upright in between gusts.

The bark was wet, slippery. I dug my toes into the deep

grooves and curled my foot arches tightly, feeling the bite of the bark. I continued down the trunk toward Bough Six. I heard a grunt and a curse above me. Bits of bark fell on my head. Sorbus had less finesse than Mangrove and me when he was climbing. He was all muscle and power. He seemed like two distinct people sometimes: hard and forceful when he was climbing, thoughtful and kind the rest of the time. Honestly, if I didn't know his other nature, I wouldn't like to climb with him.

I wrapped my legs around the tree and descended faster. I continued moving downward, feet leading fingers, my muscles stretching and flexing, performing the activity I'd been born to do. I clung to the trunk and followed Mangrove until I heard Sorbus's voice yelling from above. "Hey, guys! We should be on Bough Six by now, shouldn't we? Where is it?"

I stopped descending and looked up, and then down. Sorbus was right. We'd climbed right past Bough Six. But how? I called down to Mangrove: "Man! Stop climbing. We missed Bough Six. Where are we?"

I heard Mangrove's voice from below. "There's a huge clearing beneath me. Bough Five maybe? We must have missed Bough Six. But how?"

"Should we keep climbing down?" I yelled as loudly as I could, hoping my voice would carry so that both Mangrove and Sorbus could hear me.

"I can't go much farther," called Sorbus. "This bark is too wet. I almost lost my footing twice. I'm gonna try to go back up."

"Sorbus is climbing back up, Mangrove," I yelled. "I am, too. We'll have to find another way down."

"Wait," called Mangrove and then, "I can't see anything lower. It's too dark. I'm coming back up."

The three of us climbed up the trunk again until we met

where we'd started, water sluicing down our shoulders and backs. We rested beside the trunk, breath heaving, before we set off on the long crawl to the center of the canopy and the stairway. Along the way, we checked the few standing shanties we passed—most were missing roofs or crushed by trees—but we found no bodies—the residents seemed to have safely abandoned their dwellings. We occasionally encountered a straggler, and by the time we reached the center, ten of us crawled together.

We crawled slowly onward through the night. The wind lost strength as the sky lightened, and we were finally able to stand and stagger along, backtracking several times to find safe crossings. So many hanging bridges had been ripped clean away from the trees that there was no direct route to the central stairway. The bridges that remained had lost slats and we crossed cautiously. After several harrowing hours we reached the stairway.

Chapter Fourteen

❧

If I believed in such things, I would have thought it a miracle. The stairway connecting all the major boughs was still there. The Great Ones had protected the spiraling structure. Slats were missing here and there, but the stairway was mostly still passable. The wind was letting up now, though the rain continued. Our collection of bedraggled storm survivors drifted apart, seeking shelter in other shanties. Some, like Sorbus, Mangrove, and me, picked their way carefully down the stairs.

We finally stepped off the stairway landing on Bough Six. Sorbus pulled me into a slippery embrace. His barrel chest was comforting, and a sigh escaped me. He hugged me tighter until I rested my head on top of his, rat's nest to rat's nest. "You're something, Ostrya." His arms relaxed and I stepped back. He pecked me quickly on the cheek and stepped away. With a nod, he set off for his sister's shanty.

I looked at Mangrove. We stood for an awkward moment, and I said, "Well."

His hand leapt out and grabbed my arm. His face

blanched and he let go. I took his hand, squeezed it. "We survived."

He opened his mouth. Closed it. He put his other hand on top of mine and we stood like that for a minute, maybe two, water dripping off our heads, rolling down our shoulders. Prickles built up from my stomach and heat glowed beneath my skin. His eyes held mine, the invisible and durable spider thread that connected us. He tugged on my hand, drawing me to him, and my body obeyed. We were eye to eye, noses nearly touching, our lips a breath apart. He gulped then and dropped my hands. He stepped back, safely away from the spider girl, his eyes still connecting with mine.

You might say the moment was broken when I was shoved from behind, some oaf running past me to his girlfriend on Bough Six. But the spider thread had snapped before that, when Mangrove must have remembered that I was supposedly with Wingnut. And I remembered that Mangrove and I weren't a thing. We couldn't be a thing. Partnered. Kids. The book and the canopy forever. That wasn't what I wanted, was it?

He raised his hand in a somber salute. I inclined my head, a silent goodbye, and stepped back on to the stairway. With each step I made, the last vestiges of my adrenaline evaporated. I allowed gravity to drive me downward, closer and closer to the second bough and the comfort of my hammock.

As the storm subsided, replaced now by an unceasing rain, it occurred to me that the storm had impacted the entire canopy, not merely the highest boughs. Of course it had—it was the worst gale I'd ever experienced. Bough Seven had been nearly decimated; lower boughs would have experienced minor damage.

By the time I reached the landing at Bough Four, the entire canopy seemed to be awake. Despite the early hour—it was barely dawn, the stairway steeped in shadow—people pushed past me racing up and down. Many rushed toward the west side.

I was sucked into the mass of bodies and allowed myself to be dragged down to Bough Two. I extricated myself and stepped out onto the landing. Barely able to keep my eyes open—I didn't know when I'd ever felt so physically tired—I limped toward home. As I turned to cross the bridge to the west side, someone grabbed my elbow.

"There you are! Michelia needs you, right now!"

The man holding my arm was a gardener who lived on Bough One with his pregnant partner. Between her prenatal appointments and his skin allergies, they were frequent visitors to the clinic. Mom must have woken up while I was gone. She'd be livid that I left in the middle of the night, probably expecting the worst, that I'd shacked up with Wingnut or something.

"I'm on my way home now. Thanks." I shook my arm free.

"No! She needs you in the clinic!" His voice shook, broke. Was he crying?

"Is it your partner? Is she okay?"

He nodded. "Yes, thank the Great Ones. We live on the north side. But the others—hurry! Please!"

Energy flowed into me—other people's urgency affected me that way—and I followed him back in the direction I'd just come and down the crowded stairway to Bough One. Several women and men followed us, matching their speed to ours, and we jogged together through the rain past the nursery, the school, and the elders' community, toward the west.

A line of burned and bleeding people stretched along the pathway as we neared the clinic. The injured were mostly middle-aged, though the occasional older person or older youth or two stood out in the line. These people were from the middle boughs, usually safe places to ride out a storm.

I weaved my way with curiosity through the crowd, past the clinic and to the west side toward the bridges and skygardens. Behind me, I could still hear the sounds of the injured. Ahead of me, an unnatural stillness. A cold knot grabbed my gut. Something terrible, unspeakable—

— "Ostrya, STOP!"

Powerful arms wrapped around my torso, holding me back. I slid painfully to a halt, a splinter ripping my heel. Not five feet ahead, the great pathway stretched into the abyss, hanging on raw sinews of plant fiber. Limbs from the upper boughs lay crosswise and tangled. The bridge from the main pathway to the skygardens fell off the far side. Voices of the gravely injured, possibly dying, echoed from several platform shanties still attached, suspended from upper boughs. Embers fell, merged with the rain, and sent steam and smoke rising into the sky.

Cedrus released me and we stood together. Still. Horrified. Witnessing. A platform shanty pulled loose from its tethers and spit out a screaming soul before plummeting to the forest floor thousands of feet below.

Chapter Fifteen

I had watched Mangrove's and Sorbus's platform shanty shear off the western end of Bough Seven. Somehow the devastation that would immediately follow on the boughs beneath hadn't occurred to me.

The incendiary shanty had crashed into an uninhabited area on Bough Six and rapidly devoured the uncleared brush and the dryer needle litter protected from the rain. The upper limbs had weighed heavily upon the flame-weakened branch and snapped it off. Broken limbs gathered debris and more branches as they fell, so that by the time the wreckage landed on the western end of Bough Four, the mass was traveling with such velocity and weight that it was an unstoppable force.

The west end of Bough Three snapped under the combined weight and flames of the upper limbs and jettisoned its inhabitants. Those living on the bottom two boughs had no time to react. The debris smashed through Boughs One and Two, shearing the west ends clean away from the canopy, ripping away pathways, bridges, and humans, not stopping until it all crashed to earth thousands of feet below.

Outside of the clinic, I sorted patients by injury. People with minor scrapes and splinters, if they bothered to seek assistance, waited in the rain. Broken bones or wounds that required stitches leaned along the interior wall. Head injuries and heart pain were seen to immediately.

Inside, my mother wrapped a middle-aged woman's burned arm. Michelia was fuming. I'd get an earful later, but my mother wouldn't confront me in front of patients. She was too professional for that. I stepped to the basin, washed my hands and arms, and then set more water to boil. Michelia had already stacked the used instruments in a basin for sterilizing.

To the woman, she said, "Keep it covered and clean. Use this poultice twice a day to prevent infection and come back tomorrow for fresh dressings."

To me she hissed so only I could hear, "It's not enough that half the canopy has been destroyed in the storm, I'm supposed to worry about your antics, too?" And louder, "Dry yourself off—I don't need you dripping needles and sap all over the clinic."

I grabbed a rag and toweled off while she motioned for the next patient. A man, blood covering his face, carried a weeping boy to the examination table. A piece of wood jutted from the boy's calf muscle.

"Ostrya, you treat the man. I'll take care of his son."

Anger billowed off Michelia like the smoke off of the smoldering shanties. After the night I'd had, I was too exhausted to care. I began cleaning the man's headwound, a simple laceration, one stitch, no more. Because it was bleeding profusely, it looked worse than it was.

"A good cleaning, some antiseptic, and a stitch or two, and you'll be good as new."

He turned toward Michelia. "How's my boy?"

Out of the corner of my eye, I watched my mother extract the large splinter from the preteen's leg before placing pressure on the wound. "A puncture wound. You'll have to watch for infection as it heals. Hot to the touch, spreading redness around the outside, pus. I'll wrap it lightly at first. As with every wound, cleanliness is key. With his wound, air is essential."

Wingnut's booming voice cut through the noise of the waiting injured. "Coming through! Make room! I need to get to the clinic!"

He stomped into the small room. At more than six feet, Wingnut made me feel small and dainty, an unusual sensation for me—I'd resembled a young sapling almost from birth. Wingnut's unshaven face, generally stretched in a wide, jovial grin, was drawn with worry. He carried the bleeding body of his unconscious boss, Maestro Gardener Hamamalis, over his uninjured shoulder.

My head wound patient hopped off the examination table to make room. I threw a clean cedar mat on the table and the man and I helped Wingnut lower his burden.

"Finish bandaging this wound," ordered Michelia, patting her young patient on the shoulder before hurrying to examine Hamamalis. She pushed Wingnut away from the table.

"Is he going to be okay?" asked Wingnut, his deep voice quavering.

"That remains to be seen. Ostrya, grab me some antiseptic and spider fleece."

I gathered a large supply of both from one of the corner shelves and brought them to my mother. I squeezed Wingnut's elbow as I passed. He looked at me, startled. I gave him the hint of a smile—he looked like he needed reassurance—and his handsome face reddened.

On the other examination table, I tied off the bandage on the boy's leg. His father sat beside his son and comforted the sniffling child while I cleaned the angry wound on the man's forehead. He winced as I dabbed antiseptic on the cut.

When things were slow at the clinic, my mother forced me to practice my suturing on bits of animal flesh saved for the purpose. Some evenings we shared roasted meat stuck through with suture fibers. In the canopy, nothing went to waste. A situation like this—so many members of the community in need of stitches all at once—made all the sutures I'd picked from my teeth almost worth it.

I bent to my task. "Don't worry. I'm actually quite good at this." My patient closed his eyes and bit his lip. I listened to my mother and Wingnut, their conversation interrupted only by my patient's occasional sharp intake of breath.

"Tell me what happened." Michelia raised Hamamalis's eyelids, listened to his pulse, and examined a nasty abrasion on his head.

"We were on Bough Four checking the crossing. We're due to harvest the last of the crops and replant next week."

"And you thought that, in the middle of this disaster, when we need all able bodies to help with the rescue effort on Boughs One and Two, you should waste time checking the garden bridge on Bough Four?"

"I … I'm the trainee. I do what my Maestro says."

She sniffed. "Not all trainees do as they're told. Mine sure doesn't."

"Ma'am?" Wingnut glanced at me.

I sighed and rolled my eyes. She was pushing for a fight. It would make her angry if I pretended not to hear and I was more than happy to oblige, so I ignored her.

"So the two of you were on Bough Four, and then what?"

"The bridge was still attached on the near side and

Maestro Hamamalis wanted to secure it before its weight tore out the remaining bolts."

"And?"

"We rigged up some ropes to lash around the bridge and anchor to the trunks. We thought we could loop it around one of the planks, but we couldn't catch it from above. We tried and tried, but the rope wouldn't stick, so Maestro thought he'd climb down to attach the rope to the bridge from below."

"What are you saying?" My mother's voice was rising to the level she reserved for me and Yew when we really messed up. "You let Hamamalis climb down a tree trunk? I know that's not what I'm hearing."

"We lashed a rope around him, and he repelled down to the bridge—"

"In the pouring rain?" Her voice was beginning to screech. "He's, what? Sixty-five?"

"He's not that old—"

"He's sixty-five if he's a day."

"I should have gone, but I couldn't. My shoulder."

Wingnut was staring at his feet. My mother was in rare form, performing two examinations simultaneously: a physical exam on the Maestro and a cross examination of his trainee. I couldn't help but wonder if she was mad at me but taking it out on Wingnut. And she was getting angrier and angrier. Once started, she couldn't seem to stop. Like a snag leaning in the forest, she was going down, down, down. Fast and loud. "Why didn't you stop him? Why did your Maestro at age *sixty-five* attach a rope to his waist and repel down a cliff in the pouring rain?"

Wingnut stammered, "He's ... he's the Maestro ..."

"Where is your common sense? You knew it was a bad idea. Maestro or no, you should have prevented it."

I thought the screamy voice was for family only. In this, as in so much else, I was evidently wrong. My head wound patient and I both stared at her.

"Why didn't you stop him!" She was totally losing it.

"Michelia," I said.

I needed to distract her from Wingnut, get her anger on me, where it belonged. Wingnut didn't know how to deal with her temper. It was me she was mad at, not him.

Wingnut's eyes flickered up and he looked at his Maestro, lying pale and still on the table. Tears welled in his eyes and in his voice. "I tried. He wouldn't listen." It came out in a whisper.

I took Wingnut's hand. "Tell us exactly what happened."

He held my eyes with his own, moist and clear. "He was secured to the line. The wind grabbed the bridge and tossed it. I couldn't really tell from above, but I think the bridge struck him in the head. I hauled him back up, but it took a long time with one arm. Too long."

"Good thing you were with him, Wingnut. If he'd been alone, there would have been no one to help him, right Michelia?"

She was silent for a moment. Her eyes considered me.

"Hamamalis would have done it anyway. With or without Wingnut. If it hadn't been for Wingnut—"

Michelia's gaze softened. She rubbed her eyes and took a deep breath. "Maestro Hamamalis is a stubborn man. There's no talking to him once he's decided on something. Forgive me, Wingnut. It's been a horrible day."

"That's an understatement," mumbled my patient.

"I'm amazed you were able to carry Maestro Hamamalis here." Michelia felt Wingnut's shoulder. "Lucky that shoulder didn't pop out again. You'll be feeling it tomorrow. Have Ostrya show you where the smelling salts are. Let's see if we can wake your Maestro. I'll clean up his head abrasion, and then I'll teach you to wrap and bandage. Ostrya and I need all the help we can get today."

I smiled up at Wingnut and let go of his hand to point out the supplies he needed. The father and son lingered on the examination table. "If the bridges to the skygardens are out, how long until we run out of food?" he mumbled to no one in particular.

Chapter Sixteen

ᴥ

Dark faces, light faces, short and tall, old, young, and those in between, clustered around the central stairway from Bough One all the way to the top of the canopy at Bough Seven. In that narrow, vertical space, the silent gathering appeared vast. A light breeze rustled through the needles, the soft whoosh mixing with inhalations, exhalations, and quiet weeping.

Wingnut stood beside me along the edge of the crowd on Bough One. We'd hurried over from the clinic. My mother remained behind, monitoring Hamamalis in between sewing and bandaging the injured. I would have stayed to help, but she insisted Wingnut and I attend the Feeding Ceremony. "Their future doctor needs to be there, in community with them. Lend a shoulder to the bereaved," she said.

I glimpsed Cassia and Cedrus near the center, his arm wrapped jealously around her. Her eyes, like those of most of the crowd, were red-rimmed and swollen. Cedrus's mouth was clamped tightly in a grimace, his eyes hooded under heavy brows. The sorrow and despair weighted me down, threatened to suffocate me. My skin crawled, every nerve on alert. I bounced one leg, wiggled the other, desperate to flee, forcing myself to stay. I felt a tickle on my fingertips and glanced down. Wingnut's muscular hand brushed mine, his fingers thrummed against my palm. I looked up at him, startled by the contact. He hated this, too. Too many people. Too much emotion. Too much—everything. I wrapped my pinkie finger around his, drawing strength from his companionable discomfort. I turned my attention to the tiny white-haired woman ascending the stairs.

All eyes followed her as she climbed, her cedar rain cape flowing behind her. When she'd climbed several steps and positioned herself above the heads of the Bough One crowd, she stopped and faced us. Her intelligent brown eyes skimmed over the assembled faces. She saw me standing awkwardly beside Wingnut and her lips curved in a barely perceptible smile. My grandmother, Councilor Butia.

Barely five feet tall, her bones sharp and bent, her presence held the crowd. What she lacked in stature she more than made up for with her voice. Deep, gravelly, and resonant, it was calm and nurturing, commanding and powerful. She was cunning and politically agile. She accurately gauged the mood of the people, made difficult decisions, and somehow convinced others to live with the consequences. My mother said she was cold-blooded, a raptor feasting on the weak. I wasn't entirely sure what that meant, but I knew there was no love lost between my mother and my grandmother.

Butia had been the Councilor of the Council of Maestros for as long as I could remember. She'd outlasted plenty of powerful leaders. Despite what my mother thought of her, I supposed she must be loved by most of the climbers. Otherwise, why would they continue to select her to serve? Butia was unusual in another way. She was old, ancient by our standards. It was not only unusual for a seventy-five-year-old to be the Councilor, it was unusual for a seventy-five-year-old to be alive. If a member of the canopy lived past sixty—and with all the hazards of life in the treetops, that was a big if—they more likely than not suffered from arthritis or rheumatism, possibly even the wasting disease. Unfortunate individuals like Thevetia lost their memories or personalities. Some developed blindness, a death sentence in the canopy. A seventy-five-year-old woman with none of those ailments, fully in command of her mental faculties and as physically healthy as a woman decades younger was more than an anomaly.

Though she was my grandmother, I didn't look anything like her. Joshua had shared her brown eyes and petite build, her cunning intelligence, her unsettling ability to see and know all. I was the female version of her life partner, my grandfather, the doctor before Michelia. Tall and gangly, awkward and pale. My mother and I had inherited his heterochromia, our trademark blue eye and green eye passed down through generations along with the suffocating expectations of our ancestor Pseudotsuga.

"My fellow climbers." Her voice rang out from the central stairway. "Our canopy has sustained a tremendous, heart-rending loss. We have lost many loved and valued members of our shared family. We who are assembled here are like the First Climbers. We have survived when others have not. Let us think on that for a moment."

Around me, heads bowed and eyes closed. I bowed my head, too. Butia might call us family, but it felt weird to close my eyes even among familiar community members, so I kept them open. I tried to catch Wingnut's eye, but his eyes were shut, giving him a sweet little kid look.

"Great Ones, we thank you for our lives, for sheltering and protecting us through this latest storm and every day of our lives. We obey the commandments of *The Book of Silvanus* transcribed by that wisest of climbers, Pseudotsuga, and protected by the First Climbers, so that we all might be educated by the words. We take only what we need. We produce only to replace. We acknowledge that all spirits are equal."

Butia's voice caressed and hypnotized us. We rested in the soft cocoon she wove around us. She continued, "We offer you, in gratitude, the bodies of our loved ones, our family in the trees. As you feed and nurture us all the days of our lives, so we will feed and nurture you all the days of our death. We offer you our sustenance from the north to the south and from the east to the west."

Her rasping voice became insistent. "Everyone, let us thank the Great Ones together."

As one, we recited the words we'd all learned on the laps of our parents and teachers when we were young: "The Great Ones shelter and clothe and feed us. Protect us while we live, oh Great Ones, and when we die, we will feed you."

Everyone opened their eyes and raised their heads. The *ceremony* part of the Feeding Ceremony had ended. Now for the *feeding* part. Butia commanded, "The west side has had its fill. The storm saw to that. Maestro Hamamalis is in clinic, so we will ask only three maestros to administer the feeding. Boughs One and Two, you will feed the north side with me. Boughs Three and Four, you will feed the south side with Maestro Drypetes. Five and above, Maestro Wollemia will feed your dead to the east side."

The crowd began to disperse, moving off to gather the wrapped bodies of the storm victims. Butia cleared her throat loudly. "One last reminder. None of us has escaped this tempest unscathed. The storm was a warning to us all. The Great Ones are angry. We must all be aware of our actions and those of our fellow climbers." Her voice boomed. "The commandments must be followed!"

In all my time living in the canopy, I never witnessed so massive a Feeding Ceremony. So many bodies. So much death. All that week, we had ceremonies twice daily: one in the morning for those who had died in the night, and one in the evening for those who hadn't lasted through the day. In the extreme heat, even two feedings a day wasn't often enough.

After that first week, the feeding ceremonies were intermittent. Smaller ceremonies continued throughout the month. Many of the wounded sickened and died of secondary infections, especially those with burns and crush injuries. Michelia worked at the clinic night and day. I ran from one home visit to the next, up and down the canopy, and still the ceremonies continued. Throughout the month, we fed three corners: north, south, and east. The west had feasted during the storm. And with the bridges out, we had no way left to get there.

No matter how Michelia and I labored, no matter how many patients we treated, the feeding ceremonies didn't stop. They had scarcely begun.

From The Book

Scientists first discovered climate change in the early nineteenth century, but it took another century and a half for them to realize that humans were responsible for a large part of it. By the time the polar icecaps began to melt, two generations of children had attained adulthood and voted for the politicians who claimed it to be a fiction, a fantasy, an invention of scientists who had a cynical disregard for the economic wellbeing of the world.

When the warming of the earth accelerated, many joked that they preferred summer to winter, their gardens would be so much prettier, and finally the growing season would be long enough to feed the world. The storms grew fiercer, hurricanes and tornadoes wiped out entire towns. The politicians blamed one another: levies weren't built strongly enough, infrastructure had been allowed to deteriorate, towns and villages shouldn't have been built below sea level in the first place.

And then large cities began to flood, cities within which economic wellbeing resided. Despite the mass resettlement of urban dwellers, global warming was still not accepted by most as scientific fact. It was an accident, a mistake, a fluke of the weather, the crazy weather. Nations began to suppress immigration, becoming increasingly isolationist in their efforts to cope with the alleged non-issue of a warming planet.

Humanity began to move inland. Oceanfront property was no longer desirable as the oceans encroached, coastlines submerged, and owners were desperate to move.

Where it wasn't flooding, it was burning. Every summer the sky became choked with thick smoke. Gray ash fell from the sky like snow, coating the trees and ground, scratching skin and lungs and eyes. When the fall rains finally began, the ash washed into drains, thick like concrete, flowing into lakes and rivers and streams. As the earth continued to warm, fire season stretched longer, crossing from one season to two, and finally, lasting years, set off by any errant spark or lightning storm.

The politicians continued to crow and strut, distracting their constituents with diatribes while inventing wars with other nations over questionable ideals and diminishing resources. The adults continued to vote for the status quo, and the earth continued to warm.

We could no longer wait. We ascended into the canopy.

— PSEUDOTSUGA, *THE BOOK OF SILVANUS*

Chapter Seventeen

❧

Three months. That's all it took. Not a huge amount of time, three measly months. Ninety days, give or take. Three moon cycles. One pregnancy trimester. Three months is not so long, but sometimes it can be an eternity.

The storm had destroyed all the bridges to the west and sheared all weight-bearing branches from Bough Seven and on down. There was no way to cross the abyss, no way to reach the western skygardens. No berries, no apple trees, no greens or vegetables. Gardeners struggled to grow what they could in sunlit nooks and crannies and nurse logs, but it was never enough to satisfy the needs of the community. Climbers grazed on tiny shoots and harvested edible plants wherever they found them. They consumed fir and cedar tips, nettles and fiddlehead ferns, lichens and edible mushrooms. Spider swatters rose early in the morning, risking bites and infection to gather protein. Hunters provided as best they could, but because there was no passage to the fertile west, they soon overhunted the nearest areas with and without their trained raptors. Previously a coveted luxury, meat quickly became a precious currency, traded in the dark corners of Yew's market and elsewhere in the canopy. A replacement garden area had to be found, and quickly.

Maestros Drypetes and Hamamalis had shown foresight in their exploration of a route to the south months before the storm. Their scouts hadn't discovered an easy passage, but the two maestros thought the southern boughs might be reached by traversing the Great Ones a mile to the east and backtracking several more miles to the south. Clearing pathways and building bridges turned out to be a slow process, especially with a diminished and weakened workforce. The builders who had survived the storm and serious injuries were working on reduced rations.

Our stomachs always growled. We were hungry-angry. Mom and I argued even more than usual. We started taking turns sleeping in the clinic so we'd be available at night when people might need us. At least, that's what we told ourselves. Even after his shoulder healed, Wingnut didn't return to gardening. There was no gardening. He started showing up more frequently, learned to suture, and studied medicine alongside me. Mom started giving him jobs to do and he began working nights at the clinic. On quiet afternoons, Wingnut and I shoved spider fleece up our noses and sutured our reeking carcasses until they putrefied. The food shortage meant no fresh corpses for us to practice on.

I gave up half my rations. So did Wingnut. Everyone did. But for the young, the old, and the already fragile, three months was all it took. Three months for the first child to die of something other than storm injuries.

A frail boy, Yucca was a regular visitor to the clinic. He suffered from frequent ear infections, a near constant runny nose, and severe pollen allergies. My mother wasn't alarmed the afternoon a neighbor came to the clinic asking for a doctor visit. The family lived on Bough Three, and Mom's knees were swollen to twice their size. She didn't have to say anything. I volunteered to go.

I was surprised to see Cassia. Even with a staircase and handrail, Bough Three was a long hike for a heavily pregnant woman. Her belly was huge and she moved slowly, like an opossum with a full pouch.

"Cassia? What are you doing up here?" I asked.

She smiled at me, revealing her perfect, white teeth. "What am I doing? Right now, looking for a bathroom. These babies are sitting on my bladder."

I don't know what came over me then; I was probably dizzy from lack of food. But I surprised both of us when I took her hand. Even more when these words came out of my mouth: "I'll walk with you and you can tell me how things are going with you. You should be taking it easy."

"Yeah, yeah. I'm okay. A little tired, I suppose, but that's to be expected, right? Listen, I came up to check on one of my pupils. Do you know Yucca? He's a little brown kid, nine years old. He's got asthma and all kinds of allergies—"

"—he's the one I'm up here to visit." We were nearing the family's shanty. "Let me go in first, see how the kid's doing. Give you a chance to use the facilities. Yeah?"

I pointed to a toilet shack, a secluded tall box situated at a distance from the homes, limbs and branches below cleared away to allow the effluent to fall unobstructed to the forest floor. Cassia waddled off, leaving me alone to visit my patient.

Yucca lay listlessly on his side in a tiny hammock. His spine poked against his thin brown skin and I could count every one of his ribs. The blood had left his face, leaving his complexion gray. I knelt on the floor beside him and took his hand: cold, dry, and weak in my grasp. His brown eyes flickered up at me, apathetic. I stroked his forehead; his lips were gray and cracked. His mother stared sightlessly and picked at her fingers.

"How long has he been like this?" I asked.

She didn't answer, so I repeated the question. She looked at me then, as though alarmed that I was in her home, as though she'd been unaware that I'd entered, greeted her, and begun examining her child.

"Yucca is really sick. How long has he been like this?"

She gaped at me, began crying, and slumped bonelessly to the floor. Cassia chose that moment to walk in. One look at me bent over the sick boy, and another at the sobbing mother, and she scolded me, "What did you say to her?" She reached down and helped the woman to her feet. Embracing Yucca's mother, she frowned at me.

I pulled the stethoscope from my bag and listened to Yucca's weak, thready pulse. "When was the last time he ate?"

The woman said through tears, "I'm trying. He can't keep anything down."

"Your son is starving to death. Do you have rations?"

"Can you take him with you? Take him to the clinic? It's just, I don't have enough—" Yucca's mother broke off with a sob and covered her mouth with her hand. Her eyes filled.

"He needs food."

"But medicine? Can you give him anything?"

Cassia glared at me. "You need to do something!"

I ignored her and spoke to the boy's mother. "You need to get some food into him. Some water. Some calories. Some nutrition."

The mother was openly weeping. Cassia held her tightly and yelled at me. "You need to help him! Help his mother!"

I wanted my own mother right then. I knew there was nothing we could do. This boy was starving. Transporting him to the clinic would do nothing. He had days until his organs shut down, hours more likely. My mother had told me to be scientific, professional. I needed to separate my work from my emotions. And all I wanted to do was cry along with Yucca's mother. I wanted to yell at my sister. Instead, I tried to explain.

"His body is going to keep deteriorating. First, we digest our own fat. He's done that. There isn't any on him. Next, his body will begin consuming his own organs. And then he'll die. He needs water. He needs food."

Yucca's mother was bawling and Cassia looked like she wanted to kill me. "This woman doesn't need a lecture on science. She knows her son needs food. She needs food for her child, and more than that right now, she needs someone to reassure her."

"I can't do that," I said. "Reassurance isn't going to feed her boy."

"I gave him all I could spare. My partner and I ate less, and then we took turns skipping meals. But then he was called to bridge building in the south boughs, and now it's only Yucca and me. And it's never enough. He can't keep anything down—"

"—Soup," I said. "Fir needles will help settle his stomach. If we can get bones, we can make soup. Do you have bones? Maybe your neighbors?"

Cassia's face softened. "Spoon by spoon, we'll get him eating again."

That afternoon, Cassia and I behaved as sisters. I went doorway to doorway, collecting the odd bird or squirrel bone from the neighbors. Cassia stirred the broth over the community fire. We watched Yucca's mother spoon feed the boy.

But it had been too little, too late.

Chapter Eighteen

❧

Two days later, Mom gave me the news. I stumbled into the clinic, still waking up. It had been my night off and I slept in my own hammock on Bough Two, a well-earned respite from the unceasing demands on our tiny medical staff.

The words "Yucca died early this morning" punched me in the gut. My reaction was instantaneous. Heat burned my stomach. Tears scorched the back of my throat. I tried with everything I had to force them down, but they were choking me. My head was buzzing and then I was outside of my own body, looking at myself from the sky. A steady, unintelligible bleating was barely audible over the blood rushing in my ears. My mother's mouth opened and closed. The sound must be her voice, droning on, forever teaching. Pain in my stomach brought me back to myself. I was overwhelmed by nausea. Before my brain fully reconnected, my legs were running, stealing my body away. And then I understood where I was going. My refuge. I needed my gingko forest, my ropes, my spider nests. My legs were taking me where I needed to go.

In retrospect, I shouldn't have been surprised by his death. We'd been having Feeding Ceremonies for the past three months. In fact, the only ones getting regular meals these days were the Great Ones. But this death felt different. This death felt worse. I'd cared for this boy, my patient. But I'd also cared *about* him. I had cooked him soup, I had spoon fed him. And with each mouthful of life-giving broth he swallowed, I'd given him a little more of myself. I broke Michelia's cardinal rule of doctoring. I got emotionally involved with a patient. What was so essential for a teacher, for Cassia—establishing deep connection with her charges—was singularly hazardous for me, a medical practitioner.

By the time my brain caught up with my fleeing body, I had nearly reached the crossing to the ginkgo forests at the western end of Bough Four, and then I remembered the bridge was out.

I grabbed hold of a sturdy branch and pulled myself up into the tree limbs. I climbed up to Bough Five that way, untangling my satchel when it caught on dead twigs. Worms, flickers, and shelf fungi were busy here, breaking down sick limbs. The construction crew had roped off this area immediately after the storm. The warning rope floated in the breeze, forgotten.

Feeling my way across the limbs, I gripped the branches above my head and tapped each section carefully before resting my entire weight on it. Sunlight beamed down unbroken by overhead branches. Here was the damaged section where the upper boughs had broken through, destroying everything beneath. I tapped forward as far as I dared and peered down. The glaring sunbeam illuminated dust motes swirling in the moist air. I lowered myself gently to the rotting limb, wiped my sweating palms against my shorts, tucked my hair behind my ears, and scanned the area for a way across.

I had a tremendous arm span, enviable upper body strength, and powerful feet that gripped tree limbs like hands. Few climbers equaled me in agility. I had to admit that even I was beaten. There was no possible way I could cross into the west boughs. I guess I had known that, but I hadn't been here since the storm, and some arrogant part of me thought I could find a way across. No escape to my gingko forest, no place I could be alone. My frustration and impotence poured down my face in sloppy tears.

I thought of that little boy, Yucca, starving slowly while his mother sat weeping by his side. Even after all that had happened, Michelia never gave up on me. I doubted it had crossed her mind. She would have fought, stolen, done whatever was necessary to protect me, to feed me. She'd do the same today if I needed it.

But poor Yucca. Should I have done something more? Had I missed something? Could I have saved Yucca? His mother had as little food as everyone else. Was it her fault that her son died? Or was that simply the way life was? We all got a chance, but some kids started out healthier or stronger. Some had fiercer, more protective parents. Others had an entire family legacy behind them. Was life really that unfair? Did things just happen to us? Did none of us have any control over our fate? Or was that oversimplifying our individual choices—

—like my role in Yucca's death? Had I done everything medically I could have for the boy? I had been in charge, after all. In the course of treating the injuries, infections, and illnesses triggered by the storm, I'd been able to pretend I was only Michelia's helper. I was only her trainee, not the doctor. I'd been pretending that I wasn't making any decisions, that I wasn't in control of anything. All of those other deaths were somebody else's fault: the storm, the patient's age, the illness, maybe even Michelia. If I wasn't the boss, I had no power, no agency. But that wasn't exactly true, was it?

Because this one? This boy's death was my fault. I could have checked on him sooner. I could have made more rounds, visited more patients. Even now, other little kids probably needed food, starving like Yucca had starved. Was that my fault? I hadn't caused the storm. I hadn't ripped out the bridges to the skygardens. I wasn't taking more than I needed.

Yucca was my patient. He'd become my patient the day I helped his mother make soup. And he'd died. And when your patient dies, that's the opposite of healing. I failed Yucca and his mother. I failed Cassia and Michelia. I failed the canopy. I might be descended from Pseudotsuga and have the weird eyes to prove it, but I was a failure. I hadn't wanted to be a doctor, and I shouldn't have taken the traineeship. I was terrible at it, and now a child was dead.

I rested my head on my bent knees. Almost worse than being a failure and knowing it was the self-pity. I hated myself more for that, but I couldn't stop myself from crying. And I was pathetic: A dead child, my fault, and here I sat sniveling like I deserved frigging compassion. I wept quietly, ashamed of my emotion but unable to prevent the tears from trailing through the salt and grit on my face. I clenched my arms and dug in my nails, pinching tiny half-moons into the flesh. The self-inflicted pain calmed me. Feeling oddly empty, I wiped my face and breathed shakily.

"Ostrya? Are you okay?" The husky voice behind me was both concerned and unsure.

I spun around, startled and embarrassed that someone had seen me. Mangrove stood with head tilted and brow wrinkled, bow and quiver slung over his shoulder. His eyes evaded mine, looking down, sideways, through his eyelashes, anywhere but directly at me. His cheeks flamed and his hands fiddled with a twig, moving ceaselessly. Was he frightened for me? Or of me?

I sniffed and cleared my throat. Climbing to my feet, I tossed my hair over my shoulder. I ignored his question, feigning ironic outrage. "What are you doing here? Didn't you see the ropes? This area is unsafe."

Mangrove's warm brown eyes crinkled with humor and he cocked an eyebrow. "I could ask you the same thing."

"I'm just checking things out." I adjusted my satchel and cleared my throat of leftover tears and emotional junk. "Cassia's not getting around so well. I'm checking the area, making sure none of the little kids came over here, playing tag, getting into trouble."

"Yeah. Very convincing."

I felt suddenly shy and glanced away. I felt Mangrove's eyes on me, taking in every detail.

"So, what's the deal? You going to confess why you're over here?" Mangrove grinned. "Or will I have to bring you in front of the council?"

"The council?"

"Well, Salix. She can always get you to talk."

"Yeah, not so much. She and I aren't exactly friends anymore."

"Oh? I guess I didn't know that."

"Spreading lies, you know. Kind of ends a friendship."

"Lies?"

"Yeah, Mangrove." I spit it out and scowled at him. "Lies. Don't believe anything she says. Especially not about me."

He ran his fingers through his hair, unwittingly sculpting it into a tower of brown waves. "So ... what she said?" His fingers moved rapidly, plucking at an arrow's flocking. "About ... umm ... Wingnut?"

His eyes searched mine and I glanced away, ashamed. Why did I feel ashamed? I was so tired of feeling ashamed.

And guilty. And like a failure. And wrong. Always wrong. But I'd done nothing wrong. Wingnut was a friend. Nothing more. And besides, so what if he was? So what if we were having some torrid sexual love affair, screwing each other's brains out all over the canopy? It was no one else's business. Certainly none of Salix's business. She was a tree rat, and I was sick of the way she treated me, and Sorbus, and—

—I flicked my head up and must have glowered all my hatred at Mangrove, because he flinched. And immediately I felt guilty again.

"Is it true?"

"Is what true?"

"Are you and Wingnut—"

"No!"

"Really? You guys aren't together?"

"Of course not!"

He considered this, his eyes searching. "But he's at the clinic all the time."

"He's my mother's new favorite. I think she'd prefer him to be the next doctor," I said with more anger than I felt. I didn't care if she trained him. Part of me hoped that he would become her trainee. Take the pressure off me. "He's there because she wants him there. It's got nothing to do with me."

Mangrove's face softened. "Is that what's bothering you? That your mom is training him?"

"No."

"I know what it is." He smoothed the flocking on the arrow he'd been worrying and threaded it into the quiver on his back. "You've been missing our treks into the Outer Reaches. We haven't been out there since the traineeships started."

Leave it to Mangrove to figure it out. Sort of. Despite

myself, I had to smile. "Yeah, you're right. That's exactly what I need."

His face lit up and he puffed up a bit like a male stellar jay looking for a mate. "Hey, you know those rules don't apply to me anymore, right? I can go into the Outer Reaches anytime I want. One of the many perks of being a hunter."

"What about over there?" I pointed across the abyss. "Have you been to the west end since the storm?"

He stared at me. "Of course not!"

"Have they forbidden the hunters from going over there?"

"No, but there's no way across. You can see for yourself." He waved his arm, indicating the vast expanse where the bridge used to be.

"You really haven't been west since the storm?"

"There's no path across, Ostrya."

"That's never stopped us before. The storm damage begins where? Bough Seven? Maybe a bough or two above?"

"We've never climbed past twelve."

"Correction. You've never climbed past twelve."

He gaped at me and I smiled smugly.

"You have?"

I nodded. "Think you can handle it?"

"Lead the way."

We made our way along Bough Five toward the stairwell and scurried up the recently repaired spiral staircase to its end on Bough Seven. The area around the central Great One was eerily quiet. I reached behind and grabbed Mangrove's hand, pulling him along behind me. We ran along the southern path until we were away from a line of sight to the stairwell.

"This seems as good a spot as any," I said. I dropped Mangrove's hand, swung the satchel around my back, and grabbed a limb. The tree became an extension of my body, and I climbed, arms and legs alive with the sport. Left foot balanced on left limb, right hand hauling body upward, right foot bracing trunk, left bicep swinging out, hand grabbing neighboring limb, left leg wrapping sideways. Up, up, up, I climbed, my muscles warm and flexible, my long body swinging forward, my fingertips gripping.

I'd nearly forgotten Mangrove as I embraced the meditative motion when I heard his voice hiss from below: "Wait a sec, would you?"

I pulled both feet to one limb and crouched, my thighs burning, and grabbed an upper limb for balance. I peeked down into the tree and heard steady rustling and an occasional swallowed curse. It was several minutes before I glimpsed Mangrove's tousled hair. I plucked a tiny pinecone from a twig and aimed it at the top of his head.

"Ow! What the!" Mangrove squinted up at me through the needles. "Think you're funny, don't you?"

"Come on, slowpoke. We haven't even gotten to the twelfth bough. Can't you climb any faster?"

"My hunting gear keeps getting snagged. I thought I busted my bow string down there."

"Yeah, yeah. Likely story. Toss me your rope. I'll pull you up."

Mangrove unwrapped his climbing rope from his torso, rewrapped it into a tight hank, and tossed it up into the tree. I snagged the rope with my foot and stuffed it into my satchel.

"I think if we can get up, I don't know, maybe ten feet higher, we can toss a rope across, pull some limbs from the other side of the chasm, and climb down to the west side. If we cut in twenty-five feet or so, we'll totally miss the disaster area, and you can try your luck hunting over there."

"What? That's your grand plan? Are you trying to kill us, or are you just crazy? The limbs ten feet higher will never hold our weight. And even if we can get up that high, how are you going to throw a rope to the other side?"

"You snagged your bow string but didn't break it?"

"No … what are you thinking?"

"Are you a pretty decent shot? I mean, you haven't actually hit anything all day, but you could, right?"

"I'm a fantastic shot. I can pierce a raven's breast at twenty feet."

"Good. This will be easier. You'll be aiming at a tree. Bigger target than a raven. We're going to attach your hunting twine to one end of your climbing rope, loop the other end around a trunk, and then send your arrow into a trunk across the gap. We're going to pull the two trees together. Got it?"

"Uh, I guess it makes sense so far, if the arrow holds. That's a big if. Then what?"

"We secure the climbing rope and climb over the bridge we made out of bent tree limbs."

"Okay, you've answered my question. You really do have a death wish."

I ignored him and began climbing again. Creeping upward, I kicked bark and moss back into his face.

"Ostrya!" he yelled. "That was a total jerk move! Where are you going? You said you'd pull me up!" I moved away from him, picking up speed as I climbed.

Chapter Nineteen

❧

Above me, the sky burned blue and bright. Squinting into the sunlight, I laughed out loud. I'd never climbed this high. I was well above everyone I knew, all the climbers, the entire world. Mangrove was quivering in fear many feet below me.

I could push off this branch now, dive into the abyss, crash into the earth and disappear forever. But no, I'd rather float above the canopy with my arms spread wide, catching the updrafts, soaring among the eagles, eyes scanning the horizon. And what would I see? All the busy workers below, building bridges, weaving cedar bark, tying on bandages, growing vegetables. Working, working, working until the day their pathetic lives ended. And then feeding the Great Ones, the trees that jailed generations to come.

Better for me to climb the trees like the squirrels who jumped from branch to branch, gathering what was edible and moving on. Or to perch on the branches and rest for a while before being spirited away again on a breeze, like the crows. Far above the other climbers, and yet still belonging to them, I was burdened with responsibilities not of my choosing, weighed down by the expectations of countless others. I belonged to everyone but myself. My lungs could barely take in the oxygen required to push the weight of *others* off my chest.

I clung to the branch with my feet, curling my toes around the living wood, and released my hand grip. Balancing carefully, I raised my body high, spread my arms wide, and closed my eyes. A warm breeze caressed my face and blew the loose hair around my head. I imagined wings ruffling my biceps and triceps, lightening my load. I opened my eyes slowly and descended again, gripping the limb with my powerful fingers.

I glimpsed the tops of the conifers to the west. Several feet below me, limbs thrust out across the abyss reaching toward the Great One that cradled me. If I descended and crept toward the west, I might be able to catch a limb from the neighboring tree, pull it over the scorched gap, and tie it off to create a treacherous crossing. It would not be a crossing approved by the Council of Maestros or the builders. Not even Mangrove would dare use it. But it was the only way I would be able to return to my special place, my gingko forest. And I needed that putrid air before I suffocated in the clear air of the canopy.

I made my way back down several feet, the distance I'd estimated from above. Now I could hear Mangrove's voice, shrill and worried, carried on a breeze. He sounded farther away than I'd thought he was. I ignored him and climbed sideways, pushing low-hanging needles from my face and peering through the dense growth. I glimpsed the gaping drop to the forest floor and directly across from me, the tip of the neighboring tree. Crawling forward as far as I dared, I wrapped my legs around the limb for balance and reached for my satchel. The satchel swung forward and the front pouch opened, weighed down by my stethoscope. Before I knew what was happening, the stethoscope tumbled from the bag. I reached for it, thought better of it, and watched it gather speed as it raced through the trees for the ground.

So, that happened.

The two stethoscopes were antiques, heirlooms from the First Climbers. There had been only two, protected and cherished by the doctor and assistant since the very beginning. And now, thanks to me, only one remained. Michelia would never let me forget this.

I squeezed my eyes tightly, trying to put the loss out of my head. I wouldn't think about what a disappointment I was, breaking everything I touched ever since I was a little girl, ever since the day I climbed too high, killing that little boy. I killed both of those little boys. The stinging behind my eyelids couldn't have come at a worse time. I was dangling above everything, barely balanced on the limb. I could end it all now, let go and follow the stethoscope through the air. I'd probably pass by it on my descent; I could wave at it as I sailed past it, down, down, down.

It was morbidly funny—me sailing past my stethoscope, I could practically see it—and I knew I was being ridiculous, melodramatic again. I'd never feed the Great Ones, at least not by choice. They'd been nourished for far too long and by far too many recently, and they wouldn't be digesting my carcass anytime soon.

The rope was still in my satchel. I pulled it out, unraveled it, and quickly tied one end around my torso so I wouldn't lose it. Next, I wrapped a lasso in the other end and tossed it toward a distant tree limb. It fell short, dropped down, and I hauled it back up. I tossed harder, still too short, tried again. The fifth attempt snagged the soft end and the rope dropped off. This would have been easier with Mangrove's arrow as I'd initially planned, but he wasn't here and neither was his arrow. Besides, now I wanted to do it alone. Prove to myself that I wasn't useless. I might be a bad doctor, but I could climb. How I could climb! And it was my gingko forest. I didn't want to share that with anyone. Not even Mangrove.

I clenched my jaw, determined, and threw the lasso as hard and far as I could. The power of the shot from my right arm pushed my body to the left, and I felt my precarious balance on the limb shift. I grappled frantically with my right leg, but this propelled me even farther to the left. Bark tore at the skin on my legs as I struggled to regain my balance, and I felt a sharp tearing when my torso slid off the limb.

Joshua. A memory of his small pink mouth opening and closing. The rush of blood in my ears was deafening and my body dropped, and then I bounced and was yanked upward. I hung from a tree limb, retching and choking as the rope cut into my chest, the weight of my body squeezing my lungs. A steady ache pinched my chest, and I knew I was alive, alive and dangling in the air from Mangrove's hunting rope. My body swayed, bouncing slightly, buoyed by the tree limb above me. Good thing I'd thought to tie the rope around my torso. I hadn't wanted to lose the rope, and as it turned out, the rope had prevented me from losing myself.

I grabbed the rope with both hands and pulled my body slightly upward to relieve the pressure where the rope cut beneath my breasts. My chest ached with every indrawn breath, but a dead drop from several feet would do that to you, I supposed. I looked across the abyss and down. Far below I glimpsed a knot of debris, tree limbs and scorched structures, bits of shanties and bridge mounts. I tipped my head back and looked up. It would be quite a climb up the rope to reach the tree limb above me, not my best skill. I'd have to swing closer to the tree.

I wriggled my body to get some movement going. A wriggle to the left, a wriggle to the right, and I was swinging over the gap and toward the tree branches, over the abyss, and then safety, certain death and then not so certain life, and finally, my toes scratched against bark. One more swing out and back, and I had looped one leg around a limb, and then both legs. I tightened my core muscles and pulled my body up, grabbed the limb with my hands, and then I was crawling into the shelter of the trees, away from the clear sky as far as the rope allowed.

I dug my fingernails, short and dirty from clinging to cedar and fir, into the knot to try to extricate myself from the rope that had saved me and was now preventing my movement. It was no use; the force of the drop had tightened the knot past loosening. I pulled the rope up as high as I could, thinking I'd pull it off over my head, but I couldn't get it past my breasts.

It figured. My own small chest was going to trap me here.

I tried to push the rope down the other way over my hips, but I knew that was bound to fail. I was a classic pear shape, hips wider than breasts. The rope would never pass over my bottom half. Attached to my body like this, I couldn't reach the rope with my mouth to bite it loose. How was I going to get free?

I'd have to call for Mangrove's help. It looked like I needed him after all. Was he above me now? Or below? I took a deep breath of air and yelled. Again and again I yelled, but I heard nothing. He should have heard me. I'd heard his voice before I fell. How far would I have had to drop beneath his location for my voice to be inaudible to him? And if I were down that low, wouldn't I have seen shanties or other climbers?

I tried again, yelling in a constant stream until my throat burned with the effort. Where was he? Where was everyone else? Someone should have heard me and come to free me from the rope by now.

And then it hit me: I'd been tied to the rope while

climbing above the community. Had my lasso caught on a tree in the west before I slipped? Had the rope swung me over the abyss when I fell and left me dangling from a tree limb on the west side?

The more I considered the possibility, the more I realized that was exactly what had happened. No one had come to my rescue because—

—no one was here. No Mangrove, no community, only me. I'd done it! I'd crossed over! Hurray!

But now I was a prisoner bound by rope with a knot that couldn't be loosened. And no one was here to help me get out of the rope. I couldn't climb back up while attached to this thing.

I had my satchel, still looped miraculously across my body. I must have something squirreled away that could help.

I rummaged inside and released the breath I hadn't realized I was holding when my fingers grazed my flint. Careful not to drop it, I pulled it from the satchel and kissed it. I nicked it again and again, sparking it against the rope, charring fiber after fiber, until finally I was able to snap the frayed rope. The knot was still tied to my body—I'd need a knife to cut myself free—but the knot was no longer attached to the rope and I was no longer attached to the tree limb far above. I was free.

My head brushed against thick needles as I crawled along the limb. After a few yards, the limbs parted and I was able to stand. I stretched my aching neck and shoulders before walking to the center of the Great One. Vast empty branches stretched ahead of me. The west lay untouched, the planting beds choked with weeds and flowering and fruiting raspberry bushes. Salivating like a rabid raccoon, I ran to the bushes and, as fast as my fingers could pluck them, I crammed ripe, unripe, and rotting berries into my face. Berry juice dripped down my arms, and it occurred to me that I should pick some for Mangrove, too. I picked as many berries off the bushes as I could, dropping them into my satchel.

The gardeners should be in these tree limbs, picking raspberries for the community, training the vines and clearing the brush to allow sun to penetrate and grow the community's food. But here I was, alone. I'd gotten here only by climbing to the very heights of the trees. Not even Mangrove had managed it. The gardeners would never be able to cross that way.

I had to figure out how to return to the canopy. I'd crossed over the abyss once—well, fallen across, more like. I needed to climb back up and cross over again before Mangrove raised the alarm. This time, I couldn't fall.

Traversing the aerial pathways I hadn't climbed for three months, I reached the treetops and found the rope looped and tightened around a narrow but sturdy limb. I hauled the frayed end up, hand over hand, looped another lasso, and tossed it across the abyss. My past trial and error method had taught me how hard to throw, and I snagged a limb on the other side after a mere three tries. I leaned back, pulling against the loop with my full body weight, ensuring the knot was tight. I tugged at the limb and dragged it down across the wide gap, tightening the slack on my side. When I dragged the opposite limb down as far as I could, bowing it to a 150-degree angle, as near to horizontal as it would bend without breaking, I gathered courage into my lungs and the rope in my hands. I dropped off the branch and hung from the rope. I couldn't help myself; I glanced down. My dirty, bare feet dangled impotently in the empty air. The only thing preventing my immediate death was the strength of my handgrip and the tensile strength of the braided rope fibers.

My heart pounded in my fingertips, my toes, and my ears. I moved my body in rhythm with my hands, throwing my hips forward as I crept hand over hand. I didn't stop until my fingers felt needles, and then bark. I grabbed the limb with both of my hands, curled my body up, and looped my feet around the limb. Gathering all my strength, I pulled my body up, over, and onto the limb, and crawled slowly backward. Once I cleared the gap, I collapsed to the security of the branch and listened to my heart pound.

After I calmed down and caught my breath, I anchored my toes to the tree limb and stretched my prone body outward again, toward the rope. Taking it in both hands, I scooched my body back to the relative safety of the inner branch and leaned my weight against the rope as I had on the west side and pulled, pulled, pulled the western-growing limb mostly horizontal before tightening and tying off the rope. The two slight limbs lay on top of one another, entwined yet shyly aloof.

I stood and looked across the abyss at the bridge I had built, my own precarious pathway to my private ginkgo forest, my solitude and escape. I began my descent toward Mangrove, eager to share my bounty of berries.

Chapter Twenty

The sun was dipping below the trees by the time I made my way back across the divide. Mangrove had long since abandoned his climb. I dropped down through the branches and met him a few boughs above the safe zone. He was sweating and pacing.

"Where have you been?" he yelled. I began to answer, but he rushed me as soon as I landed, pushing me powerfully and a bit painfully against the branches in an awkward, sweaty hug. "I was so worried! I didn't hear you fall, but when you didn't come back—"

His grasp was tight, his powerful arms wrapped around my back. I was hot, thirsty, and sweaty, and the last thing I wanted was to be mauled by another warm, sweaty body. Once I got used to the warm pressure of his hands on my spine, his moist curly hair pasted to my shoulder, I realized it was kind of nice. Icky and sticky, but nice.

"I'm okay, I'm okay." I gently pushed him off me. His eyes met mine and I watched them drift down to my lips. His face reddened and he stepped away.

"Where ... where did you go?"

"Put your hand in here." I held out my satchel.

His eyes opened into two comical round balls as his fingers closed on the raspberries. "What the ... where did you ... can I—" The berries disappeared into his mouth. Juice stained his fingers and he licked them off, one by one. He grabbed another handful of the warm, sticky fruit and offered it to me.

"You can have the rest. I ate plenty already."

He crammed the fruit into his mouth and gulped it down.

"Hold out your hands." As I poured the fruit into his palms, I told him about the crossing I'd made, the berry bushes, the trees, and the untouched vegetable beds.

"You need to tell Maestro Hamamalis or maybe Maestro Drypetes. If you could get across, they can, too."

"But no, don't you see? It's so high up. You weren't even able to climb up with me. How are the builders going to construct a bridge way up there? For gardeners to travel across, back and forth. The branches barely supported me alone."

Mangrove wiped his sticky hands on his shorts. "But the food. The first little kid died today."

"I know that! Don't you think I know that?" I felt the traitorous stinging behind my eyes. "Yucca was my patient."

"Sorry. Of course. I should have realized." He was silent for a moment before he began to pace again. "If we can get to the food, we can't simply leave it. We have to tell someone."

"Who? Who are we going to tell? We're not supposed to be in the Outer Reaches—"

"It's a way to get to the food. No one will care."

"No? Will anyone care when little kids try to climb up here? What about the older climbers who don't have the skills?"

"You think everyone will try to get over there? Across your bridge?"

Yucca's apathetic eyes, his skeletal face. I saw them as clearly as if he were lying in front of me now in his hammock. His sobbing mother, Cassia's arm supporting her. Every parent who'd ever entered the clinic with a sick child. How many would die trying to get to the skygardens once they learned I'd done it?

"You've seen the desperation. What do you think? Do you honestly believe there won't be a mad rush on my bridge?"

He was silent, brow furrowed, thinking.

"And then what? A mob of starving climbers and worried parents? Can you see them trying to climb up here? They'll break all the branches, fall off the limbs, rip down my bridge—"

He nodded. "And then no one gets across. Not even you. Okay. I'm with you. We don't tell anyone."

"Not even Sorbus."

His lips twitched, drawing my eyes to his red, berry-stained lips. After a moment he said, "Not even Sorbus."

"And *definitely* not Salix."

"No. Definitely not ... but you can get to the food." He grabbed my hand, squeezed it so hard it hurt. "Don't get mad, okay? I ... I followed you once. I hid in a cluster of sword fern. You ... you didn't know I was there."

I tugged my hand back. "You spied on me? You stalked me?"

"No. Just shut up a minute. Listen to me. You scrambled into the trees, climbed like some arboreal creature. Fast as a squirrel. Strong like a raccoon. But the way you swung from limb to limb. I've never seen anyone do that. I've been hunting for months now, and I've never even seen an animal do that." His eyes were dilated in the gloom, intense. "You became something else—something beyond human." His hands were on my shoulders then and he peered into my eyes. "You're more than a bird. A tree spirit maybe, part of the Great Ones! You're the only one who can do it."

"I'm a good climber. That's all."

"We can all climb. Some of us are even good at it. But only you soar."

His eyes were too intense, fanatical even. I shrugged his hands off me and stepped back. "Whatever. I can climb. Let's not go crazy. Freaking tree spirit! Seriously Mangrove? Get a grip. I can cross to the other side and gather food. It won't be enough."

"So you'll bring back what you can. Whatever fits in your satchel."

"Then what? How do I decide who—"

"You drop it at the school. For the kids. Anonymously. Let Cassia decide. She'll make the right choice. And no one will ever know."

"No mob rush to the Outer Reaches. No destruction of the overstory. Nobody climbing too high—"

"Nobody else feeding the Great Ones."

Our eyes met and that uncomfortable sick feeling rose up from my stomach and tickled me all over. My heart beat a little faster and I was warm straight through. Was this happiness? Was this hope?

Mangrove took my hand again, gently this time, and we descended into the lower boughs as the remaining daylight faded. By the time we reached Bough Seven, our eyes were adjusted to the murky dark.

Mangrove disappeared briefly into the warm candlelight of his new living space, a shanty built for two but hung with three hammocks. Having lost their shanties during the storm, many of the men and women of the sixth and seventh boughs were tripling up. I heard snatches of good-natured ribbing waft from inside. A curious male head poked through the door, eyes squinting to catch sight of me, the woman who had kept Mangrove out so late. Mangrove elbowed his shanty mate out of the way and strutted toward me with the remains of a hazelnut loaf and a squirrel leg, a generous gift on any evening, but especially lavish in the midst of rationing. Together with the berries I gorged myself on earlier in the day, it was a healthy, balanced meal, and I felt fortunate. We nibbled the meat off the tiny leg and choked down ripped chunks of the dry loaf.

Our meal complete, we were both suddenly tongue tied. "Thanks for dinner," I said, sweeping imaginary crumbs from my thighs, faintly bluish in the gloom. When I looked up, my forehead crashed into Mangrove's chin. He yelped, then chuckled, and then his hand was stroking the hair off my face. His lips brushed lightly against mine, his tongue tasting of charred squirrel. I was startled and stiff at first, but his lips were soft and warm, so I closed my eyes and kissed him back. Behind my eyelids I saw my mother, her lips straight and stern, her forehead wrinkled in disapproval. I opened my eyes and backed away slowly.

"Gotta go," I said. "This was, um, fun." *Fun? I'm such an idiot.*

"Yeah, sure. See you tomorrow?"

"Maybe. You know where I'll be." And then, I'm ashamed to say, I realized I'd been twirling my hair. I stopped immediately.

"Clinic. Yeah." His eyes were soft and dreamy as he looked at me and it occurred to me suddenly how adorable he was.

"Um, yeah, so. Okay. Bye."

I raced toward the central Great One and ran down flight after flight of the twining staircase until I reached Bough Two. I considered a number of excuses as I hurried home: patients I'd examined, accidental injuries I'd doctored, sprained limbs I'd wrapped. It was no good, I could never explain to Mom's satisfaction where I'd been and why I'd been out past dark. My mother would assume, correctly this time, that I'd been with a man.

We'd kissed some, sure. Michelia would imagine much more. I wondered whether the fiction that I'd slept with a man, or the truth—I'd sailed over the abyss on a climbing rope—would be worse in my mother's eyes. She saw women both before and after they'd consummated their relationships with men. The wise ones, my mother told me, came to see her before. I hadn't told my mother about Mangrove, though she suspected plenty. Would she see me come in late and think I'd been unwise? Or would she assume, with my training, I'd known enough to take the appropriate precautions?

Of course, Mangrove and I weren't there yet. Nowhere even close. I wasn't ready to be partnered, and no matter what he felt, I could tell he wasn't ready either. I had no plans to be like Cassia, watching other people's kids while repopulating the canopy and living on Bough One. A woman with a pregnant belly can't climb into the Outer Reaches, can't cross the abyss, can't smuggle food from the skygardens.

If my mother discovered the truth about what I'd been doing, what would happen? Would she punish me? What would that look like? Would she denounce me to the Council of Maestros? I doubted she'd go that far, but it was interesting to consider. What would the council do if one of the climbers broke the rules? Our canopy was so intimate, our community so small that rule breaking was virtually nonexistent. Everyone belonged, every one of us vital to the lives of everyone else. Except for small misdeeds, there was no need for punishment because there was no crime.

No, my mother's disappointment and anxiety would be punishment enough. After Joshua—better that Mom suspect me of sleeping with Mangrove than that she know the truth.

I prepared myself for battle, the screaming war of words and recriminations, but when I arrived at the hanging shanty on Bough Two, the taper burned low in the candle holder, the flame nearly drowning in melted tallow. Mom lay stretched out and drooling in her hammock, unaware of my infraction. Maybe she thought I was sleeping at the clinic? Had she forgotten that it was Wingnut's turn? But if that were true, why had she left an unattended candle burning? That wasn't like her, my overcautious mother. A mystery, but not an interesting one, and I was tired. I pinched out the taper and dropped into my hammock, my head full of Mangrove's glistening berry-red lips and deep brown eyes.

Chapter Twenty-One

A dark shape hovered over me in my hammock, and then rocked me roughly until I realized I wasn't dreaming.

"Whaaa ..." I yawned, grabbing something to cover my naked body. And then I realized I'd slept in my clothes.

Cedrus grabbed my shoulder and whispered in a rough morning voice, "We need you at the school. Cassia can't teach today."

I rubbed my eyes and blinked them into focus. "Toona. Get Toona." Realizing that she'd be unable to continue teaching at the school after her twins were born, Cassia had been forced to take on a trainee. Toona had applied for and received the position, which meant I had to see both her and Salix nearly every day as I crossed Bough One to the clinic. Lucky me. But Toona's training didn't begin until afternoon. Lucky her.

"No time. Already late. Got a double shift today."

The construction of the labyrinthine bridges to the new skygardens in the south, weaving as they did through the eastern Outer Reaches before cutting back to the south, meant that the builders took turns camping away from their homes. I wasn't sure what that would eventually mean for the gardeners who worked there. Maybe they'd build shanties way out to the south for them, too.

I groaned and stretched. Today was not ideal for an early wake-up call, not after my late night with Mangrove. My skin tingled as I remembered our kiss, and I floated out of my hammock. My skin was already sticky in the moist morning air, itchy under my leather shorts and bandeau. "You can leave now," I shot at Cedrus.

"You're awake? Not going to fall asleep the minute I leave?"

"I'm a professional," I said in my best Michelia impression. "And I don't need you gawking while I change my clothes." Nailed it. He jumped down from the shanty, and I pulled off my itching clothes and grabbed one of my mother's soft cedar fiber shifts and a pair of fiber shorts. The air flowed through them and created a mild breeze around my body when I moved.

Outside, I splashed myself with tepid water from the rain barrel. It was refreshing at first, before it heated to my body temperature. We'd been skipping breakfast, saving our rations until mid-day, but my stomach wasn't feeling as empty as usual. The berries and dinner I scarfed down yesterday might have had something to do with that.

I peeked into the shanty again before I left. My mother still slept soundly. Maybe she'd taken some Passiflora tincture the night before. She was relying on it more and more these days to help her fall asleep.

Zelkova was already in the classroom when I arrived. The little redhead was curled in a fetal position on the pile of cedar mats. Her cheeks were flushed and she drooled, snoring softly. I placed my hand on her back, her bones prominent against my palm. I jostled her lightly.

"Wake up, Zelkova. Wakey, wakey."

Her eyelids drifted open and she smiled at me. Dark circles underlined the huge blue eyes in her thin face. "Hi, Ostrya."

"Hi yourself. You're early this morning."

"Yeah. Daddy had to work. Mommy is in bed. She's sick." Like Cedrus, Zelkova's father was a bridge builder. He was likely working the same shift as Cedrus.

"Did you have breakfast?"

"No."

The dull, hot throb of anger started building in me again. The same anger I had felt about Yucca. The anger I felt at the adults who were letting all this bad stuff happen. "Is there food at your house?"

"I don't think so." She stared at me with huge, hungry eyes.

I looked around the classroom. No food here and why would there be? Kids went home for lunch; they didn't eat at the school. I thought of those berries I had yesterday. Now I was angry at myself. Why hadn't I picked more? Why had I given them all to Mangrove? I should have saved them and brought them here this morning.

Mangrove was right. I had to go back across the abyss and pack all the food I could carry into my satchel. I would dig up beets and carrots, pick berries, whatever I could find. I'd replant what I could, help to feed the kids until the bridges to the new skygardens were built. I'd cross my little bridge to the west side after work today, load my satchel full of fruit and sneak it to the school. The kids would have it tomorrow.

Today, though, I would do what the adults could not. Today, I would feed Zelkova. And any other hungry little kids who came to school. But how? And then, I knew.

"Zelkova, you wait here. I'll be right back."

The door to the clinic was already open and Wingnut was wiping down the tables, preparing for the day. The key to the medical box hung around his neck. Just one lie. I was good at lying.

"Got an injury at the school. I need the key."

"Um, okay."

Wingnut unlocked the medical box. Easy. No questions asked. No Michelia to catch me out in a lie. I took the jar of apple alcohol from the lockbox and grabbed some bandages for good measure, then took off down the path toward the market.

Yew slumped in the chair at the front of the market, still waking up, picking his teeth with a stick. I glanced over my shoulder. No one around. No curious eyes. I tilted my satchel and he looked up and glanced inside. Suddenly interested, he leaned forward.

"Whatcha got there?"

"You know what I've got. Question is, what'll it get me?"

"What did you have in mind?"

"Food."

"Hmmm, that might be a tough one. We're having a famine, or didn't you hear?"

"I don't have time for this." I looked over my shoulder again. An older, tired looking guy walked by but didn't seem interested in my conversation with my loser dad. Even so, I wanted him to pass before I asked, "Have you got anything to eat, or don't you?"

"Hunters dropped off their catch yesterday. I was cleaned out almost immediately. Haven't had fruit or veg for weeks … you know that."

"Anything, anything at all." I was desperate and it showed. Not a great bargaining position.

"The entire jar."

"What?"

"For what I've got. The entire jar."

My father was an alcoholic. He was also a diabetic. A

terrible combination, and I knew I shouldn't. Especially as the doctor's trainee, I knew I shouldn't. I thought of Yucca slowly wasting away in that tiny hammock. I imagined naughty Zelkova, her mischievous grin, her red hair, all freckles and knees and toughness—she was already fading, and I couldn't. I just couldn't. I couldn't say no to Yew. I wasn't going to lose another patient.

I nodded and his dry lips twisted to reveal his teeth, yellow from chewing nicotiana. He reached forward and I placed the jar in his hands. My fingers lingered a moment as I considered the gravity of what I was doing, giving alcohol to my diabetic father. Well, he'd lived his life and made his choices. Zelkova deserved a chance to do the same. I let go.

He reached below the table and pulled out something from a hidden stash. "Put this in your bag and don't let anyone know you've got it. Or where you got it." An entire round of nut loaf. That's what my jar of alcohol bought me. Dry, tasteless nut loaf.

Yew read the look on my face and said, "Is it appetizing? No. But it's probably the most nutritious thing those little kids can eat."

I stared at him, then grabbed the nut loaf and crammed it into my satchel.

"Don't look so shocked. I know it's not for you. You're your mother's daughter." And he smiled at me, a real smile. He meant the comparison as a compliment.

Chapter Twenty-Two

❧

Deep in the satchel, my hand crumbled the dry round into several pieces as I walked back to the school. Erica sat on the doorstep nibbling a fir frond. I knelt beside her and pressed a piece of nut loaf into her palm. "Don't let anyone see you eat this." Her fingers wrapped around the morsel and she nodded her head, eyes serious, before taking a bite.

"Why are you out here? Was Zelkova picking on you again?"

She chewed her bite and swallowed before answering. "No. It smells bad in there."

I stepped in the doorway and the fecund stench of poo slammed me in the face. I gagged. "Did someone poo their pants?" That was probably not the way a teacher addressed a class, but I wasn't a teacher and—yikes! The rankness was toxic.

Though it was well past time for class to begin, only three children sat in the classroom. With Erica outside, a total of four kids had come to school. Out of the ten Cassia normally taught, not including poor Yucca, six were missing. Zelkova and a brown skinned boy whose name I couldn't remember pointed to Tung, thin, bowed, and slumped in a corner. A brown sludge ran down his leg. He didn't seem to notice.

I hadn't signed up for poo patrol; well, I hadn't signed up to sub this morning either, but you got what you got. "Tung! Go to the toilet box. I'll be there in a minute."

He moved slowly, dragging himself up from against the wall. "I'm dizzy." He wobbled across the room toward Erica on the doorsill, and then sat down abruptly.

"Okay. Rest there a minute. I'll help you." I reached into my satchel and pulled out two large hunks of nut loaf. Zelkova's eyes grew even bigger and she reached out her hand. "Eat this in here where no one can see. Then go sit outside with Erica and wait for me. Don't tease her!" I handed a piece to the other child before leaving the reeking school.

At the toilet box, I removed Tung's shorts. Luckily, they were cedar weave, which meant they were easier to clean. I wiped his bottom with the broadleaf maple leaves stacked next to the toilet for that purpose. In mid-wipe he groaned and bent double. I lifted him by the armpits. Startling how light his limp frame was. I centered his bony behind over the hole. The kid was sweaty and pale, his too-large head wobbly on his skinny neck. His skin felt clammy and hot, not warm like a healthily perspiring person. He was sick, really sick, and I hoped against hope that he hadn't infected Erica, Zelkova, and whoever that other kid was. The squirting noises stopped, and Tung collapsed his head into his two small hands.

"How do you feel?" I wiped the sweat from his brow with the side of my hand.

"Bad. Real bad." His shoulders began shaking. "Only babies cry. I'm no baby."

"It's okay, Tung. Adults cry, too. Especially when they feel bad." I stroked his head, all tight curls and tree sap and sweat. "Can you stay here? Don't move? I need to find Cassia. Then you and me, we're going to the clinic. Okay?"

I met Cassia on the path. She lumbered along, hand supporting her heavy belly. She was surprised to see me. "Why aren't you at the school? Is Toona there already?"

"No. One of the kids is sick."

"Who?" She grabbed my arm. "Is it Erica? She's so fragile, so delicate."

Cassia was always so concerned about Erica's well-being. It seemed to me that Erica was the last child in the canopy we needed to worry about. Her mother obviously doted on the girl; she was always clean, well-groomed, and despite the famine, she seemed well-fed. Clearly her parents were giving her every last morsel of their rations. Why would Cassia fret so about Erica?

And then I knew why Cassia cared so much for the girl. Why she scolded Tung for teasing her, even more than she scolded Zelkova. Suddenly, it was clear why Cassia took time to compliment the child's mother on Erica's clothing, and braids, and grooming, why she smiled so large when the girl greeted her in the morning and said goodbye in the afternoon. I saw it now, and the truth seemed so obvious. That was Cassia's secret. Erica was hers.

Almost as though she realized that I'd figured it out, that she needed to disguise her interest in Erica in case I wasn't as smart as I was, she said, "And Zelkova? Is she okay? What about Corylus?"

"That's his name! Corylus."

"What? He's sick?"

"No, no. I couldn't remember his name. Always escapes me. You only have four students today, you know."

"Well, I only had three yesterday, so that's an improvement. Who's sick?"

"Tung. He's got diarrhea. I'll take him to the clinic. Try to get some liquids into him. I needed to isolate him from the others in case he's contagious."

"Tung?" She blinked at me stupidly as though confused. "But he's never sick."

"He's a tough kid, all right. You're going to the school now?" I moved closer to her and tipped open my satchel so she could see the remains of the nut loaf. "For the kids."

"Where'd you get—"

"Shhh! Take it. Careful, so no one sees."

She looked around, but the few passersby paid no attention to us, two sisters exchanging greetings on the pathway. She snatched the remaining nut loaf from my bag and tucked it inside her bosom, one more bump on her body. "Thanks. But where?"

"Don't ask." I knew her secret, but I was keeping my own.

Chapter Twenty-Three

❧

"We're out of poultice, but I can give you more nettle tea." Wingnut glanced over Thevetia's shoulder as I entered the clinic with Tung nestled in my arms. He raised his eyebrows in an unspoken question before returning his attention to the old woman.

"Thank you, honey. I have enough tea. What I need is that potion for my fingers. So painful, they are."

"Sorry, Thevetia. We really have none left. We use fresh nettles to make it, and they've been eaten. We only have the dried tea. Would you like some of that?"

"No, honey. Wollemia and I have plenty. We won't take more than we need. Help me down." She lifted her arms up like a small child and he lifted her easily off the examination table and set her gently on her feet. "Such a good boy," she said, patting his hand. Her rheumy eyes drifted in my direction and watched me lay Tung on the second examination table. I rolled up a lightweight blanket and tucked it beneath his head.

"Poor little sprite." She shook her head and wobbled to

the doorway. "Terrible to see the little ones laid low like this."

Wingnut watched her leave, and then asked, "What's going on with Tung?"

"Diarrhea, weakness. Acute dehydration." I placed wet rags on Tung's forehead and slid one of our old mercury thermometers under his tongue. Like the alcohol we distilled for wound disinfectant, we kept our thermometers under lock and key. Michelia wasn't worried someone would steal them but locking them in our security box was our way of keeping them safe from careless breakage and loss.

The boy's temperature was elevated, not enough for panic, not under normal circumstances. But nothing was normal these days and given how the food shortage was already affecting the children, I was worried. When my mother walked in a few minutes later, I couldn't have been more relieved. She hurried to his side, took his pulse, and felt his forehead. She lightly pinched the skin on his arm and pronounced: "Elevated temp. Dehydrated. Pulse strong. We need to push fluids. Ostrya, mix a teaspoon each of lamb's quarters salt and beet sugar with eight ounces of water. Wingnut prepare some blackberry leaf packets for him. The tea will help with the diarrhea. Then you may leave, Wingnut. You've been on all night."

"It's okay, really. Thevetia was my only patient this morning."

"That may be, but I expect we'll be seeing more patients soon. Get some sleep. I need you at your best. Things will get worse before they get better."

The green salt powder and sugar mixture dissolved slowly in the warm water as I stirred. Of course! Why hadn't that occurred to me? I should have thought of making Tung an electrolyte drink first thing. That had been one of the first lessons I read at the start of my traineeship.

Nearly six months in, and there was little difference between my abilities and Wingnut's—and he'd been a trainee barely half the time I had. Maybe if I hadn't been so worried, so anxious, about Tung, I would have remembered my training. My mother was right—the more emotional I allowed myself to be, the worse doctor I was. I needed to maintain my scientific demeanor and distance myself from my patients. Even if they were funny, mischievous little boys.

I sat beside Tung on the table and cradled him in my arms. He didn't resist. Instead, he curled up beside me and gazed into my face with trusting eyes. "This will taste a little weird," I said. "Not gross exactly, but it's water with some other things in it. It's sweet and salty at the same time."

"Okay." His grubby little hands wrapped around the bowl. I helped him raise it to his lips.

"Slowly. Tiny sips."

He took a tentative taste, and then wrinkled his nose. "Weird."

"Yeah. It will give you energy. Take another sip."

"I don't want to."

"If you plug your nose, you won't taste it. Really. It works. Want to try?"

"Do I have to?"

"You don't have to plug your nose, but you do have to drink more."

"How much more?"

"Until you start to feel better. Want me to plug your nose for you? I can pinch it really gently. It won't hurt."

"Okay." He drank again, smacked his lips together, and said in a nasal voice, "I can sort of still taste it, but it's not too bad."

"Good. I knew you were a tough guy. Zelkova's right about you."

His lips curled in a self-satisfied smile before he guzzled the electrolyte liquid.

"Whoa! Whoa! Slow down!" said Michelia. "Ostrya, don't let him drink that so fast!" He sputtered and I grabbed the bowl from his mouth. "See? Too fast!"

"You startled him! He only choked because you yelled. He was doing fine!"

Tung wiped his mouth with the back of his hand, his eyes darting from my mother to me.

"Who is the doctor here? And who is the trainee?" She scowled. "I'd never hear that kind of backtalk from Wingnut!"

"Then maybe he should be your trainee. Not me!"

"Oh yeah, you think so? And what would you do then? You're unsuited for any other work."

Tung stared, fascinated. He was reprimanded so frequently that it probably amazed him to see someone else get yelled at for a change. And I knew he thought of me as a grown-up. An adult being rebuked? Fantastic entertainment.

But I stared for other reasons. It's one thing to think you're useless, but to hear your own mother confirm it? That's surreal.

What was she saying? She'd taken me on as a trainee out of what? Parental obligation? Pity? Did she honestly believe I was incapable of finding work elsewhere? Did she think no one else would want me as a trainee? It wasn't like doctoring was easy work. It demanded a huge amount of book learning, practice, and patience. Learning to be a doctor was difficult! If I could do this, I could do any of the other, less demanding jobs.

I wasn't any good at being a doctor, and my mother didn't think I would be good at any of the other jobs in the canopy either.

I put the bowl of electrolytes into Tung's hands and

stroked his unruly curls. "You've got this. Plug your nose so you can finish it."

Numbly I walked away from the clinic. If Mom truly felt that Wingnut would be a better doctor than me, she should train him to replace her. Not me. But then, what would I do?

Chapter Twenty-Four

Thundering toward me on the pathway was a bald, barrel chested man. He looked familiar, but I couldn't place him. He slowed down as he reached me.

"Ostrya! How is he? How's my boy?" And then it came to me how I knew him.

He'd been a friend of my father's when I was young. He often shared a joint with Yew on the doorstep of the hanging shanty. The two of them would smoke until they got silly-sleepy; that's what Joshua and I had called it. But he only visited when Michelia was working at the clinic. He never came around when she was home and my father never spoke of him to her.

One time she'd come home early to find the two of them laughing and teasing each other. That night, when they thought we were asleep, Michelia and Yew argued, and the friend never visited again. I had no idea this man, this old friend of Yew's, was Tung's father. But then, I only knew Tung from the few times I helped Cassia at the school, the few times I'd seen him teasing the old ladies. Tung was a healthy kid. In my six months as trainee, he never had a reason to come to the clinic. Until now.

"He's got diarrhea. A bit dehydrated. He's okay. Michelia will probably let you take him home."

"Oh, good! Good! Thank you, Ostrya. You were always my favorite, you know. So sorry about your brother. I never was able to tell you that. Your mother didn't allow me to see you kids."

"I know you, right? You were friends with Yew. You came by the shanty when we were little."

His eyebrows raised up into the middle of his forehead. He rubbed his bald head. "Shoot, Ostrya. Don't you know? I'm your uncle. Uncle Rhus. I'm Yew's brother."

What was this? I had an uncle? That meant Tung wasn't just a cute kid, another patient. He was my cousin! And Michelia had not only kept me from seeing my uncle, she'd prevented me from knowing my cousin. How had my father allowed this? I knew Yew was weak, but I had no idea how weak.

"No. I didn't know. I, umm ..." I stood awkwardly as the large, bald man wrapped his muscular arms around me and pulled me tightly against his broad chest. I stood there limply allowing myself to be embraced by this near stranger, my uncle.

"I figured you'd be lurking around. Get your paws off my daughter." My mother stood at the clinic doorway, implacable and fierce.

His arms fell away from me and his expression flattened. "Always a pleasure, Michelia. I've come to take my son home."

She stepped back and waved her arm Tung's direction. "He's all yours. Push fluids. There are some bags of blackberry tea to help with the diarrhea. Some prepared electrolyte fluid you can mix in with his water later tonight. We gave him a large dose already."

Rhus tramped into the shanty and I heard Tung's sweet voice call out with glee, "Daddy!"

"Ready to go home, Son?"

"Yeah!"

The two reappeared on the pathway, Tung resting on his father's shoulders, holding tightly to the shiny head, the father's arm wrapped awkwardly behind his back supporting the boy's back.

"Bye, Ostrya!" Tung's little voice sang out as they passed. Rhus winked at me when they walked by.

Her body stiff, her jaw set, Michelia scowled by the door until the duo was no longer visible. "Stay away from that man," she said before turning her back and returning to the clinic.

When I walked in, she was washing her hands. How was it that I had an uncle and cousin I knew nothing about? Why did my mother hate him so much? Was it his influence on Yew? The drug use? Was she afraid he'd have the same influence on me? That would be like her, thinking that I could so easily be swayed by someone else's behavior. Or that I couldn't think for myself.

I opened my mouth to complain, to tell her what I really thought, to finally get my feelings out there, when my grandmother entered the clinic.

"I saw that no-good Rhus walking down the path with his boy. Tell me he wasn't just here."

My mother sighed, a deep exhalation that communicated in one breath that she didn't have the energy today for Butia.

I wondered if I could perfect my impression of her and release a sigh of my own. Use it against her sometime. Would she understand her own message? Or would she tell me off for being disrespectful? Stupid thing to wonder about.

We get in trouble for doing the very same things our parents do, for behaving in the same way they've modeled to us from birth. Hypocrites.

Michelia said, "How many times have I told you not to chew that leaf in here? Honestly, such a disgusting habit."

Butia looked at my mother, her expression indifferent, insolent even. She cleared her throat with a guttural hack and spewed yellow-green mucus in the middle of the floor. Scarcely taller than four feet and with the girth of a large sparrow, white hair shorn so closely every bump of her skull was visible, thin blue-tinted skin stretched taut across her facial bones, she waved a fresh leaf in my mother's direction, lazily placed it on her tongue, and sucked it into her mouth. I bit the inside of my cheek to keep myself from laughing.

"Ostrya, come clean up your grandmother's mess."

There it was. I wasn't good enough to be her trainee, but I was good enough to clean the floor for her. I wouldn't do it yet, not until I gave my grandma a great big hug. I loved her, sort of, because that's how you're supposed to feel about your grandparents. But mostly, I appreciated how she always put my mom in her place. Tiny, bony, and old, she still ruled a room. And the canopy. I picked up Butia and swung her in a slow circle. Watching me totally love on the old lady would really irk my mother.

"Careful, careful. I'm getting fragile." Butia laughed. "Now wipe up my nicotiana juice before your mother has a fit."

"I'm sure you didn't come here only to flaunt your habit. Why are you here, Butia?" asked Michelia.

"Well, pleasant to see you, too, my daughter. At least my granddaughter doesn't mind my visits."

"Don't be like that, Mom. I'm sure you can imagine how busy we've been since the storm."

Butia made a big show of looking around the empty clinic.

"Yes, you look busy. What's this I hear of you having two trainees now?"

Wetting a rag to wipe the floor, I hid my face behind my hair and grinned spitefully to myself.

"You caught us at an unusual lull."

"But yes, you are right, Daughter. As much as I love seeing my granddaughter every chance I get—how is it possible for you to grow even taller, sweetheart—I am here on a council errand. As you may be aware, Hamamalis and Drypetes have directed the bridge crews to extend the pathways to the east and south—"

"Yes, Mother. Everyone is aware of that."

Butia ignored the cranky outburst and said, "Ostrya, sweetie, are you finished there? I really need to continue my conversation with your mother in private."

"Sure, Granny Butia."

"Why don't you head over to Wollemia's studio," she said. "Maybe you can help her with the sewing; it will improve your suturing skills. Give you a chance to visit with Salix, too."

As if I was going to set foot in that toxic environment.

Of course, Butia didn't know that Salix had been whispering with the other fiber workers about me for months now, giggling nastily whenever I passed. Her obvious crush on Wingnut had faded several boyfriends ago, yet she still held my one visit to his shanty against me. Now that he and I were working together at the clinic, her resentment of me only grew.

Salix was no longer my friend. It was questionable whether she ever had been. Now was not the time to tell Butia about it. Besides, it would seem petty and weak to complain, even more so in light of the sicknesses and food shortages. She'd only tell me these things would pass, to steel myself and get on with life. And she'd be right.

I grabbed my satchel off the floor and kissed my grandma on the cheek before ducking out the doorway.

"Tea?" I heard my mother ask.

"Sure," said Butia, and the clinic door slammed behind me. I heard the key turn in the lock. What was this? It wasn't enough that the door was closed, they were locking me out, too? What were they going to discuss? Was it about me? Maybe my mother had already told my grandma that she wanted Wingnut, not me, to be her trainee. Her position on the Council of Maestros gave Butia insight into the workings of the canopy that few others had. She and Mom were probably sitting there right now deciding my fate. Deciding where to move me, who to transfer me to for training. I'd have as little choice with the next traineeship as I'd been given with this one.

I crept around the back of the shanty that had been built sturdily into the trunk of a Great One. I dug my toes into the grooves of the Douglas fir and hoisted myself above the shanty. A short, sturdy limb jutted out above the roof and I stepped on to it, camouflaging myself with the needles of an adjoining branch. The cracks between the wall planks allowed breezes inside, but they also allowed sounds to reach outside. I lay across the limb, ear bent downward, and concentrated on the voices coming from within the shanty.

"Ummm. The tea smells grassy. What is it?"

"Rosemary-oregano. Gets me through the afternoons."

"Nicotiana is a surer stimulant."

"Hmmm, seems like I've heard that refrain before. Does wasting disease mean nothing to you? And next time I need an addiction, I'll let you know. Do you have any idea what that duff will do to your heart?"

"Mine's still beating, so I guess I'll survive. If I had to get by on this swill alone, I'd rather be dead."

"So, what's the news? Why'd we have to ask Ostrya to leave?"

Yes, Butia. Why'd you have to get rid of me? To what awful job detail are you and Mom going to assign me?

"The construction crews are running into difficulties. It's taking longer than Drypetes anticipated. And to get the new ground cleared, not to mention planted? Hamamalis's estimates aren't promising. Despite strict adherence to the commandments, our population has outgrown this section. Could be the past few wet seasons, or it could be your healing skills, Daughter. This cannot continue. And Drypetes is now saying the new pathways require added structural support, more materials. Hamamalis's scouts are unsure what level of agriculture the extended area can provide."

"Why are you telling me this? I'm a doctor. I have nothing to do with road building or gardening."

"Yes, but you are singularly positioned to know our current population."

There was silence then, and I wondered what was happening inside. Had they discovered they had an eavesdropper? But no, how could they know that? I glanced toward the pathway, obscured from view by the needles I'd pulled across the limb. No one could see me. I couldn't see them. I heard my mother's voice.

"No, I'm not. I report the births and the deaths to the council as I'm required. But I can only do that if patients have come through the clinic. I follow the rules. I certainly don't keep a population tally. That's your job, not mine. I've got enough to do as it is. If you're getting too old to do your job, perhaps you'd better retire. I'm sure there are plenty of underemployed climbers who would love to take your place. But I'm not one of them."

I could imagine the look on Butia's face when she said,

"Always such a hothead. Of course I know our population count. That's not the information I need."

"Then why are you here?"

"You're aware that the disaster took out all of the pathways to the western forest."

"Yes."

"And the majority of canopy soil has accumulated in the west."

"Yes. We all know this. This is not news. Why are you here?" Mom's voice was growing louder. She was getting angry, angrier than usual when she was with Butia.

"We use the pathways to get to the skygardens. We need the pathways to get the food. Is that simple enough for you to understand?"

Silence. Butia continued, "And if we can't get to the skygardens, we can neither grow nor harvest the food. Are you beginning to get the picture yet?"

"What are you saying?"

"I'm saying that we have some food in storage, but it's diminishing rapidly. We've already halved rations. We're looking at reducing even further. Our hunters must search farther afield due to overhunting. They are scouting now on average between three and five days. That's three to five days without fresh protein, and then, the quantity is simply not there."

"So we're completely writing off the west end? There must be some way to get back over there. Back to the skygardens—"

"Haven't you been listening? If there was a way, why would Drypetes and Hamamalis be focusing all their resources on the south? There is no way back to the west end."

Of course, I knew they were wrong. I'd been to the west end. I'd brought back food. But I was special. Modesty be damned, I was the best climber in the canopy. At least my long arms, long legs, and my spidery body were good for that.

My mother's voice sounded a little breathless. "The population was also reduced though, after the disaster. So we have fewer mouths to feed, right?"

"Yes, we lost members of our community. Too many. Unfortunately, we lost the wrong members. Mostly youths from the sixth and seventh boughs. Many builders. Too many gardeners. Exactly the demographic with the physical agility and strength we need to even begin thinking about crossing into the Outer Reaches. So yes, we lost some population. But not the right ones. And not enough to offset the loss in food resources."

A long silence followed her words. I thought maybe the conversation was over. They weren't going to discuss me at all. I was about to climb down when I heard my mother's voice again. "What exactly are you asking me, Butia?"

Another moment passed, and my grandmother answered, "I think you know."

"Say it. If you want me to do it, at least have the courtesy to say it."

"As you wish." I heard a spitting noise, Butia expelling her chaw on the clinic floor again. I expected to hear my mother scold her, but she didn't. "If it becomes necessary to order a cull, I'll need a list of the ill and ailing."

Why was she asking for that? We didn't keep a list of who was sick—no, that wasn't right. We had our home visit list, but that was only so Wingnut, Mom, and I could share the work.

"I'm a healer. I've sworn an oath."

"Yes, I know. I was married to a doctor for years. Your father, remember? First, do no harm. I'm not asking you to harm anyone. But as the census taker and a member of the council, I have the authority to obtain the medical records of any member of the community."

"Only in the event of grave danger to the entire community—like a viral outbreak."

"I believe the potential starvation of the entire community qualifies as grave danger, and so do the other members of the council. I expect your list by the end of the week."

"No! I can't! I won't do it!" Michelia was yelling, totally emotional, completely unscientific, utterly unprofessional.

My grandmother's voice softened, and I strained to hear. She was using her politician voice, the voice she used before every election, when she assured the canopy for the millionth time that they needed a sure, steady hand with a lifetime of experience to make the difficult decisions for them. "I know how hard this is, my dear. Who will or will not have the honor of feeding the Great Ones will be a decision for the council. It's not your decision."

"That list would be a death sentence to every person on it. The mere act of writing a name on it is the same as pushing them off a tree limb."

"I'm sorry, Michelia. This is the way it must be. Don't make me compel you. You know I can, but that will do no one any good."

Footsteps, and then Butia's voice again. "End of the week, remember."

The key turned in the lock. The door opened and closed. I climbed out of the tree and crept around the side of the shanty. From within I heard a soft weeping. My mother's.

Chapter Twenty-Five

Does the lurking spider have feelings? A conscience? Does it mourn those it kisses with numbing poison? Does it ask forgiveness for the lives it throttles in its silky embrace? Does it hate itself for its very nature? Spying from a dark, shadowy corner, does it recognize humans as kindred spirits—kissing and killing as easily as we breathe?

The story of the cull was a rite of passage, a tree top legend, a tale of horror that kids passed along to scare the younger ones. I don't remember how old I was when I first heard the story. The older kids at school had spooked Mangrove, Sorbus, Salix, and me with the tale just as those older than them had spooked them, and those older than them, and so on back through generations. The culling was a story that you outgrew—something so horrific that it could never have happened. And I, perhaps more than most, believed it was a cautionary tale meant to terrify and keep the younger ones in line. After all, I knew the cannibals and the end of the world stories in *The Book of Silvanus* were a lie. This was simply one more of those.

And yet, eavesdropping on my mother and grandmother

had rattled me. Butia had asked my mother for a list of the sick, ailing, and old. She'd asked for the least productive members of the canopy, the expendable. What names would my mother write on that list? Thevetia for sure. She forgot more and more on a daily basis. She hadn't gardened since I was a kid, and as far as I knew, she hadn't been assigned another job. But what about Wollemia? Salix and the other trainees were doing her work these days. Her mind was still solid; she must be teaching them or directing them somehow. She was contributing, at least a small amount.

Wollemia was on the Council of Maestros. None of the council would vote to sacrifice one of their own. The consummate survivor, my grandmother would never suggest a solution that put her own self at risk. That meant Butia, Drypetes, Hamamalis, and Wollemia were all safe. And Wollemia would never vote to sacrifice Thevetia, so the old woman would be safe, I reasoned.

What about little kids like Zelkova and Tung? True, they didn't eat much, but they didn't contribute to the community either. But then, they'd be strong in a few years, so they'd probably be considered worth saving. And what about Cassia and Cedrus's babies? Or the other pregnant couples? Would they have to give up their babies after they were born or abort them? What about adults with chronic diseases, mental illnesses, or addictions like Yew? They worked, but they were sick and always would be. They might even pass their genetic frailties to their descendants. Would they be considered expendable? Did they have less value as community members than others?

If only the working young, healthy or as yet undiagnosed, survived, who would teach and guide the community? Why would anyone choose to procreate if their children would be culled? Who would choose to work selflessly in a community that forgot their contributions when life became difficult, only to sacrifice them when they got old?

What about the commandment that all spirits are equal? Didn't that matter anymore? If that commandment was no longer true, what about the other commandments? What about *The Book of Silvanus,* upon which our entire canopy society was built?

Was it all a lie?

I'd been a doubter for so long—but I was a half-cynic and harbored a secret desire to be proven wrong. And now, hanging over the abyss of clarity, I clung desperately to my limb of suspicion, unwilling to know the truth.

My feet walked without my bidding to the west-facing edge of Bough Four. The tree trunk tempted me to climb. I tied down the front flap of my satchel and tightened it across my chest before I dug my fingers into the bark and lifted myself up. The gnarled crusty tree pressed into my feet and massaged them. The stretch and pull of my biceps and triceps radiated power through my thigh and calf muscles, and I lost track of time and place. My mind floated. The movement of my muscles, the expansion and contraction of my lungs, the wind in my face and the rough trunk against my skin were my entire world. Nothing else existed. I was alive. I was one with the forest.

My body took me where I needed to go, and my muscles remembered how to traverse the flimsy branches. Before my brain fully registered what I was doing, I was crossing the abyss and sailing from limb to limb toward the overgrown skygardens.

I stepped from one weedy plot to the next, harvesting dandelion greens and miner's lettuce, pressing it all into my satchel and looking for more. I foraged entire nettle plants that made my fingers tingle and burn. I stuffed myself with huckleberries and salmon berries—I could eat my fill now and give my ration to the school children tomorrow—before shaking the branches and gathering all I could to fill the space remaining in my satchel. On my way out of the skygardens, the white glow of a cluster of oyster mushrooms caught my eye. They wouldn't fill an empty stomach, but the serotonin they released in the human brain could do wonders for the community's dark mood. My bag would hold no more and I didn't know when I'd be able to cross over again. The mushrooms would disintegrate where they grew.

Some itchy fir needles had fallen into my shirt during the climb, and I reached in and brushed them out. That was my answer! I tucked my shirt into my shorts and then plucked the mushrooms from the tree and dropped as many as I could into my top. When I could carry no more, I climbed back up to my bridge. The setting sun glared an angry red and I knew I'd cut it close. Any later, and I wouldn't have been able to see my way across.

The bridge gave a sickening lurch as I started my crawl across. The satchel was thick and tight across my chest, but the items I was carrying weren't that heavy. Leaves and berries don't weigh much, and mushrooms are mostly air, but all together they increased my total weight. I tried not to think about falling and said a quick prayer to the Great Ones, though I didn't believe they'd help me, not really. The crossed branches squeaked as they rubbed against each other and I crawled faster while willing myself to weigh less.

On the other side, I loosened the satchel—it was digging into my chest and I was afraid the mushrooms would be completely squished. I climbed down to Bough Seven, and though I knew it was probably not a great idea to stop off there—Salix likely had minions eager to report back—my arms and shoulders were numb from climbing. I had done something great for the canopy, something no one else could have done. Let Salix spread all the lies about me she wanted. I wouldn't care tomorrow when the kids had full stomachs.

The thought of those full stomachs puffed me up with pride. I didn't care about the curious gazes following me as I approached the central stairway. I jogged down the stairs, my satchel banging against my stomach, not stopping until I reached our shanty. My mother lay dead to the world again, snoring in her hammock through a double dose of Passiflora. She was making this a habit, and I probably should have felt concerned, but if I'm honest, I was only relieved that I wouldn't have to explain myself.

I pulled off my satchel and dropped it in the corner under my hammock, and then stripped off my top and dumped out the mushrooms. I was bone tired. My eyes were closing as I climbed into my hammock. I would give Cassia the food in the morning.

Chapter Twenty-Six

Despite my physical exhaustion, I kept waking throughout the night. My arms and shoulders throbbed. I tossed and turned in my hammock, unable to find a comfortable position. The netting pressed into my skin. I tried to cushion my body with my squirrel skin blanket, but there was no breeze in the shanty and I was soon covered in sweat. I was tired, thirsty, and my head throbbed. I pulled on my clothes and stumbled outside to the water bucket. It had been several days since we'd had a good hard rain, and despite the frequent drizzle, the water level was low. I dipped a cup in and took a sip, warm and not very refreshing but still a welcome antidote to dry mouth.

Pressing my hands against the fir tree, I stretched my legs behind me. I leaned into the stretch, dropping my head below my shoulder blades. My arm and leg muscles tautened and I held that position a minute or two, feeling a pleasant, light burn. I released the stretch and rolled my shoulders forward and back, hearing a satisfying crack as everything dropped into place.

A shadow ran toward me. I stepped into the pathway and

he called out, "Ostrya! Is that you? Quickly, we need you at the clinic!"

Only then did I remember that it had been my turn to overnight at the clinic. Just my luck, an emergency on what should have been my watch. My mother was right: I really was terrible at this job. She would be better off with Wingnut for a trainee.

No time for self-pity though. The man had been frantic. I sped off to the stairway and flew around the spiral to Bough One and then to the clinic. My sister was waiting outside the clinic door, leaning heavily against a woman. Even in the dim light, I could see how swollen her hand was. I touched it lightly and she winced. The swelling was spongy, her lower arm angry and red. A spider bite.

She was breathing rapidly and moaning. Was she allergic? I'd never seen this reaction to a spider bite before, but I'd only treated orb weaver bites. Had she encountered a jumping spider? Or was this something else?

"We can't get in," said the woman holding Cassia. I stared stupidly. "The door is locked."

Of course, the key would be around my mother's neck. My mother, who was still asleep on Bough Two. She would have locked up the clinic when she left, when I didn't arrive to relieve her. But why hadn't she sent for Wingnut when I didn't arrive? No time to waste on questions. I had to get the key. Maybe someone else could run up to Bough Two and retrieve the key? Cassia cried out.

My mind moved slowly, sleepily, and the woman yelled, "Hurry! Her water broke!"

I looked down. The pathway was not wet. What was the woman talking about? "She's in labor?" I asked.

It was the woman's turn to stare.

"Ostrya," said Cassia in between breaths. "Babies ... are ... coming."

My sister in labor, her hand and arm swollen with spider toxin. Locked door. I set my shoulder to the door, slamming against it with an angry grunt. The man who had raced to get me joined his strength to mine. A sickening screech and the wood frame bent and splintered. One final shove, and the door hung askew on bent and rusty hinges.

"Help her to the table," I ordered, my brain now fully awake and my adrenaline pumping. I sparked a light and lit the tapers around the clinic. What was next? Cassia's babies were coming! No babies had been born since I started my traineeship. These would be the first I'd help to deliver. I was glad I read those pregnancy chapters in the ancient medical texts when I should have been doing other things for Michelia. I remembered the basics: contractions, dilation, amniotic fluid, the head and shoulders first. But what should I do now?

"When did your water break, Cassia?" I asked.

She leaned into the table and moaned with what must be a contraction building. She exhaled and relaxed again. "I don't know. Maybe an hour ago?"

"Go get my mother. I mean, Michelia," I told the man who'd helped me knock down the door. To the woman I said, "Get me some water, please."

While I waited for water, I blew the banked fire beneath the brazier to light. After I fed some sticks to the fire and began heating yesterday's water, I examined Cassia's spider bite. This I knew how to treat.

"How'd you get bitten?" I asked as I flushed the wound with a cool chamomile rinse.

"Web outside my door. Walked right into it."

I walked to the medicine box, but of course it was locked. That key would be around my mother's neck, too. I needed apple alcohol to disinfect the bite—the apple alcohol I'd traded to Yew to feed the kids. There must be more. Mom would have noticed we were out and stocked more.

Maybe I could brew a marshmallow root poultice for the bite. Better would be a raw honey swab, but our honey supply had run out a month ago. The beehives had been on the west end. Next time I went across, I'd have to see what state they were in, and then figure out how to get honey without being stung. I was no beekeeper.

I bandaged the spider bite, making a mental note to get some alcohol for it. Cassia's face went red. "Breathe through the contraction, Cassia. Inhale, exhale." She gripped my hands and exhaled a low, deep moan. The woman entered the clinic then with a large bowl of water and poured it into the brazier. "Thanks. Another bowl, please." I began washing Cassia, preparing her for the birth.

Where in the name of Pseudotsuga's balls was my mother?

"Where's Cedrus?" I asked after Cassia's contraction passed. Had he left before she'd begun laboring? Must have. He never would have left her. He was always so attentive and worried about Cassia.

"Bridge crew."

Then I remembered. He'd be gone another day.

The woman carried in a second bowl of water and I left Cassia's side to top off the pot over the brazier, and that was the end of my practical knowledge. Where was my mother? I hoped that guy would be able to wake her. I didn't know how much Passiflora she'd taken. And Wingnut? He'd know even less than me. Oh, if only Mom would hurry.

Fear climbed up from my stomach and squeezed my throat tightly as a noose. I had only ever been responsible for myself. I was well used to the heart-pounding, exhilarating sensation of climbing in the Outer Reaches when my hand slipped or I misjudged the distance from one limb to another. This was a new feeling. This feeling, a sharp-edged dread, sent bile cascading from my stomach to my ears. When I was climbing, I could self-correct; I had the strength and endurance to power through. But this situation—my sister in pain, my nieces or nephews trying to be born—I had never felt such terror.

And then I remembered, yes, I had. Only once. And that had ended badly.

I picked up the small pan of hot water. My hand shook so fiercely that I spilled some on myself and scalded my toe. I put the pan back on the brazier. Cassia was breathing rapidly and sweating profusely in the morning heat. Her contractions were growing more forceful. I stroked her brow and rubbed her back. She leaned into my palm each time she labored. "Michelia is on the way," I said. "You'll have your twins in your arms before you know it. Remember, breathe and count. Count with me—"

Her eyes locked on mine. She got to three before another labor pain grabbed her. My hand went to my neck, reaching for my stethoscope, a reflex. But it was lost forever to the forest floor. I was without my healer's lucky charm. I pressed two fingers into Cassia's abdomen, feeling in vain for a fetal heartbeat.

"What in the name of Pseudotsuga's balls happened to my door?" said Michelia. I'd never been so happy to hear her voice. "Get all the lookie-loos out of here. We have work to do."

I hadn't realized that climbers had begun to gather around the clinic door. I grabbed one of them. "Please get someone to bring Wingnut." No, he'd be a slow climber at best with that weakened shoulder. "On second thought, wake Mangrove on Bough Seven, north end. Tell him to fetch Cedrus from the bridge crew in the Outer Reaches." I hauled the broken door as best I could across the doorway in an attempt to keep some privacy for Cassia.

Mom unlocked the medical box and looked inside. "Where's the alcohol?"

Oh duff.

"We used it all," I said as casually as possible.

She pulled me aside, away from Cassia, and hissed, "What do you mean we used it all? On what?"

"Um, you know, cuts and scrapes. Disinfectant. We've got more, right?"

"We'll have to make do, somehow. Not good, not good at all. No, we don't have more. The storm cleaned us out, all the injured, the burns. It will take months before a new supply is ready." She washed her hands and arms with soap and water before approaching Cassia.

"Looks like a fine day for twins," she said with forced cheer. "Do you know what time your water broke?" She palpated Cassia's abdomen.

Cassia moaned as another pang hit, so I answered for her. "She thought an hour ago, maybe one and a half by now."

"Cassia, you're fully dilated and—Ostrya, get ready—your first baby is about to crown. Are you ready?"

Cassia curled into a ball and moaned. "Been ready— aaaahh—since—"

"Breathe, Cassia. Don't forget to breathe. One-two-three-breathe. One-two-three-breathe. Ostrya, help Cassia into an upright position. Cassia, it will be easier to push sitting up. But wait until I say."

I took Cassia by the shoulders and helped her to a sitting position, and then I climbed around behind her, rubbed her back, and coached her through her breaths. Mom positioned herself in front to help guide the first baby from the womb. Cassia grunted and pushed.

"Okay, I see a beautiful brown head. Stop pushing," said

Mom. She maneuvered the infant's shoulder through the birth canal before ordering, "One more good push."

Cassia took a deep breath and grunted. Mom scooped a tiny bundle into her waiting hands and turned around, hiding the infant from view. A few seconds later, a high-pitched wail filled the shanty and Mom said, "Thank the Great Ones. Cassia, you have a beautiful baby girl." Michelia placed the infant in her mother's arms, and then cut the umbilical cord. Cassia laughed, tears weeping from her eyes, and then groaned again. "We have more work to do," said Mom. "Brother or sister wants to come out and play."

Mom motioned to me. I squeezed my sister's shoulder and took the tiny, squirming baby from her arms. She was a warm, sticky, squirmy little thing with squished up eyes and a howling little mouth. I held her securely against my chest and carried her to the brazier. Cradling her in one arm, I gazed at the first baby I'd ever seen born. My niece. An angry red bean jutted from her belly. Her tiny face was squeezed up into a purple grimace, her mouth a tiny red O of squalls. Her itty-bitty legs and arms waved impotently in the air. Ten tiny fingers and ten tiny toes. I dipped my elbow into the water and felt the warmth drip down my arm toward my palm. It was warm but not hot.

After dipping a rag into the bowl of water, I dabbed away the blood and vernix from my niece's face. I rubbed a bit harder on her belly and legs, washed her arms and behind. Her wee fingernails and toenails were minuscule brown moons, perfect and symmetrical. I wet another clean rag and gently washed the blood from the tuft of black hair on her tiny head, careful to avoid the pulsating soft spot at the top of her forehead.

Was every human baby born this perfect? Such tiny beauty. Such potential. How did a creature this innocent and helpless turn into a nasty tree rat like Salix or a useless drunk like Yew? What happened to change this into that?

"No! The cord!"

Mesmerized by my squirming niece, I had nearly forgotten another baby was ready to be born. "Do you need my help, Mom—Michelia?"

She shook her head and blew a stray hair from her sweat-covered forehead. Cassia continued to moan softly.

"Take care of that little one."

I bent back to the bath, the splashing water and wailing baby mixing with Cassia's weak groans. My niece stared at me with serious walnut-bark eyes. I remembered reading that newborns are near-sighted, and I bent my head closer, murmuring, "I'm your auntie, beautiful little one. I love your long eyelashes and your sweet little toes and each one of your tiny ten fingers." Her eyes widened and scrunched up again. She clenched her fists and let loose again, opening and closing her hands with each shaking wail. I dabbed gently at the pinkish brown skin, removing the last stray bits of blood before swaddling her tightly in a small blanket. I was so entranced with my sister's beautiful newborn that it took me several minutes to realize that Cassia had stopped moaning.

She lay without moving on the table where my mother worked furiously. I rocked the settling baby and watched stupidly, trying to make sense of what I was seeing. Blood soaked through Cassia's shift and began to pool beneath the table.

"What ... what happened?"

"The second placenta has ruptured. I need to deliver this second baby so I can stop the hemorrhaging. I need your hands. Put the baby in the bassinet and scrub your hands. Soap and hot water—as hot as you can bear."

After placing my niece in the tiny cedar branch bassinet, I scrubbed using the water that waited on the brazier. Mom grabbed my hands and pressed them into Cassia's abdomen. Everything was red: my mother's hands, my hands, the floor, Cassia's nightdress, Mom's clothes. Terror gripped my throat and fizzed in my temple, squeezing me around the forehead, pounding through my eye sockets. A warm dizziness was building inside me. Mom was frantic and cursing and that was worse somehow than all of the red. Cassia still didn't move and the red liquid dripped, dripped, dripped to the floor, hot and sticky and reeking. I tasted the bile in my throat, acrid and stinging. I swallowed it back down.

Sweat dripped down Mom's face. She dipped her head against her shoulder, wiping her forehead dry. She bit her bottom lip, her brow furrowed in concentration, and bowed over my sister's body. Finally she straightened, holding a wrinkled, tiny body in her blood-drenched hands. A boy. Silent. Unmoving. For the briefest of moments, my mother's eyes radiated sorrow, and then it was gone, covered in a gauze of clinical detachment. "See what you can do," she said, placing the tiny boy in my hands.

What did that mean? Was there some chapter I was supposed to have read called what to do when your sister gives birth to a dead baby before bleeding to death? What did Michelia expect me to do? I held my nephew against my chest as I'd held my niece only moments ago in a moment of joy, exhilaration, love. This was—horrible.

Book learning and practice guided my movements then. I opened the tiny mouth and cleared it. I compressed the tiny sternum with my finger, puffed tiny breaths into the lungs. My niece began whimpering in the bassinet. My ear to her brother's chest, I listened for the faintest of heartbeats. I continued performing chest compressions and breathing into my nephew, his purpling body still and quiet in sharp contrast to the tiny squalling bundle in the bassinet.

Compressing and puffing, puffing and compressing, I tried beyond all hope to revive his tiny body.

A warm hand rested on my shoulder. "There's nothing else you can do," said Mom. "Stop now."

I glanced up. Mom's face was blurry and that's how I understood I'd been weeping. I dashed away the tears and looked into my mother's cold, clinical eyes.

"Wash your hands and comfort the baby. I'll take care of this."

This? My nephew. Didn't she even see his humanity?

My numb hands barely felt the water as I washed them, the red leaving my skin and turning the basin pink. I scooped my wailing niece from the bassinet and cuddled her. Was I comforting her? Or myself?

Mom swaddled my nephew in a clean blanket. Covered with a fresh blanket, my sister lay silent on the examination table, the blood under the table beneath her congealing in the warm room.

"Is she—"

"Resting," said Mom. "She's lost a lot of blood, but she'll be okay."

A warmth cradled my brain then, fuzzy and comforting. My sister was okay. The adrenaline drained from me and the dizziness filled the empty spaces. I knew I was about to faint, but no way was I dropping this baby. I leaned into the wall as the deep, dark veil billowed down over my vision. I slumped to the floor, unseeing yet hearing all, my niece unharmed in my loosening grip. My mother cursed. The broken door scratched and creaked and heaved open. I heard the soul-piercing howl of a man who believes his beloved is dead.

Chapter Twenty-Seven

What happened next was a blur, a passing of shadows before my closed eyelids. Cedrus shouting, my mother yelling, my niece squalling, and two more male voices arguing. Feet thundered past me, too many for the small space. Cedrus's sobbing and shouting faded away. Mom cursed and my niece was lifted from my arms.

"Ostrya? Honey? Can you hear me?"

And Wingnut's voice, "Pseudotsuga's balls! He really hit you hard, Michelia."

"Don't worry about that right now. Rouse Ostrya. She fainted. Get the peppermint oil."

"But Michelia, you're bleeding all over!"

"Wingnut, who's the doctor here? It's only a little graze. Wake Ostrya."

A sharp, cold, minty odor, a clearing of fog, Wingnut's wrinkled brow. "Welcome back, Ostrya."

My brain wobbled inside my head. I gripped my skull in two hands and willed the spinning to stop. "I'm okay. Lost it there for a minute. Too much blood."

He helped me sit up and held a bowl of water to my lips. "What happened in here?"

The water was lukewarm and I wondered if he'd taken it from the brazier. Remembering the pink wash water, I pushed the bowl away from my face and tried to stand.

"Careful, careful," said Wingnut, grabbing my arm.

I looked at Cassia, asleep on the table, a dozing baby curled against her breast, the red pool beneath the table, and the still bundle in the second bassinet. My mother held a crimson rag to her face. "Mom! What happened? Let me look!" Still woozy, I nearly tipped over.

"Ostrya, sit back down. I've got this," said Wingnut. He helped my mother to the second examination table and winced as he examined her wound beneath the cloth.

"Cedrus struck me. He thought I'd killed Cassia. Sorbus and Mangrove dragged him out. How is he?"

"He'll be okay. Sorbus will see to him." Wingnut's large frame bent over the medical chest. "Where's the alcohol?"

I gulped. "It's gone. We used it."

He glanced at Cassia's sleeping form on the table. He probably thought I meant we used it on her. I imagined Yew, drunk on our medical supply. I'd been so stupid. "Do we have more?" he asked.

"No," said my mother. "Use soap and water."

Ashamed of my terrible judgment, I looked at the floor. The flies had found the half-congealed blood. The buzzing, disgusting mess needed to be dealt with. I might be the worst medical trainee in the entire history of the canopy, but I could certainly clean a floor.

By the time Mangrove stepped into the clinic, I was on all fours mopping up blood. He took a tentative step in my direction, and then took a rag and knelt beside me.

"Where's Cedrus now?" Wingnut asked as he stitched the wound above Michelia's eye.

Mangrove glanced up at Wingnut. "I told him he'd better stay away for now. Thought we should clean up in here first. No one wants to see their partner's blood all over the floor." He rinsed the red from his rag and continued scrubbing the floorboards.

"Ostrya, check Cassia's pulse," said my mother. I rinsed my hands in the pink water before standing. My niece slumbered peacefully on her mother's chest, moving up and down with each of Cassia's breaths. How was I going to fake this? My stethoscope was gone—more proof that my mother had chosen the wrong trainee. I could see Wingnut was better at this than me as he calmly sutured my mother's forehead with his quick, even stitches.

I laid my fingers against Cassia's right wrist—her left was wrapped, the swelling flesh around the spider bite pushed against the rags—when her eyes flickered open. She smiled drowsily. "I'm so tired," she said. She kissed the top of her daughter's head. "Where's my other baby? Boy or girl? I can't remember."

She didn't know! Her mind had been unconscious as her body had birthed her son. She didn't know he had been stillborn, or that his body awaited burial in the bassinet in the corner of the clinic. I opened and closed my mouth. No words came out. Standing there, useless, I burst into tears.

Mangrove's arms were around me then, pulling me away. My mother's voice rose in the small room. "Get her out of here!" Cassia was crying, my mother explaining, my niece wailing.

Chapter Twenty-Eight

How does a doctor recover from the death of a patient? Do they get used to it? At some point, do they become anesthetized against it? Would I ever get used to it? How could I, especially when the dead patient was my infant nephew? And if I got used to the death of others, what kind of person would I be?

My mother had lost many patients. Illnesses and accidents were plentiful in the canopy. Old age was largely unheard of. The few who made it that far, especially if they'd held on to their minds—Butia, Wollemia, Drypetes—were kind of miraculous. In a community that depended upon physical strength and balance, the common malady of arthritis was the beginning of the end. Yucca had been the first patient I lost to starvation, but young children had been succumbing to malnutrition and disease long before we lost the western skygardens. Learning to walk was an adventure that many didn't survive, even on the lower boughs.

Intellectually, I knew the life of a doctor would be challenging; there was only so much we could do. My mother preached stoic acceptance. If I couldn't harden my heart against adversity, if I continued to feel too much, I would never survive this job and my patients would ultimately suffer.

Mom told me once she learned this early on in her own traineeship. Her father had taught her—maybe too well, I often thought—how to distance herself emotionally from those she doctored. He had taught her to focus on the science of the healing and to leave the bedside manner on the ground with the earthwalkers. Bedside manner didn't save lives. Science and toughness did.

When the time had come for Michelia to take over the duties of doctor to the canopy, she had chewed on his words, digested them fully, and she had bid her maestro-father goodbye as he made his plunge to feed the Great Ones. She had not shed a single tear for him, or so she claimed, and she knew this had been the best way to honor him.

But I'd seen her cry about a death. Once. One life taken too soon and felt too deeply. I'd seen those blue and green eyes shed tears once, and I'd never forgotten.

Having cried myself into numb apathy, I curled on my hammock and stared at the wall of the hanging shanty. Mangrove sat on the floor beside me, saying nothing. I thought he'd fallen asleep, but when I turned to look, he was awake and watchful. My mother called out and Mangrove lifted Michelia easily into the shanty before leaving me to her care.

She sat on the edge of my hammock, rocking me downward so my body pressed against her back. She rested her hand on my arm, absently stroked my skin. I waited for the lecture, but she was silent.

Minutes passed before she sighed and stood. She walked to Joshua's shelf and lit his candle. "I'm sorry," she said. "I'm sorry this was your first birthing experience. I'm sorry this happened to your sister. I'm sorry about all of it."

An apology? From my mother? For what? She hadn't killed anyone. That had been me, all me. I had let my nephew die. I had given the alcohol to Yew. I was inadequate. If I'd read more of the medical texts, if I'd only studied harder.

"Your connection to your patient was too close, too personal. You were too young for this birth experience."

And there it was. My fault. Even my mother acknowledged it. I was too young. Too close. Too emotional. I had plenty of remorse but no more tears. I said, "I should have saved the baby. I should have tried harder."

The light from Joshua's candle flickered when my mother turned. "Stop it. I will not have you blaming yourself. That child's fate was determined long before you laid hands on him. You did all you could, everything that could be expected of a doctor under these conditions. And I will not have anyone in this canopy questioning your skill, not even you."

She didn't have to say what I already knew: My inadequacy would reflect poorly on her. My deficiencies were hers. My admission of fault would be blamed on her.

"You stopped being a silly, emotional teenager when you became my trainee." Her eyes glittered in the candlelight. "You were entitled to your feelings when you were Ostrya, daughter of the doctor. You belong to the canopy now and have since you became a medical trainee. Any hindsight you have now won't change the past or infuse breath into the still lungs of that baby. You use what you've learned on the next patient and the next and the next. Your emotions are useless to that dead baby. And they're downright dangerous to the well-being of this canopy." She turned her back to me, her voice quieter now. I strained to hear her. "Grief and guilt are luxuries we can't afford. We have a community to care for, sicknesses to heal, injuries to mend. Today we had a stillborn child. Tomorrow we'll have a malnourished five-year-old."

She turned back and embraced me. I mean, she really

hugged me. An arm-wrapping, boob-smashing mother-daughter squish like none she'd ever given me before. Not even when I was a child, at least, not that I could remember. Her actions didn't fit with the lecture she'd just given, and it made me wonder. Had Mom been talking to me? Or to herself? Were these her words? Or was she repeating words spoken to her by the doctor who had trained her, her father, telling her to push down her emotions, not to acknowledge her feelings, to believe only in the science.

Whose impractical, unprofessional, unscientific emotions were we talking about here?

Early the next morning, Mom and I attended the feeding ceremony for Cassia's baby. Not all the assembled mourners could fit on the branches that surrounded the feeding altar; Cassia's role as teacher of the young children had earned her the love and respect of the canopy. Residents of all seven boughs attended the ceremony. Cedrus was close to the front, flanked by Sorbus and several other builders on their day away from the bridge site. The four elders hovered at the edge of the feeding altar. Butia wore the ceremonial cape.

I glimpsed Yew on the eastern side of the crowd. Of course, he would be here—he was Cassia's father, after all. The baby would have been his first grandson. Mangrove stood behind him and craned his neck, obviously searching for someone. I lifted my hand tentatively and he saw me. He smiled encouragingly. I dropped my hand and smiled back. Briefly. This wasn't the place or the occasion for smiles.

Even Salix was there, cozied up with her group. She glared at me, and when she caught my eye, her lips curled into a mean smirk. She whispered something to the girl beside her. It must have been a whopper—the girl gasped, shook her head, and stared at me. Cassia was noticeably absent from her son's feeding ceremony. She and her daughter were at the clinic with a vigilant Wingnut.

Beside me, my mother gingerly touched her eye, swollen shut, a bandage positioned over her eyebrow. And beneath it, I knew, was a beautiful example of the continuous suture technique, courtesy of Wingnut.

"Does it hurt much?" I asked.

Mom looked at me. She cocked her head and asked, "Where's your satchel?"

I looked down. She was right. I'd forgotten my satchel. With all that had happened yesterday, I'd forgotten to put it on this morning. I never went anywhere without it, and now that she mentioned it, I felt naked. As if I needed more evidence that I wasn't thinking straight.

Butia performed the ceremony with all the gravity and emotion expected of her. Raising her hands to the sky and tipping her head back, cape flowing behind her, she led us in a tearful lullaby for the stillborn child and called for the Feeding of the Great Ones. The tiny, swaddled body was raised over the Altar of Earth and released to the forest floor.

After this latest innocent had been fed to the trees, we all scattered to our duties. My mother hurried off to relieve Wingnut. I returned to our shanty to retrieve my satchel.

When I got there, my satchel wasn't beneath my hammock. Had I forgotten it at the clinic yesterday? I reached back in my memory. No, I hadn't brought it to the clinic. Cassia's neighbor had met me outside when I was washing my face. I'd gone to the clinic without my satchel, full of food for the children. Lettuce leaves would be wilted. Berries would be hot, fermenting juice. Where was my satchel?

Chapter Twenty-Nine

The small clinic was full of women when I returned. I'd know the back of Salix's curly head anywhere. I'd spent more hours than I cared to remember combing the needles out of her thick black hair. Beside her, Wollemia's silver braid lay down the back of her soft cedar tunic. My mother had an odd expression on her face. Cassia reclined in a chair nursing her daughter. Wingnut's large frame hovered in the back of the clinic as though he were trying to escape this assemblage of women.

"Here she is now," said my mother as I stepped inside. "I'm sure she can explain everything."

Nearly in unison, Wollemia and Salix turned to face me. My former friend looked pleased with herself but not as though proud of a personal achievement. She looked more like she'd won some prize that had long been denied her, the victor in a competition against a hated adversary. I'd have to be an idiot not to know that the adversary was me. Wollemia's face was stern and searching.

"Hi, Wollemia. Salix," I said. Neither of them responded.

Predictable that Salix wouldn't say hello, but Wollemia's silence was perplexing.

"Ostrya, it seems that Salix has found your satchel," said Mom.

My overstuffed bag lay on the floor at my mother's feet. Who told Salix I'd lost my satchel? She'd be the last person to help me find it. I didn't even remember having worn it since the night before the birthing. How had she found it?

"Thanks, Salix," I said. "I've been looking for that."

"Don't thank me just yet."

"So you acknowledge this is your bag?" asked Wollemia.

A movement at the back of the clinic caught my eye. Wingnut tried to get my attention. He shook his head as I answered, "Yes. Where'd you find it?"

"Not important," said Wollemia.

"Ostrya, what did you—"

"Quiet, Michelia." What was this? Wollemia was telling my mother to shut up, and my mother stopped talking? Mom shook her head and turned away. What was going on? "Open it." Wollemia pointed at me. "Let's see what's inside."

I was confused for a second, and then I wasn't. Wingnut and my mother huddled together in the rear of the clinic. He put a strong arm around her shoulders, squeezed. She let him! Salix stood with her hands on hips, an ugly sneer distorting her face. I bent and picked up my satchel and plopped it on the examination table. My mother didn't scold me or tell me not to put my dirty things on the clean patient surfaces. I unfastened the front flap.

"Show us. Empty it."

Wollemia ordered me to empty my bag on the clean examination table. I glanced at my mother. She watched me sadly. She was saying nothing. I reached into the inside pocket and pulled out my flint, the rusting knife I'd traded for at the market years ago, some spider fleece, a couple of pinecones, and a few packets of random teas I kept with me for home visits.

"We already know what's in there, Ostrya," jeered Salix.

"Silence," commanded Wollemia. Salix crossed her arms and closed her mouth, but not before throwing me an evil look. "Show us what else is in your bag."

Reaching into my satchel, I pulled out the greens I'd gathered for the kids, limp and shriveled now. The berries on the top of the pile were still okay, but the deeper I dug, the worse was their condition. My fingertips, red and sticky with warm berry juice, plucked the tiny apples from the bottom of my bag. They were almost ripe when I picked them. I also brought back mushrooms, but I'd stuffed those in my shirt, so I suspected they were—

I'd put down my satchel in our shanty, my mother's and mine. Our hanging shanty. On the floor. Beneath the hammock. My hammock. And then I'd dumped the mushrooms out of my shirt before falling asleep. The mushrooms had been there. In our shanty. I hadn't taken the satchel anywhere. I hadn't lost it. It had been in our hanging shanty the entire time. Which meant—

"You went into our home. You took my satchel from my shanty. You stole my bag!"

Salix grinned at me. "So what if I did? Doesn't change any facts. You were hoarding food."

"How dare you? How dare you take what doesn't belong to you!" I shouted, spitting my frustration. My nephew was dead. And this, this, this—tree rat—had stolen my satchel from my shanty. "You entered our home without invitation and stole my bag? What else have you stolen?"

"Nowhere near as much as you've stolen! How many boys do you need, Ostrya? Take only what you need! That's the law! It applies to all of us, even you!"

"That's enough. Salix, outside. Ostrya, I want all the contents of your satchel on the table, now."

Strawberries. Salmonberries. Huckleberries. Raspberries. A few apples. It all rolled across the table when I upended my satchel. The inside was red and sticky from their combined juices and now the table was red, too.

"Did you get all this at the market?" asked Wollemia.

I glanced at my mother, but she wouldn't meet my eyes. Even Wingnut was looking at the floor.

"No."

"Yew didn't sell this to you? Give you extra? Did you bribe him?"

"No!" *Not for this.* I knew Mom and Wingnut thought I was lying. They were thinking about the missing alcohol. They both suspected me. Mom might accuse me later, when we were alone together, but she'd never say anything in front of an outsider. What about Wingnut? Why wasn't he telling Wollemia what he knew? He wanted my traineeship—he'd be certain to get it if I was no longer in the picture.

"If you didn't get the food from Yew, where did you get it? This wasn't part of your allotment. Michelia, did you have anything to do with this?"

"No!" I shouted. "She knows nothing about it. She's innocent. I did this alone. I'm guilty."

Wollemia considered this, her face an unreadable mask. She nodded once. "Okay, then. You've been under a lot of strain lately. So have we all. I will take this food and distribute it as I deem fit. This will serve as your one and only warning. A second infraction, and I will take this to the council."

"Thank you, Wollemia." I didn't feel thankful though. There was no space for that, not when my heart was full of rage and resentment against Salix. Thieving tree rat.

"Don't thank me. Thank your mother. Her good name has

saved you this time. But next time—Salix! Come gather this food."

I watched as the food I'd harvested at my own peril for the starving school children was gathered up by my enemy and taken away. Alone, I'd found a way to the skygardens. Alone, I'd risked my life to cross the abyss. And it would be up to Wollemia and the council to determine who would receive the fruits of my life-threatening labor. It was all so unfair, I thought I would scream or cry. I could almost kill someone. Salix jeered at me as she stole my harvest.

From The Book

It is unclear when the cannibalism began.

What has been agreed upon is that both traditional food sources and alternative food sources disappeared for all but the wealthiest. Governments collapsed, and along with them, the fragile remnants of the social order. A fraction of one percent of the global population controlled the wealth, the remaining foodstuffs, and the private militias to hoard them. The most plentiful, indeed the only source of nutrition remaining for the rest of humanity, was other humans.

We not only decided to remain within the safety of the boughs thousands of feet above the earth, but we swore an oath never to descend during our lifetimes. One living soul, hunted and tortured by a tribe of cannibals, could reveal our civilization above, sentencing us all to the death and destruction of the earthbound masses. Now that we are established in the canopy, we will never return to the earth alive.

— PSEUDOTSUGA, *THE BOOK OF SILVANUS*

Chapter Thirty

❧

One of the many problems of living in a small community is that rumors spread faster than bindweed. Within twenty-four hours, everyone knew about my so-called hoarding of resources during a famine. Salix was no friend of mine and even before I'd been caught with the food in my satchel, she'd been working hard at turning everyone against me. Not that it was much of a loss—I'd been set apart from the other climbers long before this all happened.

Given enough time, maybe people would have forgotten or at least have chocked up my "theft" to youthful stupidity. I'm sure many would have sided with me over Salix. She'd made a lot of enemies over the years—I certainly wasn't the first "friend" she turned against.

But something else happened. Zelkova's best friend, that naughty little imp who kept Cassia's classroom lively and the older folks on their toes, my recently discovered cousin Tung died. The day after we buried Cassia's baby, the very day after, not even twenty-four hours after we lost a member of our family, the gluttonous Great Ones decided they still hadn't had enough to eat. Selfish. Greedy. They were taking way more than they needed. And they took Tung. Though I hadn't killed him, everyone behaved as though I had.

His father, my Uncle Rhus, carried his son's limp body to the clinic as I was brewing tea for myself and Cassia. Cassia was dozing in a chair, her baby cradled in her arms. It had been my turn to sleep at the clinic and having been woken every two hours by my niece's vocal appetite, I was tired and grouchy.

"Help him!" His eyes wild and desperate, Rhus lay the boy on the examination table and stepped back. The pungent smell of feces filled the room. A thin, brown ooze covered Rhus's chest and arms where Tung's body had pressed against his father. The boy's bottom and legs were covered in excrement. His face was lifeless and gray. I pulled open his eyelids. The whites of his eyes were tinged a dirty yellow, his breathing ragged.

I poured the water I'd been boiling for tea into a basin and began washing Tung's limp frame. "When did he last eat?"

"Dinner. I gave him the last of the horsetail."

I paused mid-scrub. We dried horsetail for respiratory teas. It was a useful herb to alleviate asthma attacks and our go-to remedy for bronchial infections. The gardeners had grown it for us on the west end. Because it grew so well in the shade, our respiratory patients never ran short. But I'd never heard of anyone eating it. "Where did you find horsetail?"

"There's a crop growing just behind our shanty. The Great Ones have provided well for me and Tung. Since we have so much horsetail, I've been giving our rations to our neighbors. A lot of children not getting enough to eat these days." *How could you steal food from the mouths of babes?* He didn't have to say it. I knew what he was thinking, what everyone was thinking. His eyes flickered over to Cassia, still asleep and blissfully unaware of the awful stench permeating the clinic. "How ... how is your sister doing?"

I'd forgotten—he was her uncle, too. We shared a father, so of course we shared this uncle. Why hadn't I thought of that before? Did she know that Rhus was her uncle? That Tung was her cousin? She must know—Michelia wasn't her mother. Cassia hadn't been prevented from knowing her family.

I dipped a cloth into the warm water and washed Tung's face. "Physically, better. Emotionally? You know. Not great."

"Terrible thing, to lose a child." The way he said it. Dismissive. Bitter almost. "But the other one, she's got her mother. That's more than my boy has ever had."

Cassia' eyes fluttered open. "What are you doing here?" She pushed against the chair and struggled to her feet, clutching her daughter to her chest. "Get out! Get out!" Her face was a mask of fear.

Startled, I looked from her to our uncle. "Cassia calm down. It's our Uncle Rhus. Tung's father. It's okay, he's family. Don't you know him?"

She was shaking yet fierce, the baby wailing in her arms. "Get. Him. Out."

Uncle Rhus was an immovable rock, all smooth muscled body and clenched jaw. If she was a picture of terror, he was the very image of hatred. His demeanor was beginning to frighten me. I gently touched his arm. He shuddered and looked me in the eye. His gaze softened. "Please fetch Michelia," I said. "She should be in our shanty on Bough Two. I don't know what's wrong with Tung. I can make him comfortable, but nothing else."

When he left the room, I turned and stared at Cassia. She was rocking back and forth, whether to soothe the crying infant or herself, I didn't know. "What was that about?" I said. "Why did you treat our uncle like that?" I laid my hand on Tung's forehead, even hotter now than it had been the first time I'd treated him.

My sister took a deep, quavering breath. "Why is Tung here?"

"He's sick. I don't know what's wrong. Why did you yell at his father?"

Tears welled in her eyes as she looked at the dreadfully thin, feverish body on the table. "He doesn't look right."

"No, he doesn't. He's quite ill. I'm sure his father is worried about him. And you screamed at him to get out. Why did you do that?"

"He's going to die." She said it just like that. Blunt, those words I'd been trying to banish from my own mind. And once she'd uttered them, she began to cry, ugly gasping sobs. "It's my fault. I'm going to lose them all. All my fault."

Those startling words lay in the dank air. What was she talking about? She was going to lose all of her young students? Why would she think the famine was her fault? It was a result of the storm, nothing more, nothing less.

I didn't get a chance to calm her down though because right then Tung's body began convulsing. Unsure what to do in the moment, I tried to hold down his arms, hold down his legs. His body was releasing its fluids, fetid browns and yellows. By the time Uncle Rhus returned with my mother, Cassia had fled the clinic with my niece and I stood help-lessly by, watching my cousin die.

Michelia explained later. Scientifically. Tung had succumbed to beriberi, the result of eating too much raw horsetail. After a month of consuming the plant and nothing else, Tung's thiamine stores had been depleted, his small organs destroyed. Uncle Rhus would not suffer the same fate as his son; his body was larger, and Michelia ordered him to replenish the missing nutrient by eating all the dandelion greens he could find. Scientific answers would restore my uncle's health. Tung and Rhus were not the first climbers to be poisoned by eating the wrong wild plant nor would they be the last. But science had been too late to save Tung, and Rhus would never forgive himself.

The rest of the community would never forgive me. I missed the symptoms of poisoning the first time I treated Tung. I had been alone with Tung when he died. Salix already had their ears; it didn't take much for her to spin up the story. Like bindweed, the rumors were growing and spreading, strangling the life out of the truth.

Chapter Thirty-One

Two days after I'd been nabbed with the food and one day after Tung died, the bridge crew reached the new skygardens. Sure, it would take some time for Hamamalis and his gardeners to clear the area for sun crops, but self-sown berry bushes and wild greens had been found in tree crotches in the south and were already being harvested. The food shortage was nearing its end. Irony.

The agriculture crew reabsorbed Wingnut and my mother missed him dearly. There was so much work to be done in the south that the gardeners and trainees camped there as the builders had done. He popped by the clinic on his off days, which amounted to once every other week or so. Mom suspected he was passing his time away from the garden with a new girl, but I knew better. He wasn't avoiding the clinic; he was avoiding me. He didn't want to be guilty by association with the food hoarder, the ration breaker, the baby killer. Me.

Sorbus had disappeared, too. Now that the bridges were built, I didn't know why I hadn't even seen him in passing. He might have been avoiding me out of loyalty to his sister, but I doubted it. He wasn't the type to take sides in a fight or judge another person. Don't get me wrong: He followed canopy laws and prayed to the Great Ones. He believed everything *The Book of Silvanus* taught, or at least, he gave no one cause to suspect he didn't believe. He didn't have any great conviction; he simply didn't see the point in expending energy to disobey the laws. Too much energy and no point.

He might be chasing along after Cedrus, all eager trainee with baby squirrel eyes.

The only friend I could still count on was Mangrove. He alone knew where the food had come from and for whom it had been intended—but he'd left for an extended hunting trip immediately following my nephew's feeding ceremony. I didn't know if he was even aware of Salix's betrayal and Wollemia's warning.

My sister had been absent ever since Tung died. Michelia said it was normal for new mothers to nest, to focus all their attention on their new baby, and it came as no surprise to her that Cassia was staying away from the clinic. She'd experienced a trauma within these walls and probably had no desire to pass through our doorway again. But after several days had gone by with no word, Michelia urged me to look in on my sister. Michelia didn't say it out loud, but I knew she had no desire to set foot inside Cassia's shanty. After the beating she'd sustained, even though she'd not denounced him to the Council of Maestros, it was obvious that she was afraid of Cedrus. If Cassia refused to visit the clinic, it would be up to me to visit Cassia at her home. One of us needed to ensure the baby was thriving and that Cassia was healing.

Though it was mid-morning and Bough One was bustling with activity, my sister's shanty was silent. When I stepped inside and saw my niece dozing peacefully against Cassia's bared breast, my initial impression was that all was fine. Mother and infant were napping together. But my nose picked up a faintly cloying, rotten smell. When my eyes fully adjusted to the inner gloom, I was able to see my sister's hand and arm. I lightly touched the dark, soft, swollen flesh, and her eyes jerked open. She cried out and the baby wailed in protest at being awakened so abruptly.

Cassia uttered soothing noises and the baby found her breast again, suckled, and drifted off. "It's bad," she said.

My thoughts exactly. "It's infected, Cassia."

"I know."

"Why didn't you come to the clinic?" I rested the back of my hand against her forehead. As I suspected, she was running a temperature. "Why didn't you send Cedrus?" The bones of her hand and wrist were engulfed by the swelling.

"He hasn't been here. Not since—" She bit her lip and looked away. "Since Tung died."

"Where's he been? I thought they finished work on the bridge."

Cassia shook her head and wiped away a tear. "My fault. It's all my fault. He left because of what I did."

"What did you do?" I glanced around the small room. It was clean and tidy. "Have you been eating?"

"Yes. Thevetia's been taking care of us."

"Thevetia? She's barely cogent." For some unknown reason, my sister had been abandoned by her partner and was being looked after by a senile elder. If only I'd known! I'd been caught up in my own drama when I should have looked in on my sister, my patient.

"She brings me food. Tidies up. Sits with Naria."

"Naria? You named the baby?"

She nodded. "Pulmonaria."

"Lungwort? That's an awful name!"

"She's got a set of lungs on her."

"Okay, that's almost funny. But I need to check that arm, Cassia. Then you can tell me about Cedrus."

"I don't want to wake Naria when I get up. We had a rough night."

"I'm here now. I can help." I gently took my niece from her mother's breast, swaddled her tightly in a fiber bundle, and watched as Cassia crawled out of the hammock. I placed the tiny bundle in the center of the hammock, a hazelnut weight on a breeze-kissed leaf. Naria whimpered lightly but didn't wake. I guided Cassia to a stool by the light-filled doorway.

My stomach turned when I got a good look at the arm. The swelling had spread outward toward her elbow. A putrid smell came from beneath the wrapping. I loosened and removed the bandages. The spongy flesh was black and swollen, saturated with blood. I turned my head away and gulped to clear my nausea. "We need to go to the clinic, right now."

"I can't go back there! I—I won't!"

"Michelia needs to see this arm. I don't have the training. Cassia." I held her face between my hands and forced her to meet my eyes. "What happened in the clinic was bad. It was awful. There are no words ... It haunts me every night. I have nightmares during the day. I get it! But you need to go to the clinic. To Michelia. Now."

Her eyes filled. "It was my fault. My fault the baby died. My fault Tung died."

I gaped at her. How could she possibly think the stillbirth was her fault? I hadn't been able to revive the infant, my mother hadn't been able to deliver it, but Cassia? She'd been lying on the examination table bleeding to death. And Tung? Where had that notion come from?

"None of this is your fault. Not your baby boy. And certainly not Tung. Now tell me, where has Cedrus gone?"

"Produce to replace. I'd already borne one healthy child. I

broke the law." A shuddering sob escaped her then. "The Great Ones punished me for twins."

"The Great Ones didn't punish you. The Great Ones are trees! Trees that we live in—not gods!"

It was Cassia's turn to be shocked. Her eyes went wide. "Don't say that! Don't even think it! They're listening!"

"They aren't listening, and do you know why not? Because they don't have EARS! They don't cause the storms or the sicknesses. They didn't make the laws. Pseudotsuga did that, we did that. Now tell me. Where is Cedrus? How could he leave you alone like this?"

"Ostrya, you must repent. They will punish you, too."

Didn't she realize I lived my penance daily? My punishment was delivered by the other climbers, not by the trees. Besides, my infraction was far worse than a few negative words about a cluster of trees or squirreling away food for children. I'd be making amends for Joshua as long as I lived. And I didn't need magical trees or spiteful climbers for that. My self-loathing was more than enough. But I didn't tell her any of that. Instead, I said, "We need to get you to the clinic. We need to do something about your infected arm. Your daughter Naria needs her mama healthy and strong." And then I blurted, "And your other daughter, Erica, does, too."

She looked at me blankly. "What?"

"Um, your daughter. Erica. I figured it out. She was your first baby. I don't know why I didn't see it before. She's your favorite; anyone can see how much you love her. And she looks just like you."

"She looks just like me? She looks nothing like me."

Did I have it wrong? Two brown children attended Cassia's school. Erica and that other little boy whose name I always forgot. But that other little boy—Corylus—looked nothing at all like her, while Erica … Erica was long and thin. Cassia was short. She'd had round curves always, not the sharp edges that Erica did. Cassia had never been shy or soft-spoken. She was right. Erica was nothing like her. "I'm sorry, I thought—"

"You thought, because Erica has brown skin, I have brown skin, she must be my child, the one I told you about?" She shook her head and I didn't like the look she gave me. "You're my sister, with your white skin and your light-colored eyes, the green one and the blue one, and your straight hair. But you're still my sister! How can the first thing you see be skin color? You know me better than that. I've been a part of your life since your first day in these trees! All this time, he's been right in front of you with his curly head and those awful stick-out ears you and I both got from Yew. And that personality—it was all you, he was just like you, all the time like my sister. My son and my sister—and you never could see it."

My vision blurred and I wiped at my eyes, whisking away more traitorous tears.

"He was your favorite, Ostrya. And now you know why."

"But he was—"

"Fair? Yes, that surprised me, too. Michelia said he had a pigment difference. Something called albinism. That was the only way we could keep it a secret." Her eyes gleamed. "Oh, how I loved that boy. But every time I looked at him, I had to remember. And I couldn't do that to him, hold it against him."

"Hold what against him?"

"His father. Your Uncle Rhus."

"Yours, too."

"No. Never. He is no uncle of mine!"

"He's our father's brother."

"Our father. Yew. Who left my mother, left me, as soon as something better came along. Your mother, and then you and Joshua. That's why he wasn't there to take care of me. To protect me. When his brother—" She threw her hand over her mouth, trying to catch the words before they spilled across her lips. The secret she'd kept so well, that others had held for her for six years.

"Our Uncle Rhus. He, he … and Tung—Tung's your son. Oh, Cassia!" I threw my arms around her, pulled her to me, cried with her. My cousin and my nephew, my favorite, and I'd never known. "But why didn't you denounce him to the council? He would have been punished—"

"Banished, yes. And then what? Everyone would have known. What would that burden have done to Tung? Unprotected from the gossips in this canopy, damned to live beneath a shadow cast before he was born."

Emotion overwhelmed me now. She was the best one, the best sister. The best mother. "Cassia, I'm … I'm … so sorry." I turned my face away so she couldn't see me cry. She wrapped her arms around me, put her forehead to mine, now forcing me to face her.

"I don't regret Tung. He was a ray of sunshine—" Tears spilled down her cheeks. "Now you know."

I pulled away, brushing away more teardrops from my eyes. I cleared my throat, professional now. "Cedrus should be here. Where is he? Does he know?"

She nodded and sniffed. "All my fault."

"What?"

She met my gaze. Silent. Solemn. Once again accepting her fate, a fate determined by a man.

"You've got to be kidding me! That's why he left? Because of … because of what was done to you when you were—" She would have been the same age as me when Rhus raped her. I could barely kiss Mangrove. I couldn't imagine … that … and then having to hide the pregnancy … what my sister had gone through. Was going through. And the unfairness of, of, everything. Her partner walked out on her when she finally found the courage to tell him.

"He was so mad when he found out. Because I didn't tell him before. He said I was dishonest. But, how could I? If he'd known, he would have kept my secret. And that would have made him guilty. How could I? I was trying to protect him."

"Guilty? Guilty of what?"

"Produce only to replace. I'd already had a child. I'm only allowed to produce two: One to replace me and one to replace Cedrus. If he'd known and not told the council, he would have been just as guilty as me."

"Yew had three children! You, me, Joshua. And that was worse! Me and Joshua weren't twins."

She was silent, and I could hear the words she didn't say. *Yeah. And look how that turned out. The Great Ones took the extra child.*

"Okay, so you didn't tell him before. And now he thinks you deceived him. But he can't blame you, can he?"

She shrugged. "It's my fault."

"No! It's not! We will talk about this more, but first, we need to go to the clinic. I'm sorry, but your arm is bad, Cassia. Really bad."

"I can't." She shook her head. "That's where I lost both my boys."

"Cassia, we have to. I'll be there with you. The whole time. We need to go."

"I won't take my daughter there. I need to keep Naria safe. The Great Ones—they will take her, too!" The swaddled infant twitched and whimpered but didn't wake.

A shadow blotted out the sunlight for a moment. As if summoned, Thevetia stepped into the shanty.

"Hello, Ostrya. I thought I'd stop by, see if the new mother needs anything."

"Yes! She does," I said. "Would you please stay with Naria?"

"Of course, I will! There's nothing I'd like more. You know, I never had children of my own."

I looked triumphantly at Cassia. "See? Naria is well cared for. I will take you to the clinic, assist Michelia, and then hurry back for my niece. Okay?"

"Thank you," said Cassia. She kissed the old woman on a wrinkled cheek. Thevetia glowed with happiness. It was difficult to imagine this gentle, caring soul partnered with Wollemia for a lifetime, but perhaps it was true what they said about opposites attracting. I guided Cassia out the door.

My mother's face when she saw my sister told me everything I needed to know. I'd feared wet gangrene when I smelled the arm, and when Mom sent me off to Hamamalis to beg for apple cider—"We don't have time to wait for it to fully ferment"—I knew I'd be assisting in an amputation before the day was out. When I returned with a jug of newly turned apple alcohol, Mom had already boiled and prepared the amputation tools, scrubbed Cassia's arm, changed into a surgical cape and head wrap, and dosed Cassia with a triple Passiflora tincture to relax her. The apple alcohol would do double duty as both anesthesia and surgical sterilization.

I gave my sister several sips of the alcohol before securing her to the table. My mother said she'd perform a circular amputation below the elbow. It was simpler than a flap method and would require less dressing. What I knew from reading, what she wouldn't say in front of my partially conscious though quite drugged sister, was that we didn't have enough anesthesia for the more elegant, prolonged surgery that most amputees received.

Cassia dozed off; the alcohol was working now. Mom picked up the surgical blade. "First, I'm going to teach you to tie off blood vessels to prevent hemorrhaging."

The scalpel sliced straight through my sister's soft walnut-colored flesh, the crimson blood bright and stark against her skin. A clammy dizziness crept from the pit of my stomach to the base of my neck, and I knew it was about to happen again. I was fainting.

Chapter Thirty-Two

The week following the surgery, I moved in with Cassia. Day and night, I cared for my sister and my niece. Thevetia stopped by several times a day to sit with the baby. With Wingnut working the skygardens again, my mother worked alone at the clinic. My last fainting spell had proven to both of us that the clinic was no place for me. She seemed relieved not to have me there. I changed my sister's dressings, attempted to reduce her pain with Passiflora tinctures and willow bark teas, helped her when Naria wanted to nurse, and kept her, the baby, and the shanty as clean as I could. Together, we waited for Cedrus to return.

One afternoon while Cassia was sleeping—part new mother exhaustion, part healing from surgery, part analgesic daze—my mother stopped in for a visit. She gazed down at the drowsy infant cradled in my arms. Naria's head, a lovely soft oval, rocked slightly forward on her young neck. Her eyelashes curled back from eyes the same amber hue as her father's. Mom reached out a tender finger and stroked the baby's velvety brown skin. I touched my lips to Naria's thick head of hair and inhaled. "Mmmmm. Baby head."

"That's from mother's milk. They smell sweetest while they're nursing."

Mom pulled the second chair out from under the table where I sat. She glanced quickly at napping Cassia before sitting. "Ostrya, this needs to stop."

"Hmm? I'm not sure what you're saying."

"I need my trainee back."

"Really?" The word was out of my mouth before I realized I'd spoken.

"Of course! What are you thinking?" Her initial confusion was soon replaced by more typical irritation.

"I haven't gone anywhere. I'm right here. On an extended home visit." *I'm probably less dangerous to everyone this way.*

"Yes. I understand why you might think that's what you're doing. And I do find it admirable that you're taking such fine care of your sister."

"Really? Wow. Thank you."

"But Cassia is asleep now. You've checked her temperature, cleaned her wound and changed her dressing, provided her with medicine. Your home visit is finished. We do have other patients, you know. I need your help to visit the homebound. And when that's done, you should be at the clinic, preparing medicines, practicing your sutures, and continuing your medical studies."

"I can't leave right now. Thevetia isn't here yet."

"And Thevetia won't be coming today. Wollemia thinks Thevetia has been taking on too much. She can watch the baby occasionally, but she's not a young woman. Or even a healthy old woman."

"I can't leave! What if Naria needs something? Cassia won't hear her if she cries. And she needs to rest. Her wound—"

"Don't overreact. I'm not suggesting you leave the child unattended." She shook her head. "This damn canopy." She took a deep breath and pressed her fingertips into the pressure points of her temples. Must be a headache starting. Furrowing her brow, she began: "Ostrya ... how do I put this?" Crossed arms and squared shoulders, she looked me dead in the eye. "I see a young woman crushed beneath a grown adult's responsibility, protecting a woman who is not her partner and a baby who is not her child. And again, another healthy, able man taking advantage. Story of my life. I won't let it be yours. What you are doing is noble. But it is not your duty. It belongs to someone else."

"You're talking about Cedrus."

"Obviously, I'm talking about Cedrus. He is doing the exact same thing to Cassia that Yew did to her mother. And you have been filling in for him. You are Cassia's sister, not her partner."

"I don't mind."

"I know you don't. And that's a wonderful sentiment. But you are my trainee, and I require your assistance. Nursing an infant is not part of the training to be a doctor. Your destiny lies elsewhere."

My destiny lies elsewhere? That was rich. Like I'd ever had the opportunity to think about my destiny. And anyway, what did she expect me to do? Abandon my sister in her time of need?

It wasn't my fault Cedrus left his family. And I suppose, as Mom kept trying to convince me, it wasn't my fault that my nephew died, that both of my nephews died. But her words meant nothing, because I knew beyond an inkling of doubt that Cassia had lost an arm because of me. There was no one else to blame. If I hadn't traded the alcohol to Yew. If I had disinfected the spider bite properly. If I had checked on Cassia. So many ifs. If I left this baby now, whatever happened to her and Cassia would be my fault.

"I need to protect Naria."

"No, her parents need to protect Naria. We need to find Cedrus."

"But Cassia hasn't seen him since—I haven't seen him since the baby's feeding ceremony. I don't even know where to look."

"Salix told Wollemia that he's been staying with Sorbus."

"With Sorbus?"

That puzzled me. Sure, Sorbus was Cedrus's trainee, but the two weren't friends, were they? Why would Cedrus stay with him? And how? Sorbus was already bunking with two other trainees. Had they crammed a fourth body into one of those tiny shanties?

"Supposedly, he lies in a hammock all day, crying."

"What! That can't be true. You know Salix is a liar."

"I'm well-aware she likely embellished the truth for effect. But no matter. He needs to care for his family. Someone has to convince him to do the right thing." She pushed away from the table and stood, looking down at me. "If you don't go, I will."

The bruise around my mother's eye was fading, a pale green-yellow now. The stitches across her temple were removed, but an ugly red scar distorted her eyebrow. I shook my head. "No. I've got this."

Chapter Thirty-Three

❧❦❧

Sweat trickled down my chest, tickling the sensitive skin between my breasts. The sensation was weird and gross, but I was getting used to it. Naria was a tiny ball of heat slumbering against my ribcage, and the colorful sling Mom had given me held her body temperature tightly against me. Wollemia's fiber trainees had designed, sewn, and dyed this baby carrier. Despite my loathing of Wollemia and her team of malicious workers, even I had to admit the sling was beautifully crafted. Mom had secured my niece tightly to my front and she was in no danger of slipping out.

Mom refused to watch the baby while I was gone. She told me to take Naria along to show Cedrus who he'd left behind. Without the baby, Mom thought my words would be unlikely to have much effect on Cedrus. She was probably right. Long before Salix began spreading rumors about me, Cedrus had disliked me. I doubted recent events would have improved his opinion of me.

I climbed the stairs slowly so as not to rouse the baby. If Naria woke, she would want to eat. And seeing as I had no milk to offer her, it would be a noisy trip all the way back to her mother. It was mid-morning and the stairway was mostly quiet. I walked slowly, methodically, round and round the spiral. On any other day, I would have climbed through the trees, stretching my muscles and exercising my brain. Walking the staircase like an ordinary climber was boring in the extreme.

Even when I was on rounds for the clinic and forced to walk the stairway, I would run, skipping every second or third step in a race against myself. Tied to Naria by fiber strings and responsible for her safety, I was forced to take care. The world is a terrifying place full of hidden dangers when you're holding an infant in your arms.

What would I say to Cedrus when I saw him? What would he say to me? Did he even know that Cassia's arm had been amputated? I mean, he must. Right? The way the gossip in this canopy flew from mouth to mouth, there's no way he could have missed it. And though it was my fault I hadn't checked on her, he more than shared the guilt. If he'd been helping her with the baby, taking care of her after her terrible birth experience, he would have noticed her arm wasn't healing properly. He could have alerted us before an amputation became necessary. And knowing about the amputation now, why hadn't he returned to help her?

The more I thought about it, the angrier I got. His behavior was totally inexcusable. I actually had to go hunting for him—to ask him to take care of his partner and his child. Between the tiny heater tied to my chest and my burning rage, it was miraculous that I didn't self-combust.

I didn't know where I was going. Cedrus was somewhere on Bough Seven, but Michelia didn't know who he was staying with. I hadn't talked to Sorbus in ages, and though I suspected he was sharing space with two other men like Mangrove was, Salix hadn't told Wollemia where that was. Mangrove wasn't around to ask.

So that was another thing I was terrible at—being a good friend. I only had three friends—Mangrove, Sorbus, Wingnut —and I didn't even know where one of them lived. Now, halfway up the stairway, I had no idea where to begin looking for Cedrus.

I suppose the wise thing to do would have been to ask Salix, but I wasn't going to go there. It was a huge assumption that Salix was even telling the truth that Cedrus was staying with Sorbus. No way was I going to give her the satisfaction of asking for her help. Never.

When I got to Bough Seven, I poked my head into shanty after shanty, looking for someone who could tell me where Sorbus lived. The bough seemed deserted with most everyone at work. All the gardeners and builders were hard at work building up the new skygardens, repairing bridges, and repairing shanties. Hunters were far afield scaring up prey. And the other trades were working with skeleton crews; those who could be spared were helping at the skygardens. How would I know when I found the shanty Cedrus was staying in with no one around to ask. Besides, he would be at work, so what was the point?

And the more I thought about it, the stupider I felt. Obviously, Salix had been lying about Cedrus. No way was he lying around all day crying in a hammock. That would have been ridiculous at any time, but especially now when there was so much work to do, so much at stake for all of us. This entire excursion was a waste of time. Michelia was a human lie detector—she couldn't have been taken in by Salix. So why had she sent me and Naria away from my sister and Bough One? What was Michelia up to?

If nothing else, walking up the central staircase gave me a chance to stretch my legs and get some air after all the sitting and rocking I'd been doing lately. That was probably why

Michelia made up this whole story—to make me get some exercise, to get Naria some fresh air.

Now that I was at the top of the canopy, I played along. I might as well. Michelia had played me for a fool so I kept up the pretense, peeking into one empty shanty after another. Two hammocks, two hammocks, two hammocks. Occasionally, I saw a bedroll on the floor where a displaced climber was bunking until the new shanties were constructed.

If I moved outward from the center, I'd probably come across some builders repairing storm-damaged shanties and building new ones. The builders would know where Cedrus was working. I kept looking into empty shanties. I had climbed all the way up to the top of the canopy with a baby; I might as well do what I'd been sent to do. I'd have to hurry to find someone though. I didn't know how much longer I had before my niece woke hungry for another meal.

Nothing to do but walk the entire bough, branch by branch, shanty by shanty, and continue searching for builders. I walked as quickly as I dared without waking Naria. I checked five or six, maybe seven offshoots on the east side, and then circled a tree to a north-facing pathway and crossed into a newer section of shanties. I poked my head into eight, nine, ten newly constructed shanties with no signs of life. I walked around another tree and the pathway pointed east again. On the upper boughs, pathways were built like labyrinths growing around secondary and tertiary trunks. At the far end of the path, a lone shanty was set back into a slender trunk. It looked unfinished and uninhabited. I thought about retracing my steps through the labyrinth, but there was something about that shanty.

Naria stirred and cracked one eye open, and then the other. Her amber eyes wavered before focusing on me and I held my breath. She sighed once, moaned lightly, and her eyes drooped shut again. I stood frozen, my chest nearly bursting with captive air. Naria snored softly and I exhaled in relief, and then tiptoed gingerly toward the shanty at the end of the path.

"Ostrya, what are you doing here?" Sorbus called out from behind me. I turned my head and smiled at my friend who held a basin of fir resin. The acrid smell of the sticky material tickled my nose. As soon as he saw Naria in the sling across my chest, his eyes grew hooded and suspicious.

"Hi Sorbus! I haven't seen you in—"

"Yeah, you shouldn't be up here." His voice was gruff, his body language … different.

"I'm looking for Cedrus. Do you know where he's working today?"

He strode to my side. "You can't be here. You have to leave. It's not safe." He grabbed me by the elbow and tugged, hard.

I shook him off and brushed at the sticky handprint on my arm. "Pseudotsuga's balls! Hands OFF! Where's Cedrus?"

"How should I know?" He grabbed at me again but I was ready for him and pushed his hand out of my way.

Gossip thrived in this closed community, and lazy thinkers were eager to believe the worst about their neighbors. Salix was an expert at convincing gullible climbers that her lies were true. And I had been in Salix's crosshairs for a while now. Many climbers believed Salix's stories, and considering recent events, those who hadn't hated me before certainly did now. But I never suspected that my friend Sorbus would be one of them. If he didn't want to be my friend anymore, I'd learn to live with that, but only after I got what I came for.

"What is with you? Get off me. Look, your freaking sister says Cedrus is living up here now. I've come to get him.

Cassia, his *life partner*, needs him. And his *baby*." I thrust my sling-wrapped chest in his general direction.

"You need to go, NOW!" Sorbus dropped the resin and lunged for me, grabbing me around the waist and wrestling me backwards.

"GET OFF!" I yelled. From the sling came a tearful whimper. The noise and fight had woken Naria. She let loose a shrieking wail.

"Shut her up," hissed Sorbus, his eyes flicking fearfully toward the shanty at the end of the path.

"Why are you acting like this?"

Naria was awake now and screaming her displeasure. My eyes stayed locked on Sorbus who'd become jumpy and frantic. "You need to go. Now. Get out of here!"

"I'll leave as soon as you tell me where Cedrus is. This baby needs her father."

Naria's crying grew increasingly strident. Knowing it was useless, I bounced and jostled her. She needed her mother, she needed milk, and I was in danger of returning to Bough One no wiser about the whereabouts of her father.

A movement at the end of the path caught my eye. "Who's that?" I said and pushed past Sorbus who put up no resistance but silently followed me. I strode to the unfinished shanty and stepped through the doorway, my niece wailing the entire way. A shadow moved in the dim interior, staggered backward, and fell. I waited for my eyes to adjust in the stale darkness, but I already knew.

The voice in the darkness said, "Is that—"

"Your daughter. Naria."

The shadow approached me and resolved into the body of an unwashed man, stinking of body odor and despair. His eyes were bloodshot and red-rimmed, his beard and hair dirty and unkempt. Naria wailed without end, gasping for air in between shrieks. A tentative hand reached for the infant but drew back, leaving the baby untouched.

"No. I can't."

I stared at my half-sister's life partner. His muscular shoulders shook silently. Why was he crying? His daughter was alive! His life partner was alive!

"Have you been here this entire time?"

"Go. Just leave me."

I glanced back at my friend. His face was solemn, his eyes weary. "Cedrus, your daughter needs her father. Cassia can't do this alone. Not with one arm."

At the mention of Cassia's name, Cedrus shuddered. "What did you say about Cassia?"

"She needs your help. You need to go home. I've been taking care of her and your baby since the amputation."

"Amputation?" His wild eyes bored into me. "What amputation?"

It was unbelievable to me that he hadn't heard. "The spider bite. Her arm got infected. Went septic. We took it off a week ago. Didn't you know?"

Naria shrieked, tears running down her face. I bounced and danced, caught between sympathy for my innocent and hungry niece and self-righteous anger at her loser father.

"A week ago?" He stared at a stricken Sorbus. "You didn't tell me."

"You said I shouldn't mention her name."

"But an amputation—"

Sorbus shrugged.

I needed to get Naria to her mother, but I was riveted. And furious. So very, very furious. "How could you leave your partner? After she almost died in childbirth. After she lost a baby." I shook my head. "If I didn't know it had happened, I'd never believe it of anyone. Not even Yew would do something like that!"

"You don't know everything." He recognized the truth in my eyes, raised his eyebrows, and sighed. "How long have you known?"

"About as long as you. And that was no reason to leave her."

"I didn't leave her. I needed to have space. Think about things for a while."

"Well, do you have enough space now?" I spat it at him.

"I have to go to her." He turned and ran from the shanty.

Naria needed her mother, but first, I needed to yell at someone else. I rocked from foot to foot and rubbed the baby's bottom through the sling. Naria wailed for food, but I wasn't leaving this place until I got some answers. "Sorbus, by the Great Ones! Why didn't you kick him out? Tell him to get his sorry butt back to his partner and child?"

"You ruined it." His face crumpled.

"Ruined what?"

"He was so angry. Punching things. He needed to be away from people."

"So you brought him here to this new build site, where he'd be away from everyone?"

"You know what he did to Michelia when he thought Cassia was dead. Even after he learned she survived, he was still so upset. I didn't think it was safe, him raging down there on Bough One."

I searched his face. "And you wanted him all to yourself for a few days, didn't you?"

He reddened. "It's not like that."

"No, but you'd like it to be."

His bottom lip quivered and I squeezed his shoulder. "You aren't his family. Cassia and Naria are. You can't get in the middle of that."

He blinked away tears and met my eyes. "I wanted to feel what it would be like. To have someone."

I wanted to hug him, but squalling Naria was attached to my front, so I took his hand instead and squeezed it. "You're crushing on him. I get it. But you know it's never going to happen. Not with him. Even if he left Cassia. He doesn't love … you."

"Yeah." He nodded. "But … you don't know … Wingnut … he's … I just wanted … he doesn't even see me."

I pushed Sorbus's coils away from his face. Slow drops slid down his cheeks. I pulled him against me, squishing Naria between us, and let them both cry.

Chapter Thirty-Four

My triad of medical fiascos—the baby's death, Tung's death, my sister's amputation—had done nothing to increase my reputation among the climbers. The storm, the famine, anything remotely negative that happened in the canopy called for a scapegoat, and there I was.

It started with home visits. All of a sudden, patients I'd visited faithfully for months were never at home when I stopped by for their routine visits. Others pretended to have healed from chronic ailments and no longer needed ongoing treatments. Some patients ignored me as though I were a nonentity when I called at their open doorways. Still others loudly told me to leave; they would not allow *The Blight* into their homes.

Oh yeah, did I not mention that Salix and her imaginative minions had dubbed me *The Blight*? The moniker stuck.

My mother insisted I continue visiting the patients on the upper boughs as I'd always done, convinced they would eventually come around. But after several weeks of active resistance from the wounded and the ill, she realized the problem wasn't going away anytime soon. She began taking double doses of her arthritis tincture and climbing the stairways early in the morning, making the routine house calls that previously served as my training ground.

Tired and irritable, she arrived at the clinic in the afternoons, her knees in agony, only to find more patients waiting for her at the clinic. Cuts and burns, simple stitches, insect bites, and runny noses—the simple procedures that I helped with formerly—were now impatiently lined up, waiting. No one would allow *The Blight* to treat them.

Useless to my mother now, I spent my time making poultices and medicines until our herbs ran out. I practiced my suturing religiously, though I had serious doubts my needle would approach a patient ever again. If things didn't improve soon, I knew Mom would need to find another trainee. What use to her was an assistant who couldn't assist?

The morning Yew limped into the clinic I was ripping bandages. I glanced up briefly. "Didn't you hear? The doctor does home visits all morning. She won't be in clinic until this afternoon." I stretched my hands apart and listened to the satisfying sound of the cedar fabric tearing in two.

"That's why I'm here now. Rather have you clean out my foot than Michelia."

"Really?"

"Don't look so surprised. No such thing as a blight. Least not a human one. So long as you save me the lecture I'd hear from her." He hopped up on the examination table and showed me the sole of his foot. An angry wound oozed pus. I wrinkled my nose in distaste.

"I think you know what I'd say. And you know it yourself already."

I gently washed Yew's foot, and then I pulled on a clean pair of well-used fiber gloves. Gathering a handful of fly larvae from their lined cedar box, I arranged them around Yew's diabetic foot ulcer. Maggot debridement was one of my favorite treatments. It never ceased to amaze me how these tiny creatures could clean a wound so completely with no discomfort to the patient. We carefully disinfected the wiggling creatures after each treatment to remove microbes and the maggots could be used again and again. I sat alongside my father and watched the maggots at work, occasionally picking them up and moving them to other areas of his foot in need of a gentle munching.

"Yew? Can I ask you something?" I chewed my lip. He didn't respond. "You knew about Cassia and Rhus, didn't you?"

He was silent for so long I thought he hadn't heard my question. Finally, he said, "Ostrya, I don't know what your mother has told you about me—I didn't know. Not until after Cassia had the baby—Tung."

"Mom told me she didn't know."

"Oh? Did she? That's interesting, seeing as she delivered the baby. I guess she needs to keep that a secret. Since she never officially reported the birth to the council. Butia loves nothing as much as her ridiculous laws. For my part, I knew nothing about it until after the baby was born. The whole time Cassia was pregnant. No one told me anything. Not Cassia. Not her mother. Definitely not my brother. If I'd known—"

"You didn't tell me I had an uncle."

"You don't remember? He and I used to sit outside the shanty in the evenings when your mom was in clinic. You and your brother were asleep inside. It never occurred to me that you wouldn't remember him."

"I guess I don't remember much from—before."

"Before?"

"Joshua."

"Oh." He was quiet again. I focused on the squirming larvae on his foot and picked up one to move it to a new spot.

He broke the silence. "Ostrya, if I'd known what Rhus had done to Cassia, was doing to her back then, believe me—if I'd known what he was capable of—but he was my brother. You never think—oh Great Ones. I was blind. Your mother never liked him. She always had a sixth sense about people, you know?"

"She was blind where you were concerned though, wasn't she?"

"What's that supposed to mean?"

"You left us. Just like you left Cassia and her mom. She should have realized you'd leave us eventually."

"Ostrya, look at me!" He grabbed my chin, forcing me to turn my head. I shook his hand off but I met his eyes. "Ostrya, I didn't leave. At least, I didn't leave you and your mom. Don't you know? She kicked me out."

"She never did!"

"Oh yes, she did. Don't look so surprised. I loved your mother. She's not an easy woman—and her family—don't even get me started. But I loved her with everything I had. Part of me probably still does. I never would have left her—or you."

"But why? Because of Rhus?"

He rubbed his hand over his face. "Oh, Great Ones. In part, I guess, but not how you think. She didn't blame me for what he did to Cassia. She blamed me for my blindness. I was different when he was around. Reckless. Irresponsible. If we hadn't been high that night—"

"What night?"

He exhaled and shook his head, and then pointed at his foot. "How much longer?"

"We're about done." I tweezed out a few maggots and dropped them back into the box. "What night?"

"You know what night. I should have been watching. You kids crept out when I was high. I didn't realize you'd gone."

I gaped. He was talking about Joshua. "I thought you left because of what I did."

It was his turn to be surprised. "What did you do? You were a kid. I should have been watching you. You're better off without me. I am a bum, a loser. I would have ruined you if I stayed. Michelia and Butia were both right about that."

What did Butia have to do with any of this?

"I mean, look at me." He waggled his foot.

The debridement complete, I wrapped one of the bandages I'd just ripped around the clean wound. Yew clasped my hand.

"Ostrya, you and Cassia are the best of me. I've near ruined both your lives, in different ways. Best if I stay out of them now."

He leaned on my shoulder and slid off the table, and then hobbled out of the clinic.

Chapter Thirty-Five

Following Yew's revelation, I was left alone with the medicines, medical texts, and my thoughts. Thoughts floated through my head without end lately, clouds of hazy images and ideas filling up my empty hours.

The fact was, early in my traineeship I had bitterly wanted my solitude. Now that I had it, there was nothing I wanted less.

I'd be the first to admit I wasn't a natural healer. Despite our family lineage and my mother's highest hopes, this traineeship was a failure. I kept fainting at the sight of blood, and more than that, most of the canopy despised me. My mother seemed to think I'd grow into the job and the community would give me a second chance, but I doubted it.

In the beginning, I hadn't wanted to become a doctor although the entire canopy expected it. And now that the canopy wanted nothing to do with me, my contrary self wanted only to heal them.

"Hey, Ostrya. You got a sec?" Mangrove stepped into the empty room, all wiry muscles and hunting gear. My heart beat a little faster.

Besides Yew, Mangrove was the only patient I'd treated in days. Since his return to the canopy from the hunt, I was seeing more of him than ever; he showed up every few days when Mom was out for one minor injury after another. It was almost like he stood sentry waiting for her to leave. I suspected he purposefully injured himself again to spend time with me.

"For you? Always." I was glad to see him. His brown hair curled tightly against his scalp in the humid air, and I imagined how the ringlets would feel twisted around my fingers. The rest of the canopy might call me *The Blight*, but as long as my wiry hunter liked me, I could muddle through.

He held up a bloodied hand. A piece of bark jutted out from beneath a fingernail.

"Yikes! I'll bet that one hurt." I took him by the hand and brought him to the washbasin. I washed his hand as though he were a young child. I picked up the tweezers in one hand and held his injured hand in the other. I squinted, concentrating on the large splinter. With his free hand, he pushed my hair to my shoulder. I felt his warm breath tickling the little hairs on the back of my neck. I aimed for the bark at the same moment his lips caressed the soft skin at my hairline. My knees quaked and I jabbed the end of the tweezers into the tender skin under his fingernail.

"Ouch! Dang it, Ostrya," he yelped into my neck.

"It's your fault. You can't be doing that when I've got medical instruments in my hands. Hold on a second. I've almost got it. There!" Triumphantly, I brandished the tweezers, the large splinter captured between the points.

"Wow. That was a big one."

"Sure was. Hold still now. Let me dab a little astringent on that. And a little wrap ... all set." I grinned, proud of myself.

Mangrove pulled my face to his and our lips merged. He

tasted of salt and pine resin, his tongue so soft. His fingers stroked my head, tangling my hair—

"Ahem."

Of course, the one and only time Mangrove kissed me in the clinic, my mother showed up.

"Sorry, Michelia," said Mangrove. "Your trainee did such a fine job of removing a splinter, I was simply overcome with gratitude."

To my surprise, Mom snorted in amusement. "Why don't you two go spend the afternoon together? Someplace that's not my clinic."

"But Mom-Michelia. It's early. Don't you need my help?" I knew the words were ridiculous even as I uttered them. My presence merely lengthened her day, keeping away the patients who summoned her later, after clinic hours.

"Mangrove, would you please wait outside for a moment?"

A fleeting glance at my mother, and then at me, and Mangrove left the clinic without a word. What had I done wrong now?

"Ostrya, I need to tell you before you find out on your own ..."

That didn't sound great.

"Wingnut is coming back."

"But that's great, Mom! That's what you wanted."

"Mmmm hmmm." She looked at the floor. "Wingnut has requested a change and with Hamamalis's approval, he'll begin his formal traineeship with me this afternoon."

"He'll be a great help to you."

"Ostrya, I'm not sure you understand." She lowered her voice as she raised her eyes. "He will be my trainee."

"Good. I like Wingnut. It will be good to have the help."

The strange quaver in my commanding mother's voice was my first indication that I wasn't getting it. "You'll find another maestro, another job. We both know this is not your calling."

You could have knocked me over with a feather. I was dumbfounded. The level of my dumbfoundedness surpassed all previously known levels.

I heard myself arguing stupidly about a job I'd never wanted in the first place. "I'm a direct descendant of Pseudotsuga. It's in my DNA to be a doctor. You can't singlehandedly make that decision! It's not fair!"

Her blue and green eyes met mine, deep sadness mixed with her characteristic resolve. "I haven't made the decision. Our community decided when they began avoiding you and calling you *The Blight*. The Council of Maestros decided—an hour ago—when they ruled you would no longer train with me. And you decided. A long time ago."

She was right. I'd made no secret of the fact that I didn't want to follow in the family footsteps. I'd announced my intentions to Sorbus and Mangrove, and of course, Salix, way before any of this started, before the storm and the food shortage and everything that followed. In retrospect, I'd been rude and condescending to many of my patients in the early days. But I'd changed, hadn't I? I really had been trying these last few months. "I want to be a doctor. I changed my mind. I want to take care of the climbers the way you and Grandpa and all of our ancestors have done."

"Ostrya. The council is correct on this point. This is not your calling."

"But—I can work harder. I can learn! Isn't that the whole point of a traineeship?"

"Yes. You are smart. You are a quick study and a hard worker. If book learning and suture practice and poultice making were all that you needed to be an adequate doctor, maybe this could work. You might even learn bedside manner, given time. But Ostrya, a doctor who experiences vasovagal syncope at the sight of blood cannot be effective. Not in the canopy."

Vasovagal syncope was a fancy term for fainting. "But I'm not grossed out by pus or maggots or spiders. I extracted a huge splinter from Mangrove's hand, and I didn't faint—"

"And that's wonderful. You can perform first aid, and that's a vital skill in whatever profession you choose. But blood phobia is nothing to take lightly. Twice, during dire medical situations, you fainted. I couldn't count on you in an emergency, and if I'm honest, I have no business training you to be my successor. Your auto-responses are simply too unpredictable. In this job, you are a danger to the canopy."

I was a danger to the canopy. She had said it.

My past, my ten-year old self, my sin. I would never be clear of it, no matter how I tried. I would never be forgiven. Tears sprang to my eyes and I scooped my satchel off the floor before walking stiffly from the clinic. I didn't want her to see my defeat, to see how much I had wanted this, to see my shame.

What was to come next was a fluke. It had to be.

Because if I believed the Great Ones had any power over us, were anything more than the giant trees we lived in, I would have thought they were inflicting their justice. If I believed in *The Book of Silvanus*, I would have accepted what came next as my penance.

If I had known what was coming next, I never would have broken another commandment.

Chapter Thirty-Six

❧

Mangrove's rough, strong hand gripped my thin, bony one and we set off along Bough One. "Want to climb up through the limbs?" he asked.

I shook my head. "No. Let all the haters see me leave the clinic. Screw them. Screw them all!"

"You're being paranoid, Ostrya. No one hates you." But I saw the looks aimed at me as we walked along. I heard the hushed whispers. I even saw a mother drag her child out of my path. They were all afraid I was going to infect them. *The Blight*. I'd done nothing wrong, not this time. And I refused to be cowed by them. I shook off Mangrove's hand. I would do this alone. I held my head high and looked at each and every face staring at me as I passed.

Soon I was to endure the final insult. Though they had nothing in common and fought constantly, Salix and Toona seemed to be following the philosophy that the enemy of my enemy is my friend. They stood together outside the school where Toona now instructed the children. Salix sniffed and made a show of whispering to Toona. And Toona, who was responsible for the education and moral guidance of the canopy's children, spat at me as I marched by. I saw Maestro Wollemia take this in, watching as she was from the bench outside the elder shanty. She turned her back on the coarseness of her trainee, turned her back on the injustice of the council's decision, and she turned her back on me.

I bit my tongue, gritted my teeth, and thrust my chin out and my shoulders back. They would not rattle me. They could judge me and taunt me and tell lies about me. Their judgments would never change who I was. I would have to care about them and their opinions for their opinions to matter or to injure me.

And then Thevetia, that sweet, senile, oblivious old woman, greeted me. "Hi, sweetie! That knee potion of yours is a real marvel. When can I get some more?"

I burst into tears and raced for the stairway, climbing two stairs at a time. "Hold up!" called Mangrove behind me. At Bough Two, I stepped onto the landing and waited for him to catch up to me.

"Why'd you run away from me?"

"I didn't. I want to go somewhere. I don't know. Get out of here for a while." If I'd been alone, I might have ventured across to the west side again, across my perilous bridge and down to my gingko forest. It had been a while since I'd worked on my rope. Maybe that was what I needed.

"Hey, I've got an idea," said Mangrove. "Want to try something new?"

I shook my head, felt tears prickling, and turned my back to him. He caught me gently around the waist and turned me toward him. He brushed the hair from my eyes and stroked a thumb across my cheek, catching a stray tear. He set his jaw and met my eyes. No pity softened them. He stepped back, and then pulled the bow off his shoulder and handed it to me. I took it in my two hands. The smooth, softly sanded surface invited a caress. It was lighter than I'd expected. I raised an eyebrow and looked at him.

"We're going hunting," he said. It wasn't a question.

Early in my traineeship, I toyed with the idea of becoming a hunter. Now I looked at it as a real possibility. I'd be able to do two things I loved: be alone and climb in the Outer Reaches.

"Is that even legal? Am I allowed to hunt? The council—"

All spirits are equal. That was one of the three inviolable commandments. That meant no killing any creature that didn't pose a threat or wouldn't be eaten—though we all turned a blind eye to the clubbing of spiders. The only weapons in the canopy were the bows and arrows, slings and raptors used by the hunters. Before wielding a weapon, potential hunters were required to register with the Council of Maestros.

"No. But when have the rules stopped you before?"

Chapter Thirty-Seven

❧

A raspy cackle came from the eastern boundary, a raven clearing its throat in the camouflage of soft fir branchs. Mangrove tucked himself quietly and securely into the crevice made by the young tree sprouting from the nurse limb, and then pulled me in beside him.

"You can't shoot with that satchel hanging off your chest."

I pulled the strap over my head and looped it over his. He wrapped the satchel crosswise across his body as he'd seen me do, then handed me his bow. He tied one end of his security rope around my waist and tethered the other end to the stout limb. I gripped his bow in my hands and looked at him. He closed his eyes and listened intently. The forest was silent except for the lonesome call of the raven.

The raven cackled and waited, cackled and waited. There was no response to its call for a friend, a member of its avian community.

"It's probably searching for a mate," whispered Mangrove.

"No one's answering," I whispered back. "Do you think it's lost?"

"Maybe. Separated from its group somehow. Easier to hunt them when they're alone. They sometimes mob a hunter when they're together."

"Maybe the group abandoned it?" I asked. Perhaps this raven had offended the rest of its species and was ostracized from the group.

"No, they don't do that. It might be the sentry, calling danger, telling the others about the hunter in the trees and to stay hidden."

"Poor thing," I said. "What if it's lovelorn, looking for its mate? And we kill it?"

Mangrove grinned at me. "You're so soft. A raven wooing a beautiful girl bird."

"Who knows? Maybe he's a strong, handsome, eligible bachelor of a raven who all the lady ravens would be proud to marry."

"But he has his beady black eye on one special bird with feathers blacker, glossier than any of the other fowl, legs longer than any of the other lady ravens, brown hair that flows over her slender shoulders, a soft, raspy voice—"

I blushed. "Are we still talking about the raven?"

The raven's call drew nearer, moving, approaching our hiding spot. I scanned the sky. A glimmer caught my eye; the black-purple plumage of the bird glistened in the branches of a tree less than twenty feet away. I elbowed Mangrove and he nodded. Slowly, stealthily so as not to attract our prey's notice, Mangrove slipped an arrow from his quiver. He took my hand and helped me loop the finely spun hunters' twine around the middle of the arrow, careful not to disturb the flocking. Together we nocked his arrow, stretched the bow, and sited the quarry.

At the very moment we shot the arrow, the raven tilted its head, called one more time for its beloved, and stretched its wings to fly. Mangrove's arrow grazed the bird's wing, scraping away feathers and skin, and the bird screeched, flapping frantically and careening toward the forest floor. Mangrove cursed as the arrow dropped impotently into the tree, snagging on a branch. He yanked at the twine once, twice, trying to work it free.

"Stay here a second," he said and stretched his body as far along the nurse log as he dared. My satchel dragged against the bark beneath him. He flapped the twine, attempting to wriggle the arrow from the branches of the adjacent tree. The log groaned beneath his weight. I felt the tree shudder and shouted. Mangrove scrambled back towards the crevice too quickly. A sickening crack, a shudder, and all sound vanished.

His mouth stretched wide in silent horror. His eyes dilated into deep wells of terror. His arms flung up and out toward the trees, toward the heavens, toward salvation. My friend had tied his rope to my waist, not to his own. The twine wrapped around his leg, snapping the arrow in two as he fell.

My disbelieving eyes followed the broken arrow as it dropped. The forest floor so far beneath was invisible from this height, divorced from view by mammoth tree limbs, leaf detritus, parasitic and symbiotic plants, and the hazy mist of low-lying clouds. The injured raven and the tool of its death would rot together out of my reach. *Mangrove.*

Sound returned. The branches creaked, rubbing against one another. In the distance, a raven called—too late. Its partner was gone now.

Mangrove had told me how he tried never to lose an arrow. Making them was a tedious, thankless task. I'd have to learn how to make arrows if I were to be a hunter. I looked witlessly at the bow in my numb hand, my fingers caressing the two names his fingers had carved side by side into the smooth wood. Mangrove Ostrya. Our names together. I slung the bow across my back as I'd seen Mangrove do hundreds of times. His quiver was gone.

"We lost the arrow," I said to the empty sky.

Chapter Thirty-Eight

My brain was shrouded in a deep forest mist, a heavy gray cloud cover of regret and remorse, a thick fog of denial. The heavy, wet, dripping gunk enveloped my mind and my spirit. The weighted mist throbbed within my skull, making coherent thought difficult, memory painful, the future inconceivable.

Death followed life, another stage of the human life cycle that awaited the elderly, the sick, and the infirm. Anticipated by the middle aged. Startling and tragic among the youthful and healthy.

I'd witnessed more death in the past six months than in all the years of my life before the storm. As a trainee, I'd not handled the death of my patients stoically or professionally, but I handled them. Each of them left a visceral scar deep within my soul. The stinging pain of Joshua's death so many years ago had faded, leaving the ceaseless, unavoidable prickle of guilt. The deaths of Yucca and Tung were dull aches in my ribcage. Cassia's unnamed son was a bad tooth radiating into my skull.

Mangrove—my hunter. The silky skin of those earlier

scars was torn open, flayed and raw, the truth bleeding forth: my fault. I am to blame for all the bad things.

I lay in the hammock of the grieving shanty. Its existence was known by only two other climbers: Sorbus and Cedrus. One of them had built it, a lonely trainee practicing his trade. One of them had mourned in it, a distressed father trying to regain self-control.

The construction was crude. Daylight peeked through the ceiling joins; a heavy rainstorm would produce a good-sized waterfall in the center of the room. My brain welcomed the brief distraction of noting deficiencies in the structure, but I couldn't banish the image from my mind. The moment I closed my eyes, I was right back with Mangrove. The branch, snapping.

Mangrove's eyes.

His eyes. Such terror.

I had panicked. Frozen. I knew it. I was as useless to him in his need as I'd been to Michelia in the clinic. I should have grabbed him. I could have saved him. We shouldn't have been there in the first place. I shouldn't have been hunting. I shot the fatal arrow. The Great Ones punished him because of me. All my fault. Useless. Useless. Useless.

And now he's dead. Because of me.

His eyes. He knew he was dead before he died.

He knew.

The gray fog in my head crushed me, suffocated me, but I couldn't break free. I don't know how much time passed. Hours? Days? I ventured into the drizzle to pee, crawling back into the dark embrace of the hammock like a spider cowering from sunlight. I felt neither hunger nor thirst; every cell of my body was numb—except for the blazing, rending stab through my center. I curled in upon myself, focusing on the pain within my core, willing it to grow, willing it to devour me. I wanted to disappear, to die, to cease existing.

To never have been born.

A pressure on my shoulder, a dark brown hand, gentle eyes in a familiar face. Sorbus. "Ostrya? Are you all right? We've been searching for you and Mangrove for two days."

A rag wiped my eyes, my face, my nose. Arms around me, lifting my long body as though it weighed nothing. The warmth of another body. The tickle of long, twisted, wiry hair against my neck, down my shoulder, intermingled with my own, unwashed, a greasy tangle.

Wingnut's voice: "It's Mangrove's bow. Where is he, Ostrya?"

Large hands tenderly rubbing my back. Broad chest accepting my sobs. Whispering voices buzzing around my head.

"Did he—"

"That wouldn't be like him—"

Wingnut's voice, direct, breaking through: "What happened, Ostrya? Did Mangrove lay hands on you?"

"I'll kill him!" Yew's voice?

What were they asking? What were they thinking? Mangrove, my hunter. So loyal, so kind. I realized he'd been my best friend. In the last few days, he'd been my only friend.

I realized what they were suggesting. "No! Never! He did not hurt me!"

Sorbus held me, supported me, lending me his strength. Someone else's voice, strident and commanding filtered through the room. Cedrus. "Where is Mangrove? Ostrya!"

Sorbus's hand stroking my hair. He put his fingers under my chin and raised my head, his eyes troubled and questioning. Mangrove was his friend, too. His best friend, too. I looked into those humane dark eyes peering out from his gentle bear face. I needed to tell him. He deserved to know.

Sorbus's eyes welled. He knew. He'd known his best friend was dead the moment he saw me in that hammock.

"My fault. My crime." I pulled away from Sorbus. My touch was defiling him. I covered my face in my hands. "He took my punishment. He fed the Great Ones."

Sorbus's face melted. His shoulders slumped. He didn't resist as rough hands pushed him away and forced me to my feet. Sorbus's eyes stayed on me, not angry, not accusing. His sadness matched my own. Wingnut embraced him, absorbing his emotion, while I was dragged from the shanty.

Chapter Thirty-Nine

I was brought before the Council of Maestros: Butia, Wollemia, Hamamalis, and Drypetes. Butia wasn't allowed a vote. They thought her too emotionally involved, though I could have disabused them of that notion if only they'd asked me. Nothing emotional about her, and certainly no emotional involvement on my part. Not anymore.

I was charged, convicted, and sentenced in a single hour. I'd broken two of the three commandments. Wollemia told the council about my alleged hoarding of food during the famine. The severity with which I'd supposedly violated the first commandment—take only what you need—was sufficient on its own to punish me with banishment from the canopy. But combined with the second commandment—all spirits are equal—my sentence was to be much worse. According to the council, I'd broken the second commandment twice: I loosed an arrow upon a forest creature as a non-hunter, and I caused the death of another climber. Mangrove.

The vote was unanimous. I was not to be exiled; that punishment was too lenient for a murderer. It was decided that I must be sacrificed to cleanse the canopy, my actions too offensive for mere banishment. All spirits were not equal after all, especially if the spirit in question belongs to a murderer. The irony was not lost on me: I'd been convicted of feeding Mangrove to the Great Ones and my punishment was to be fed to the Great Ones.

The council house on the north side of Bough Two was the only shanty besides the clinic that had a locked door. I never understood the purpose of the lock before, but now that I'd been sentenced, it made perfect sense. This is where they imprisoned criminals before feeding them to the Great Ones.

We had all heard the story about a mass feeding, a time when a brazen few endangered the survival of the many and paid for their transgression with their lives. Like the story of the cull, this story was handed down from one generation to the next. Like the story of the cull, I assumed it was a myth.

No one had been executed in my lifetime, not in my mother's lifetime, not in my grandparent's lifetime. I would be the first punishment feeding in living memory.

It had all happened so fast, Cedrus and his crew hauling me away, the rapid assemblage of the council, the charges against me listed, and my fate announced before I realized what was happening to me. I'd been mourning and confused, sleepwalking. Nothing like a death sentence to wake you right up.

No one had spoken up for me, to tell my side of events. Neither my mother nor my father, not Sorbus or Wingnut. The climbers dragged my mother away yelling and fighting. At least she'd tried. But there was nothing to be done. The council had voted: No more blight in the canopy.

Immediately after uttering my death sentence, Wollemia turned her back on me and exited the council house. As far as she was concerned, I was dead already. Never let a silly detail like a beating heart prove otherwise. Butia shook her head at me and followed Wollemia out of the door without saying a word. My own grandmother. Compared to her cruel silence, having my hands and feet bound by Hamamalis and the door locked by Drypetes was a mercy. My time in the canopy would end at dawn. No way to empty my bladder. No water to drink. The final insults against my body before killing me.

The joke was on them. I was already dead.

My heart had died twice: once with the death of my brother, and again with the death of Mangrove. Tomorrow my heart would die a third and final time, along with the rest of my body.

I listened in the darkness. This was my last night to listen to the nocturnal creatures, the whoosh of the wind through the fir needles, the creaking of branch against branch, the popping and clicking of carpenter ants in the wall. Now that my life was to be stolen from me, I regretted all of the thoughts I'd ever had of jumping and every moment I'd pitied myself.

I regretted all the times I'd avoided Mangrove.

A rustle at the door, some metallic clicks, and the door to my prison opened. A body entered, the flash as a flint was struck, and then a taper burned in the center of the room, lighting up the interior and my father's face.

"Yew!"

"Shhh. Don't need any nosy climbers hearing us."

My father, my good-for-nothing, alcohol-addled, loser of a father, had found a way to see me before I was executed.

"Stop crying, Ostrya. You're not dying tomorrow." He untied my hands and feet, muttering to himself. "Lawless savages. Tying up my little girl. Treating her worse than an animal."

"What are you doing here?"

"Breaking you out, of course." He crouched down and began picking a lock on a standing metal box. The lockbox was like the medical supply cabinet in the clinic but at least twice the size and made of metal, not wood. I heard a click and Yew chuckled softly.

"Never been a lock made I couldn't pick." His gaze flickered over my feet. "These should fit." He held two heavy leather blocks laced with thin pieces of rope. I watched as he turned them upside down and slapped them on the bottom. "Always check them for spiders or other biting creatures before you put them on your feet. Don't look so confused. These are boots. The earth dwellers wear them."

So many questions ... I didn't know where to begin. I started with the *boots* in my hand. "What ... why ... how ... what's the point of breaking in to show me these ... these ... *boots*?"

"What's the point? What's the point! Kid, you're getting out of here, out of this canopy. If I'd had any guts in my whole rotten life, I would have gotten you out of here years ago. But no way are these hypocrites, this council, killing my daughter. Not when she can climb like you can climb! You're getting out of here and this is the gear you need to do it."

I poked my toes tentatively into the holes at the top of the *boots* and pulled until my foot rested inside. I wiggled my toes, pressing my feet against the heavy leather on all sides. "Why do I need coverings for my feet? They'll prevent me from feeling the bark."

"You'll need them so you can wear the gaffs. Don't put the boots on yet, though. Carry them until you get where you're going."

I pulled my foot out of the boot, tied the laces of both boots together, and hung the heavy leather boots around my neck. Yew gave me two strange looking pieces of equipment made of a heavy fiber tube connected to metal spikes. "These are your gaffs. Only use them when you're on the trunk. You put the boots on first before buckling these over the top, like this." He held one over my foot and said, "The brace goes against your inside calf like this, the spike on the inside. This is called a buckle. You slide one end through the other, like so."

"But these are sharp. They'll stab the Great Ones!"

"Don't worry, you won't hurt them. Their bark is plenty thick. These gaffs were used by the First Climbers to ascend. The spikes never penetrate the cambium; the outer layer is far too thick. You'll need them so you can descend. You'll never get down thousands of feet of trunk without them."

"Down? You want me to go down?"

"Of course. Why do you think I gave you the boots? What do you think I'm doing here? Don't you want to see what's down there, on the forest floor? Haven't you always wondered?"

How did my father, so long absent from my life, know this about me? I was sure I'd never told him, and I knew Mangrove never would have said anything—

Mangrove.

I couldn't allow my mind to go there. Not now. Later, after I'd escaped. His crooked smile, warm brown eyes, curly head, soft lips—I swallowed all of the images, buried them deep in the acid of my churning stomach.

I focused on my unlikely rescuer. Yew. Too many unanswered questions, too much information to unpack, and no time. "All of this belonged to the First Climbers?"

"Yes. This entire cabinet is full of their original climbing gear. You'll need this, too—a saddle." He handed me another leather and fiber garment with metal rings on the side. "I'd like you to put it on now. One leg through each side, yes, like that. Tighten it around your hips. Comfortable? Good. Your safety line goes up top through these rings." He pointed to the front rings. "Your flip line attaches to these side ones. You wrap the lines around the trunk like a lasso and hook yourself to the tree with the safety line. You thrust your body up and down with the flip line, adjusting your safety line as you go down. Got it?"

I nodded, amazed that this gear had been hidden away in the council house all this time and stunned that Yew knew how to use it. He poked deeper through the cabinet before pulling out a stiff, heavy rope. "That's your flip line. No safety lines here as far as I can tell. Probably used them for bridges early on."

He rested on his heels and looked at me. "Pseudotsuga's balls. I forgot rope. I don't know who we'll steal it from—"

My rope in the gingko tree. "Don't worry about that. I have a secret stash."

"That's my girl." He grinned.

"How did you know all of this was here? Or how to use it?"

"They haven't told you yet?"

"Who? Told me what?"

"You're in Pseudotsuga's line. You and your mom and your grandfather. The council passes it down to all of the descendants of the First Council of Maestros."

"You mean Mom knows about this stuff?"

"Back in the day, I wasn't the only one who liked the cannabis. Got your mom baked one time and she let a few things slip. I figured out the rest on my own."

"How? By breaking in? Picking locks?"

He smirked. "What can I say? It's a gift. But this isn't the only thing I discovered."

"Yeah? What else?"

He bit his lip and looked at me a moment. He shook his head and said, "Naw. There's no point. You'll be out of here before morning. It won't matter."

"Tell me! What else don't I know?"

He bent close and whispered, two conspirators in the middle of a dark night. "They've got books in here. Everything you ever wanted to know about the before times. About the earthwalkers. About the climbing gear. And *The Book of Silvanus*—"

"So? Who cares about *The Book of Silvanus*? They teach all of us that duff, those lies. The end of the world. Cannibals. Snow."

He quirked his lips. "What's this, Ostrya? You doubt the almighty book? Perhaps you are like your old man after all."

"Wait—you don't think it's true either?"

"I don't know a thing about the world down there. Don't know if earthwalkers are still alive or ate each other long ago. What I do know is this—there are pages we've never seen locked up in here. Pages written by the First Climbers. Books written before the First Climbers. So much to read, so much we don't know."

"So that's curious because?"

"Why does the council keep all of this knowledge to themselves? What do Butia, Hamamalis, Drypetes, and Wollemia know that we don't? They teach us about oxygen saturation levels, the lifecycle of an orb weaver, the protein content of a squirrel. What aren't they teaching us?"

"I don't know. The truth? They've been lying to us for years."

The laces of the heavy boots cut into my neck. I moved the string to a fresh spot. I didn't care about any of this. I hadn't believed *The Book of Silvanus* for years. To find out now that we didn't know something, or that some of us didn't know, only confirmed my disbelief. Butia's involvement didn't even surprise me. Nothing surprised me. I was ready to be gone.

"You're right. They don't share the books precisely

because they don't want us to know the truth. Ever since the First Climbers, the council has handed down secrets from one generation to the next. These books are just the tip of the conspiracy."

Yew's eyes gleamed, pupils huge in his gray face, and I realized he was drunk. I'd briefly glimpsed the father I once had. For the first time in years, he'd helped me as a father should. He'd taught me a few things and we shared a moment, but abuse of drugs and booze had addled his brain. He was paranoid and suspicious. And my time was limited.

"I need to go."

He looked away and when he turned back to face me, the candlelight glinted off his wet eyes. For the first time in eight years, I reached out and hugged my father.

"I love you, baby girl. My fierce climber. You'll never know how much."

"I love you, too, Dad." I grabbed the climbing gear and didn't look back.

Chapter Forty

For seventeen years I lived under the eyes and control of my mother—my authority figure both at home and at work. I could have moved out at sixteen, gotten myself a roommate, and taken a hammock on Bough Six. I had no reason to continue living with her, but without me, I knew that my mother would have only her sick patients and Joshua's doll to keep her company. She would have been compelled to relinquish our hanging shanty to a family and move to Bough One or Bough Two with another single adult, torture in the trees for a woman like Michelia.

I'd believed that I was responsible for my mother's solitude, responsible for Joshua's death and Yew's abandonment, and I considered it my duty to save my mother from the indignity of a shared shanty. But along with this living situation had come the burden of perpetual childhood and, I now understood, my unspoken resentment.

As I hovered in the shadows outside of our hanging shanty, the only home I'd ever known, an aching sorrow built inside me. A dim light oozed through the wall cracks: Joshua's light kept Mom company tonight. My eyes, hot and aching from so many tears, welled up again. I readjusted the climbing gear across my shoulders and turned away when the muffled sound of secret weeping stopped me.

I crept to the doorway of the hanging shanty, tossed my climbing gear to the branch pathway, and hoisted myself up. I heard a gasp as arms wrapped around me, a wet face nestled against mine, and soft kisses rained over my cheeks and forehead. Not since I was a small child had my mother caressed me so, and soon I began to cry, too.

"Shhh, shhh. The neighbors are close," said Mom. "Who was it?" And then she answered her own question. "Yew. That man was always good with locks."

She held me at arms-length and scrutinized my face. She ran her fingers over my eyebrows, my eyelashes, my nose, my cheeks, memorizing me. "My darling daughter. Ostrya. You were named for the ironwood tree. Your grandpa said it was no name for a child, but I knew the moment I laid eyes on you. Yew and I both knew that your will would be unbendable. You've always known your mind, never allowed anyone to sway you—you are a true descendant of Pseudotsuga. You would have been a powerful councilor. You would have replaced Butia, in time. But the Great Ones have other plans for you."

"If trees were capable of thought, I'd say the Great Ones made up their minds about me long ago." I took a deep breath. If I didn't tell her now, I never would. "When I killed my brother."

Her gaze was direct, serious, not shocked. She *knew* what I had done.

"How long have you known? Did Yew tell you?"

She shook her head. "No. He told me you'd been asleep that entire night, that Joshua crept out on his own. But I knew. Deep down. A mother knows her own child. Like I knew you shouldn't be the next doctor. But I forced it. I thought healing others would help you heal yourself."

"But … you never said anything … you never let on …"

"Ostrya, you were my long-limbed girl, always hanging upside down from the tree limbs like an orb weaver, your arms and braids dangling." She walked to the shelf and picked up Joshua's doll. Her eyes glittered in the candlelight. "You didn't see him like I did. Joshua, my beautiful boy. He watched you, those brown eyes of his. The way your father looked at you. Joshua adored you. They both did. Joshua was your shadow."

I saw him then as he'd been eight years ago, his thin frame, dark brown hair, eyes framed by curling eyelashes and a flawless pale complexion.

"He'd run after you, his little legs struggling to keep up with your stride."

"I teased him."

"Yes. You did."

"I was mean and sarcastic."

"You were."

His face appeared before me in the dim room. Big eyes questioning, a hint of a smile on his lips, always desperately wanting to be in on the joke and not realizing he was the butt of it. So much shame. Such regret. "I didn't want him following me. I wanted to be alone." I covered my mouth, dashing away more tears. "That night, I knew he was awake. I knew he was following me. I climbed too high. I thought he'd stop when he realized he couldn't keep up with me. He kept following, kept climbing. And then, he couldn't climb any higher. He was stuck. He couldn't climb up, but he was too scared to climb down. He froze." The words spilled out of my mouth, my long-held confession. Tears mixed with saliva as I spoke the truth. "I taunted him. I teased him for being scared. I told him he was a big baby. I wanted him to fall. I didn't want him to fall far, but I wanted the climbing to be for me—I didn't want to share it with him. I was already sharing everything else. I was the climber. The trees were mine!"

Mom watched me. Cool. Scientific. Reserved.

"Say something! Forgive me! I'm sorry, so sorry. I never meant it to happen. I loved him. I didn't realize until after, but I loved him. My little brother. I'm so, so sorry. Forgive me, Mom. Please. Please, forgive me."

"I forgave you eight years ago, Ostrya. I forgave you before it ever happened. You were cruel to your brother. You never thought of his feelings or his emotions. And you've spent the last eight years punishing yourself in a way no one else ever could."

"But … but don't you wonder, if Joshua had lived, would you and my father still be together? If Joshua had lived, he'd be your trainee."

"What good does that do? If Joshua had lived, who would be his best friend, would he have a sweetheart, would he still look like Yew or more like me? You think I haven't asked myself those questions every day for the last eight years? It doesn't change the past. It only makes it more difficult to live in the present." She crossed the room and wrapped her arms around me again. "Ostrya, the grief you feel—the death of your brother, and now Mangrove, the many tragedies over these past months—I'm sorry that you've experienced so much loss so young. But I pray to the Great Ones that you never outlive your own child. I pray you never suffer that loss."

She kissed my forehead again and I squeezed her tight, absorbing her essence. She stepped away from me and gathered a breath. "I've made mistakes. Too many. My worst one was to imagine I knew what you needed. Everything that led up to your trial—my fault."

"No! I won't let you take the blame."

"You're right." She chewed her lip. "There's been enough blame and shame in our family. Personality interwoven with dreadful events. Our family history is full of it." She reached out and touched my hair, tucking it behind my ear. "You need something other than what I gave you. I don't know what that is. I probably couldn't have given it to you even if I had known, but I pray you find it wherever you're going." She took her flint and our knife off the shelf, tied them in a squirrel pelt, and handed them to me. "I notice you don't have your satchel. You'll need these where you're going."

I tied the package around my waist and then reached for her hands. "I love you, Mom."

"You must leave now, Ostrya." Her voice was firm. "Climb to the Outer Reaches. Cross to the west—and yes, I know about that. Your hunter told me. He didn't want me to believe the lies Salix told about you. We both know that no one can follow you across—please take care. Use the sacred tools Yew gave you. Leave this place."

I squeezed her in a hug and allowed myself one last unscientific, unprofessional display of emotion. Except for one lone tear, her face was a stoic mask.

"Go now. Give me the chance to imagine what your life is going to be like. Don't let them catch you. I can't mourn the death of my last child. Please go."

I gathered the climbing tools and climbed out of the shanty, my heart full and breaking at the same time.

Her voice was barely audible. "I love you, Ostrya, my iron-willed child."

Chapter Forty-One

In retrospect, it was an idiotic decision, but I was carrying ten-pound boots, gaffs, and the metal-core flip line. It might have been safer to climb up to Bough Seven through the interior limbs, but the mere thought of lugging all of that heavy, awkward gear through the foliage exhausted me. The night wasn't pitch dark but it wasn't a full moon either. Five boughs up the stairway. That's all. How was I to know that Salix was sneaking around the canopy after a nocturnal tryst?

I heard the hiss of her voice as I stepped off the stairway. "What's this? The condemned murderer has escaped? Not in my canopy."

My hackles rose. All I wanted at this moment was to slap her across her smug face and knock her off the tree limb; I'd been convicted for murder anyway, might as well commit the crime. But I thought of my mother, her grief if I were caught and fed to the Great Ones. I thought of Yew, his attempt to atone for his part in Joshua's death by freeing me, and I knew that revenge wasn't part of the plan. Not if I wanted to live. I was faster than Salix and, if I weren't hauling so much gear, I could have outrun her easily. But even if I did run, all she needed to do was raise the alarm by yelling and all the youth of Bough Seven would capture me in seconds.

"Salix, haven't you done enough? Why do you have to be like this?" I spun around to see Sorbus on the north-facing limb.

"Stay out of this," she growled.

"I will not. I've kept my mouth shut too long. Why must you continue to torment our friend? Ostrya, go."

"Don't you dare move! I'll scream! How can you take her side? She's a criminal. A murderer."

"She's as much a murderer as I am. You know she could never have hurt Mangrove."

"She's a food hoarder and a thief."

"That food was for Cassia's kids," I said. "Mangrove would have told you that."

"But he's dead, isn't he, Ostrya?" She sneered. "Convenient for you. Not enough for you to kill your brother. You had to kill my friend, too."

"Salix, shut up," said Sorbus. "Ostrya, Mangrove told me. And I told Salix. She knows about the food. Don't you, Salix?"

Salix crossed her arms and glared at me. "It wasn't enough that you had Mangrove. You had to take Wingnut, too. You knew how I felt about him."

"And it wouldn't have mattered." A third voice chimed in. Wingnut stepped over to me, handed me Mangrove's bow, and then stood behind Sorbus. He wrapped his two arms around the shorter man's shoulders. "I only wanted your brother."

Salix's face registered shock. "Pseudotsuga's balls! But Wingnut—you're not gay!"

Wingnut shrugged. "Gay, straight—what difference do words make? I love Sorbus." He winked at me. "Go, Ostrya. Quickly."

"Take care of my mom," I said. "She chose the best trainee."

He nodded solemnly, and then held Salix with a look. I turned and ran to the edge of Bough Seven.

It was a slow, arduous climb through the canopy to the twelfth bough. The boots got hung up in the trees so many times I thought I'd never reach my crossing—if there were still a crossing to reach. Day was dawning by the time I reached the treetops. A blue sky beckoned and my bridge to the west side stretched in front of me.

If my climbing gear added too much weight to the slender limbs, I could break through and plummet a half mile to the forest floor. But if I retreated, I'd take the plunge in front of an audience and my parents would know forever how I died. No matter what happened now, I needed to continue forward. I owed it to Michelia and Yew. They needed to believe that one of their children was alive and well. I gathered courage into my lungs and set off across my makeshift bridge.

The branches I tied together had abraded each other, leaving open wounds and those wounds had begun fusing. In a few years, the trees would grow together, creating a natural bridge to the west side. If the climbers moved into the higher reaches of the canopy, they'd discover what I had left them.

But I wouldn't be here to cross it with them.

I reached the west side and climbed down, gathering what food I could in the old skygardens. I stopped at my gingko forest, inhaled the vomit smell of the gingko fruit, and retrieved my cedar rope. I swung into the Outer Reaches, gathering breath, gathering courage, willing myself to climb down to discover what lies on the floor beneath the canopy.

The Present

I didn't ask to be born into this family. I never wanted to live in the canopy. I certainly never wanted to be a healer. I didn't want Mangrove. Not at first. But after everything you think you don't want is taken away, you're left with yourself.

Better hope that's enough.

The Book of Silvanus describes an ocean of water to the west. I know that's a lie, like all the rest of the lies. Even so, maybe I'll walk toward the setting sun. What would it be like to bathe in a body of water? To taste salt water on my lips? After that, I might just look for snow.

I tighten my climbing harness, fasten my boots and gaffs, and tie up my safety rope and flip line. I descend, like an orb weaver on its dropline. I am the solitary spider. I am silent and alert. I am stealthy and agile. I am gentle, but don't mess with me, or you'll get my fangs.

Acknowledgments

The Silvanus Saga, especially this first book, has been percolating in my creative coffee pot for years. I started writing it and then parked it several times, waiting for my storytelling skills to develop. Ostrya's story felt compelling and important, and I wanted to do her justice. I needed more practice.

At some point I realized that I simply needed to get out of the way and let Ostrya speak. I was helped along the way by some wonderful folks.

Rachel Barnard and Jenn Hotes, my insightful beta readers, helped ensure that Ostrya's story was as honest and real as I could make it. Canth! Decided-Baldwin, my force-of-nature muse, taught me a few things about climate change and quite a few more about spiders. Leslie Cole, my unrelenting and eagle-eyed editor, held my feet to the fire and my nose to the grindstone. (Leslie, those clichés were specially chosen just for you.) For all the years of love, support, and OMG delicious cooking, Matt Conners, my phenomenal spouse, I thank you.

www.ingramcontent.com/pod-product-compliance
Lightning Source LLC
Chambersburg PA
CBHW010551170726
48285CB00011B/2856